# $\mathcal{A}$ CANDLELIGHT INTRIGUE

# CANDLELIGHT INTRIGUES

# DARK LEGACY

formerly *The Red Turrets of Orne*

## Candace Connell

*A Candlelight Intrigue*

Published by
Dell Publishing Co., Inc.
1 Dag Hammarskjold Plaza
New York, New York 10017

*To Dorothy*

Originally published under the title *The Red Turrets of Orne.*

For information address Doubleday & Company, Inc.,
New York, New York.

Dell ® TM 755118, Dell Publishing Co., Inc.

ISBN 0-440-11771-2

Reprinted by arrangement with Doubleday & Company, Inc.
Printed in the United States of America
First Dell printing—February 1980

# Chapter I

I was going to Orne Hall.

Every threatening clack of the train's iron wheels rolling over the railroad tracks increased my feeling of sick fear and irresolution. The dusty three-car train clattered and swayed its noisy, protesting way toward Pykerie Junction. My empty stomach—for I'd eaten nothing all day—lurched with the train's ceaseless clacking and jerking, but I forced myself to sit stiffly erect, my head up, one hand grasping the armrest, no matter how weary I might become. Plain I might be, but I had my pride! Nor did I turn away from the curious stare of the skinny man who had come from the end of the car to sit down facing me.

"Going far, ma'am?" he asked in an oily voice. He leaned forward and a smirking smile touched his thin lips.

"No," I said briefly, and turned away to look out of the window.

"You travelin' alone?" he went on.

He'd left his seat only shortly before, and had chosen to sit down opposite me. Only two other men shared the car, sitting together at the far end.

"I do not talk to strangers," I said crisply. "I beg of you, please leave me be."

A sneer lifted one corner of his thin lips. "If'en I'd seen how homely you are, I'd not sat down," he said, and got to his feet.

I stared back at him, my face frozen so he'd see no emotion in it. "The pot calls the kettle black," I said tartly, and turned away a second time. I knew he walked back to the end of the car, and I knew my face felt warm and tears stung my eyes—and I told myself they were tears of pure anger.

I watched through the railroad car's dirty windows at the stark, leafless trees which swept by in ranks like stern sentinels marching on the slopes of the molded bleak hills. At times the huffing and hooting engine's black smoke swirled and twisted over the sinuous windings of the famous Erie Canal, and I frequently saw poking-slow gray barges drawn by weary spans of plodding mules. I saw the animals strain, leaning heavily into the yokes as they trudged along the waterway's towpath. On one barge I glimpsed a woman who wore a windblown apron and red-and-white bonnet. She fought the cold wind as she hung her wash of flapping sheets and pillowcases strung out on lines to dry—or perhaps to freeze, for it was a cold fall day.

I wished miserably that I was on one of those slow-moving barges, going nowhere instead of traveling at this terrific and frightening speed by train across upper New York State, heading to a fearful and unknown future which lay in wait for me at Orne Hall.

Orne Hall! The very name seemed fearsome to me. And there would be people there ready to stare at me. I had no idea what my future would be except I knew that I would see in their eyes and in their actions the inevitable pity which it had been my lot to see in everyone's eyes since Mamma died. But what other choice did I have? Who, in this Centennial year of 1876, was going to care what happens to a dowdy, homely female like me? Who would want a woman who was already an old maid at twenty, one who had no dowry and whose only talent was pecking with tired fingers at the keys of the newfangled invention called a "type-writer" and writing gossipy church items for a small-town weekly newspaper? I knew the only reason my father forced me to learn to work the type-writer keys was that he had no need to pay me wages, and he was too stingy to pay good money to anybody.

I suppose I could have gone to work in one of the many factories I'd seen spreading in confusion near the train tracks as the train moved through cities. I knew that the factories' spinning and weaving machines had to have girls operating them but I'd heard of the deplorable conditions under which they were forced to work for terribly long hours. I was good with a needle, but I hated to think of sitting before one of those sewing machines, stitching up the ready-made garments for the stores to put in their show windows.

The train began to slow, and finally shrieked to a protesting stop at some little town—I saw by the sign on the end of the bright red station that its name was Weggner— and as I stared out of the car's dingy window, I could see high on a hill one of the wooden windmills so like the one we had at home before Mamma died. I'd been ten then, and when my beautiful, sad mother was laid away in her grave, I think I died somewhat with her. After she was lowered into that awful gaping hole in the earth of the cemetery, there wasn't anybody left to stand between me and my father, for he loved me not at all. After Mamma was laid away he became even meaner and more strict. My conviction that he hated me grew stronger with each passing year. Even up to the day he shot himself, he kept saying bad things about Mamma and me. Not a day passed but that my father would tell me no man would ever look at me twice.

"You're ugly," he'd say. "Get out of my sight! I don't want to have to look at your homely face. All any man is going to feel for you is disgust and pity!"

I thought of the repulsive man who had spoken to me earlier, and I glanced toward the end of the car, from where he watched me out of small eyes. Was that the only kind of a man who would ever seek after me? I'd rather die.

The train stopped again at some little village, and a tall fair-haired man got on. He was uncommonly handsome with bold blue eyes. His roving eyes glanced around the car, and for a moment rested on me, and I felt my face flush, though I still sat stiffly erect.

But I saw his interest fade quickly. He walked on down the aisle past me. I blinked quickly; would the pain never cease? I could never really become used to pity; I'd seen it so often in people's eyes after my father's cowardly suicide.

7

I'd sworn, then, to myself that in my whole life I'd never cower. I'd hold my head high. Perhaps I *was* homely, but I would not cringe! Nor had I. Even though I was drab and dowdy, and the daughter of a self-convicted schemer, hypocrite, and embezzler, no man would ever see me cringe outwardly, no matter how much I might do so inwardly!

The rest of the train trip to Pykerie Junction lasted forever. I grew more hungry and I felt exhausted and fearful. At various stations more passengers got on, and others left. I saw the tall blond man had put his hat over his face and had leaned back, apparently asleep, and I did as I had so often before: I played games with my imagination—games in which a man like that tall one would smile at me, and I'd be a beautiful woman of polish and breeding—and we'd fall in love. For a while I forgot the dark, forbidding skies out the car window, and that a late-fall chill mixed with cigar smoke filled the car.

The old conductor who'd spoken kindly to me stopped beside my seat and startled me by reaching across for the ticket stub in the clip on the window frame. He'd asked my name before, and now he used it.

"Miss Dorsey," he said, his voice friendly, "the next stop is Pykerie Junction. 'Bout fifteen-twenty minutes," he murmured as he pulled out his big railroad pocket watch and glanced at it. He put it back in his vest pocket; the silver chain swung with the lurching of the train. He glanced out the dirty window. "It sure do look they's goin' t'be a storm. I sure hope it don't snow! Will there be people meeting you?"

"I expect to be met. Thank you for being so kindly."

He smiled back and touched the brim of his cap. Then he went on down the aisle, swaying with the train's jerky movements.

The coming of early evening made it difficult to see clearly as I peered out of the sooty windows. My cloth suitcase rested on the dusty red plush seat beside me—I held my bulky handbag in my lap, and I discovered that my fingers were gripping the leather handle so hard my wrist and hand ached. But still I held up my head as I told myself for the thousandth time not to be a coward, and that, after all, no matter what my father had said about the people at Orne Hall, I really didn't have any other choice. Mamma had been an Orne, hadn't she? Her father, Joshua Orne, had been John Orne's brother, and Jewel Avigny Orne was John Orne's wife, which made her my great-aunt, didn't it? If she hadn't written to me—my great-aunt Jewel, I mean—what would have happened to me? I'd tried to find work in Newton after they found out about my father's embezzlement at the bank and he'd killed himself with his pistol, but no one would employ me.

Once I went into Mr. Osborne's dry-goods store and asked if he needed a clerk. He looked at me, his mustached lips curling, and he suggested that I get a job at that awful house on B Street.

"Maybelle might hire you," he said bitterly. "To wash floors!"

Maybelle and her girls were notorious in Newton, but to be told that even there all I could do would be to wash floors was a final insult! Blinded by the tears of fury that gathered in my eyes, I turned away quickly and walked out of the store. But I held my head stiffly erect, and my shoulders back—though perhaps my corset stays had something to do with that!

Mr. Osborne called after me, "And if'en you make any money you might pay me what your lying father owes me!"

I didn't turn back or answer. Instead I walked down the plank sidewalk away from the dreadful man, not knowing what to do next. All I had was a few dollars after the sheriff had sold off the newspaper and paid the money out to greedy creditors. It was barely enough to pay the train fare from Newton to Pykerie Junction.

I was on the train the day after I received Aunt Jewel's answering letter, telling me to come at once.

The train began to slow in jolting jerks, and suddenly the rain came down out of the dark sky in great sheets, hammering on the window and making it impossible to see out. The conductor came by again and picked up my cloth suitcase.

"Ma'am, it's goin' to be a wet one," he said. "You're

goin' t'get soaked. You run to the station, soon's the cars stop. I'll fetch your bag."

I stood up, smoothing the dark shawl over my unfashionably plain gray day dress and then lifted it up over my head, drawing it tightly—it didn't even have a bustle! The three petticoats did give some fullness and the long hem did touch the floor behind me. I followed the conductor to the end of the car, clutching each seat for balance.

The brakes screamed and the train jerked heavily and lurched to a jangling, huffing stop. The conductor handed me down to the board platform into the stinging rain and a howling wind which picked up my skirt and tugged at it; I lifted up my petticoats and skirt in my two hands and ran for the small unpainted station, shamelessly disregarding my exposed limbs. My heavy handbag swung from my elbow, banging against my hips.

Under the station's narrow eaves I stopped, breathless because of the tightness of my corset stays. I was barely sheltered against the wind and slanting cold rain.

"Sorry, ma'am," the old conductor said as he put my bag down beside me. "Don't seem like they's anybody here t'meet you," he added as he glanced toward the far end of the planked platform.

I saw pity in his eyes, and, as usual, I cringed inwardly though I forced myself to hold up my head and to smile. "Someone will be here," I assured him confidently, with far more certainty than I actually felt. "I am expected, thank you," I added firmly.

He touched the hard bill of his dark blue cap and trotted back to the train. No one got on, and with a long hoot and several huffs, the train started up, letting out huge billowing puffs of smoke and steam.

Seconds later fear gripped me anew as I stood there watching the disappearing cars. The station door behind me opened, giving me a new start. A little bald-headed man peered up at me over pince-nez glasses. "Come on inside, 'fore you get yourself soaked," he commanded sharply in a high, squeaky voice.

I heaved a quick sigh of relief; at least I wasn't stranded all alone. "Thank you," I murmured, and picked up my suitcase. I stepped through the door into the tiny unpainted waiting room with its raw plank benches bolted to three walls. On the fourth side I saw the grilled ticket window and I heard the telegraph instrument clattering in a staccato frenzy inside the station agent's office.

"Somebody meetin' you?" the agent asked in a more friendly tone while he continued to peer up at me. "I'm the station agent."

"Yes," I answered his question as confidently and firmly as I could. "Someone from Orne Hall will be here for me," I added.

The station agent's watery blue eyes showed considerable curiosity as he continued to examine me, though when I'd mentioned Orne Hall, it seemed to me that a change came over his countenance, and his lips curled.

"So, you're old Joshua's granddaughter," he said as if he spoke to himself. I heard the thin note of pity in his tone of voice—and something else, the meaning of which I failed to fathom. He turned away as if his examination had given him all the information needed—or wanted—dismissing me as not being worthy of another look. "I sent old Pete Barnes out to deliver that telegram saying you was comin'," he said. Suddenly he cackled with laughter as if it was a great joke. The loudness and abruptness made me jump. He went into his cubicle of an office as the telegraph instrument continued to clatter impatiently.

My knees trembled from the wet cold that seeped into my body from the soaked clothing, which had received a drenching, even though my dash to the depot had been brief and quick. I sank down onto one of the unpainted benches. A zigzag flash of lightning seemed to split the clouds apart and the sound of the rain hammering on the roof and cascading water from the eaves worsened, if that was possible, sounding like countless demons. A second later a crack of thunder shook the small building and I couldn't repress a cry as I put my hands to my ears to block the sound. But when it was over and the rumbling gone, I put my hands again in my lap. I glared at the agent as his face reappeared in the window, daring him to say anything about my foolish cry of fear.

11

"That was a bad'n," he muttered. "Must have hit close by." He glanced at me again. "Where're you-all goin' to stay if'en nobody comes in from Orne Hall?" he asked sharply, somewhat as if he relished the straits in which I found myself.

"Isn't there a hotel?" I asked.

"In Pykerie Junction, ma'am?" he said, and laughed briefly. "There ain't nothin' here but this here station. Pykerie Junction ain't no town!"

The sheets of drenching rain had kept me from discovering what he said was true, for I'd seen nothing during the quick dash from the train. What *would* I do if no one arrived? Would I have to sleep in the station? And I felt as if I would starve if I was unable to obtain something to eat before long.

My question, fortunately, was answered at once, for suddenly the depot door banged open and a tow-headed boy about eight years old bounced in, wet to the skin through his gray denim work shirt and knee-length trousers. His wide blue eyes glanced around and settled on me immediately. "You be Miss Adelia Dorsey?" he asked in a high, breathless voice. Rain glistened on his freckled, round face and dripped from his wind-whipped hair. "If'en you is, come on. They's the buggy outside." He looked at me more closely. "Ain't you got no coat?"

My jacket and shawl weren't much and I had to admit I had nothing else. "No," I said as I rose to my feet. "It was warm when I started but it doesn't matter, because I'm already soaked."

"You sit," he broke in, and disappeared out through the door.

"Who—who is he?" I asked the agent.

"That there's Harlan Wiley," the agent answered with a slightly twisted grin. "His granddaddy is that uppity Paul Wiley. He is the butler at Orne Hall; his grandmamma, Charity Wiley, she's the cook."

"Oh . . ."

"You best watch out for him, Miss Dorsey," the agent went on. "I wouldn't trust him no further than I could toss a rattlesnake."

12

The boy burst in again before I could ask why. Rain shone on his round face, dripping from his turned-up pug nose. He carried a black woolen blanket bunched carelessly in his arms. "Toby says you should wrap up in this," he said breathlessly as he pushed the blanket at me, "so's you don't get no more wet."

His cheerful smile and tone of voice warmed me more than the blanket would. I instinctively liked the boy in spite of the agent's comment and my spirits lifted a little.

"Thank you," I said, and did as he directed, lifting the blanket, even over my head. He picked up the heavy suitcase by the round wooden handle and headed out the door, the big bag banging against his skinny knees. I followed him as he ran toward the two-seated buggy at the end of the building. I saw that curtains with isinglass windows protected the inside from the rain and I gave an inward sigh of relief; at least I'd keep reasonably dry during the trip. The buggy door swung open and I quickly clambered inside. Harlan put the suitcase on the seat beside me and then climbed up to sit beside the burly driver, yanking the door shut.

"Miss, you shore did get yourself terrible wet," the driver said, turning his head so he could examine me, his bold but kindly blue eyes taking in every part of my body, making me aware of the way my wet clothing clung to my limbs. Despite my chill, I felt my face flush. I saw that he had a weather-beaten Irish countenance wreathed in a friendly smile. His large nose shone with a bit of redness which indicated that he might be a man who enjoyed tippling.

"I surely did," I answered, and forced a smile to my lips.

He turned away, shook the reins, and yelled, "Git up!" at the team. The buggy began to move as the two dappled grays leaned into the harness. The driver called over his shoulder, "I'm Toby Muller, ma'am." His voice had to be a shout against the wind and the hammering rain on the buggy top. "It ain't no fit day to be out, it surely ain't!"

In only a few minutes, due to the storm and wetness, the air had become much colder. I couldn't repress a shiver as

**13**

the chill settled in my bones. "It surely isn't," I repeated. "Is—is it far?"

"No, ma'am," he assured me over his shoulder. "No more'n four mile," he added, and touched the flanks of the horses with the tip of his whip, so that they broke into a sluggish trot.

"Like I said, ma'am, I'm Toby. I take care of the stables, mostly—me and Aaron Forrester, leastwise when Aaron ain't . . ." He stopped as if he had said too much. "This here is Harlan, and he's Paul Wiley's and Charity's grandson. He ain't got no pa." Toby broke into a laughter that was both kindly and harsh. "He never did have no pa!"

The boy, Harlan, turned around in the front seat to look at me with frank curiosity on his round, cheerful face. "I'm a bastard," he said with childlike innocence. "Was old Joshua really your grandpapa?"

There did seem to be more than mere child's curiosity behind his question, and I hesitated a moment before I answered.

"Yes," I said with a forced smile even as my teeth chattered. "What do you know about him, Harlan?" I asked, curious myself. My grandfather died of consumption many years before Harlan could have been born.

"Him and old John Orne had a fight over a woman, and John licked him and kicked him out, only Joshua swore he'd get even, only he never did because he never came back," Harlan answered as if it were an oft-told tale.

It was a new story to me, though. I felt a quick astonishment. Nothing I'd ever heard about my grandfather made the story of a fight over a woman seem likely. I'd been little when my grandfather, Joshua Orne, had died, but I had heard him curse his brother John with terrible words of eternal damnation, though I'd never known why. Nor would my mother ever tell me.

But thinking back now, and after hearing Harlan's story, I realized how very little I actually knew about the Ornes who lived in Orne Hall. All I knew was that the Ornes owned countless barges that moved up and down the Erie Canal, and that they were so very rich.

A fresh gust of wind and storm made the buggy sway

14

dangerously as the span of horses slogged heavily through the muck of the lane. Harlan turned to stare ahead into the growing darkness at the narrow winding road that led through a narrow valley which separated high tree-covered hills on either side. The wind became slightly less violent, though jagged flashes of bright lightning still occasionally illuminated the muddy road, followed by sharp cracks of thunder.

I forced myself from habit to sit erect on the hard, barely padded bench of the two-seated buggy, still clutching the black woolen blanket closely about my body, but even so, I shivered with the wet cold and my teeth chattered in spite of everything I could do to prevent it.

The boy in the front seat turned back to look at me, his face nearly hidden in the lowering darkness, but his voice expressed concern. "Ma'am," he asked, "are you gettin' awful cold? Your teeth's clacking."

His solicitude touched me; he was too young, perhaps, to see me as the plain person I knew myself to be. I wondered if he wasn't colder than I was, in his wet shirt, for, after all, he wore no jacket.

"I'm all right," I answered as cheerfully as I could. "But how about you, Harlan? Aren't you chilled?" It occurred to me that he required the blanket more than I did, but I suspected it would hurt his pride if I attempted to return it to him.

"I'm used to it," he answered manfully.

Suddenly I felt the buggy turning sharply and I glanced out of the isinglass, but in the growing darkness I saw nothing but the dim, naked arms of trees that lined the lonely, muddy lane. For just a moment the rain hammered a little less violently on the buggy's tightly stretched top.

"Are we nearly there?" I asked, as brightly as I could to hide my misery and coldness.

"Yes'm," Toby answered without turning his head. Just as he spoke several jagged flashes of lightning made the countryside seem as bright as noon.

In those brief instants I saw that the lane led up a hill, and I gasped as I saw at the top a huge building that looked almost like one of those castles along the Rhine

River in Europe which I once had seen pictured in a history book. It squatted at the top of the hill as if it clutched the earth with claws from two wings that reached toward us from each side; at the center a high-pitched roof slanted deeply above the wide expanse of gray stone punctuated by slender, tall, dark windows. At the outer corner of the wings I saw bright red turrets with conical, pointed spires. From the steeply pitched roofs of the wings and from the central roof, too, I saw tall black chimneys reaching toward the dark clouds; black smoke, streaked by the wild wind, fled eastward from each of them.

Wide, low steps led to the large Gothic-shaped door at the center of the morosely imposing mansion, an expanse of glistening black. Then the sight disappeared as if by black magic, as the narrowed pupils of my eyes failed to adjust to the darkness. A heavy fear settled over me. I saw no warmth or welcome in that bleak first sight of Orne Hall. No warmly lighted windows betrayed the presence of anyone within; only the smoke from the tall stacks indicated that the place wasn't deserted.

"It's so big," I murmured to myself, but Harlan heard me above the sounds of the storm.

"It sure is, ma'am," he responded. "There's a big cellar you can't see, too, under the east wing." He glanced at Toby quickly. "Only, I can't ever go down there," he added, complaint in his young voice.

"How many rooms are there?" I asked.

It was Toby who answered. "Probably thirty-five, if you don't count them that's on the third floor. Nobody goes up there no more."

Thirty-five rooms! It had to be a castle.

The mud of the lane gave way to gravel as the team drew the buggy past the empty-eyed gargoyles which guarded Orne Hall's wide, almost barren grounds. I saw dimly a small stone building, and then a door opened, and against the dim light of candles, I saw a man come out.

"That you, Toby?"

"Who'd you expect, Bob?" Toby retorted.

"Can't be too careful, Toby," the one called Bob answered. "You know how Mr. Orne is . . ."

"Mind your mouth," Toby said briefly, and touched the flanks of the grays, urging them on to the top of the hill. Stones crackled and growled beneath the buggy's iron-shaped wheels, as if they complained reluctantly against our going up to the mansion.

The lane made a circle around what appeared to be a dark stone fountain; another flash of lightning let me see briefly the unclothed nymph of bronze standing proudly, naked breasts upthrust, glistening in the wetness of the rain. Then the darkness descended again as Toby guided the team around the fountain to the far side and up before the dimly seen wide circular steps which in turn led to the main Gothic entrance.

"Whoa there," he called to the team, hauling back on the reins as he did so.

The downpour had lessened, though the wind still blew furiously. Toby got out of the buggy and opened the rear door for me to alight. "You best run," he suggested as he held out a big work-coarsened hand to assist me. I took it and then did as he said, running up the steps to the glistening black door which opened inward just as I reached it.

An old, lean white-haired man in black livery stood there in the doorway, stiffly erect, his narrow face expressionless, and certainly no welcoming smile on the thin lips or from the large black eyes.

"We got her, Grandpa," the boy, Harlan, shouted. "This here's her. She ain't like you said, at all, Grandpa!"

His words startled me; what had the butler told his grandson about me? What could he possibly know to tell? The old man inclined his white head slightly and glanced at Harlan disapprovingly.

"Welcome to Orne Hall, Miss Adelia," he said coldly, and then stepped back, gesturing for me to enter. "Toby," he called back to the buggy, "bring Miss Adelia's bags, and then take the team to the stables. Harlan," he added sharply, "go with Toby."

Harlan seemed almost to shrink under the grandfather's cold glance. Without a word he trotted back to the buggy.

"Miss Dorsey," the old man murmured with a slight

bow, "I am Wiley, the butler. Madame Orne is expecting you."

His greeting failed to warm me as I entered the mansion's foyer.

My first impression was of a wide expanse of white marble, for all of the walls gleamed coldly from the coal-oil lamps with painted spherical chimneys set in brackets high on the side walls. There were but two windows. I understood why I'd seen no light, for heavy black drapes kept the rays within the room. The polished surfaces of the marble walls reflected back the countless rays of light which came from the candles in the chandelier overhead. I looked up at the many crystal pendants which still moved slightly from the gusts of wind from the now closed door.

A sculptured head, cast bronze, of a bearded, angry-looking man rested on a stone pedestal in one corner while seeming to stare at me with disapproval in the blank eyes as well as at the statue of a naked woman—I guessed it to be that of Diana, goddess of the Roman hunt—which stood in another corner. Her empty eyes ignored me, but stared motionless as if at some prey of the hunt.

"This way, Miss Adelia," the butler, Wiley, suggested from thin, unsmiling lips as he gestured toward the open, arched doorway directly opposite the Gothic entrance. I saw that it must lead into a very large room.

I walked through and I barely repressed a gasp of astonishment.

Across the Great Hall stood a large, glistening black-marble-faced fireplace in which the embers of a fire glowed, and directly above the high mantel a large scroll of gold letters reflected the yellow lights of bracketed, ornate coal-oil lamps.

It read: DEATH IS THE REWARD FOR ALL WHO ENTER HERE.

# Chapter II

I felt a coldness even greater than the chill of the large room which seemed to stretch so distantly to the left and right of the large fireplace. I drew my attention away from the scrolled legend as the impression of bigness flooded over me.

I'd seen pictures of English manors, and I knew that the builder of this mansion must have faithfully copied one of them. I stared in startled awe at the curved and painted ceiling, which must have reached up the full three stories. The painted glass chimneys of the bracketed lamps enhanced the brightness of the flaming wicks, bringing out so clearly the brightly painted scenes of the plastered and scrolled ceiling, yet scarcely reached the far corners, leaving them in darkness.

I saw that two settees of brocaded silk supported by Empire-design legs flanked the fireplace, and that drapes of dark velvet closely covered the many high and narrow casement windows. Many Empire-style small tables and chairs rested against the walls between the windows; rich, heavy carpets of black and white in an ornate leaf design covered the polished oaken floors.

To my left a wide carpeted staircase with broad polished banisters was supported by intricately carved balustrades. The first steps led to a wide landing, and then turned upward to a balcony which ran the length of the wall. I saw, too, that a heavy railing protected one from falling from the balcony—and from a kind of gallery which stretched the width of the big hall at each end.

A dark-haired, dark-eyed girl whose loveliness was marred only by sullen lips appeared in a hallway at my left.

She wore the blue-and-white garment and apron of a servant. Her tiny waist and proudly uplifted bust betrayed tightly drawn corset stays. No welcoming smile touched her lips as she came down the three steps with deliberate grace. She approached me and gave a tiny, reluctant curtsy as she stopped a short distance away.

"Ellen," Harlan's butler grandfather said in a cold, authoritative voice, "show Miss Adelia to the room Madame had you prepare for her. You will assist her in unpacking." He turned back to me. "I will tell Madame Orne that you have arrived," he said in the same cold voice which still carried no welcoming warmth to me, but I scarcely noticed as I continued to stare about at the huge hall.

It nearly overwhelmed me, such a huge hall. In my life I'd never seen, even in my dreams, a house like this. Nor had I ever had a servant to help me unpack, and I suddenly saw in my mind's eye the shabby underclothing and petticoats which filled my suitcase and which were hidden by my gray wool skirt and plain shirtwaist, and I cringed inside. A fresh terror swept over me; how could I cope with everything here? There'd been no welcome; no Orne had yet greeted me. Where were they? How could I deal with a great-aunt who cared so little she didn't even come to greet me? It seemed to me that the big room mocked me and made me feel small, unwanted, and helpless.

Ellen's lips curved in a smile that mocked me, too. "This way, Miss Adelia," she said coldly, her tone expressing derision as her quick glance took in every part of my unbecoming and unfashionable gray skirt. She took the suitcase from the floor at my feet, and led the way toward the wide staircase, her heels clicking a staccato rhythm on the highly polished dark oak floor. She went up the carpeted staircase and I followed her, the wool blanket still drawn about my shoulders, for the hall hadn't warmed me.

Ellen waited until I reached the balcony, and then led the way down a wide hallway lit by a single dim lamp in a wall bracket. I more sensed than saw the row of portraits hung at eye level in heavy frames. At the end of the hallway she turned to the right down a much narrower and darker hallway which I supposed was in the west wing. In almost total darkness she stopped and pushed open a rather small door and then gestured me to enter.

I did so. I saw that two coal-oil lamps in high wall brackets illuminated the room. I stopped just within the small heavy door, and I now saw it had broad straps of steel which reminded me of a door leading to a prison dungeon, rather than a bedroom. I turned my attention to the room, and I gasped at the strangeness of it, for on two sides it was curved. I knew that I must be standing below one of the red turreted towers I'd seen in the glimpse from the lane below.

The room's gray and red-figured wall covering was far from cheerful, but the heavy oaken chest of drawers and the mirrored dresser appeared strong though stiffly unyielding; not even the one straight-backed chair appeared to give me any welcome. The canopied Empire bed looked hard and uncomfortable. Only one small carpet adorned the narrow oak flooring, and its sullen black-and-red figures expressed harsh disapproval, too.

"Shall I unpack for you, Miss Adelia?" Ellen asked, a sly look in her black eyes, one eyebrow cocking up expressively.

Again, I felt embarrassed, ashamed at the worn cheapness of the few belongings. I couldn't bear the thought of the contemptuous smile which would certainly wreathe Ellen's derisive lips if she unpacked my few and miserable pieces of clothing.

"Thank you, no," I said as firmly as I could. But I forced myself to give her a smile, for I desperately wished for someone to think well of me.

I still dripped rainwater and coldness still enveloped me. I asked, surprised at my own boldness, "Would it be possible for me to have a hot bath?" I felt both miserably wet and soiled from the long train ride and the storm.

"Yes, Miss Adelia," she said, and walked to a narrow door on my right—one that I hadn't noticed. Her smile widened and I noted derision again in the shape of her lips and in her tone of voice. "This is the water closet," she added as she drew open the door and gestured for me to

21

look. Her tone suggested I might well be more used to an outhouse.

Again my eyes opened with astonishment, for I'd never seen a bath like this! It was so big, with a huge porcelain tub of cast iron resting on clawed feet. The paneled walls of dark mahogany gleamed at me. The beautiful mahogany washstand had two bowls resting in it, and I saw the receptacle above which held the tank of water for my ablutions.

There wasn't a bathroom like this in all of Newton—and I'd never had a bath except in an ugly zinc tub in all my life.

"I will tell Wiley you wish to have hot water for a bath and it will be brought up," Ellen said, and turned to leave.

In no time, it seemed to me, Ellen reappeared with two pails of water. She was followed by a younger girl with a moon-shaped face also carrying two pails, who peered at me hesitantly; it seemed to me her blue-eyed glance was peculiarly innocent and oddly vacant. But the third person was a young man of perhaps eighteen, with bold eyes that glanced at me once and then discarded me as if after a quick taste of bad wine.

Then, when enough trips had been made and the tub was nearly full, they left, and I undressed hurriedly and slid under the hot water, letting the heat sink into my weary bones. I began to relax. I stayed in the bath an almost indecent length of time, but finally I climbed to my knees, soaped my body heavily, and washed away the grime laid on me by the trip.

Finally I got out of the tub, toweled myself dry, feeling the pleasure of the towel's roughness against my body's moist skin. And I thought, as I sometimes did, that without my awful clothing my body seemed nice and rounded and soft. If only my face wasn't so plain! And my hair so ordinary a brown, although at least it was of full body and shiny.

So often I'd heard it said that beauty is only skin deep, and, oh, how I had prayed that I might have some of that skin-deep beauty on my face, but of course I never would. My features, with my so wide-set gray-blue eyes, straight

22

nose, and square, stubborn-looking chin, simply weren't pretty, and nothing could make them so. After all, my father had pointed it out often enough.

Still, by the time I'd dressed in my second skirt and bodice jacket—I only had two—which was dark blue instead of a mousy gray, I felt I was better able to face whatever the future might hold for me. But what was I supposed to do now? Should I wait until somebody came for me, or should I go down the dark hallway to the stairs and into the Great Hall? Where was my great-aunt Jewel? I wondered again what she would be like, and I wanted to read again what she'd written; I got out the letter from my bag and opened it. Under the yellow light from the bracketed lamps I reread the spidery script.

> My dear Adelia,
> We are so sorry to learn of your father's untimely death. Although your grandfather and my husband have been dead for many years, you are still part of the family. Of course you will be very welcome at Orne Hall, dear Adelia.
> Do come at once. Send a telegram to tell me when you will arrive at Pykerie Junction and Toby, our coachman, will meet you.
> You will also be of great help to me, and need not feel that your sudden arrival is a burden to the family. I am writing my memoirs and look forward to your aid, particularly since you have written that you can use the machine they call a type-writer. I have directed my grandson, John Orne III, to procure one immediately.
> Please do come at once.
>
> Yours,
> Jewel Orne

That was all. The letter was succinct and to the point. If great-aunt Jewel didn't want me to feel like a burden on them, she was making sure I wouldn't be. I had no way of knowing how she really felt or if I was being too sensitive. I folded the letter and put in back in my bag. Just then a light knock sounded on the heavy door of my round room. It startled me, almost as if I'd been guilty of something. I caught my breath and answered.

"Come in," I said primly, and Ellen pushed open the door and stepped inside. Her face seemed flushed but not as if she was angry; her black hair appeared to be in some disarray, her cap not neatly centered, and her apron not precisely tied around her slender waist. Did her duties include an assignation with a lover? It was quite silly—or bold—of her to appear this way.

"Madame would like for you to come to her sitting room," she said after her tiny, perfunctory curtsy. She seemed a little breathless. "You can go through there," she added, and pointed to the third door. "That leads to Madame's sitting room." With a slight toss of her dark head, she disappeared back through the door by which she'd entered.

Other than that she was my great-aunt, I knew nothing about Madame Jewel Avigny Orne, wife of my dead great-uncle. What was she going to be like? Somehow, I visualized a tall, angular woman without knowing why that pictured vision satisfied. What if she didn't like me and sent me away? Where could I go? But I had my pride—what was left of it. I stiffened my spine, lifted my head, and told myself not to be a foolish coward. My great-aunt would scarcely turn me out into the storm . . . but the reluctance to go to that closed door and to open it still stayed with me.

"This will not do, Adelia!" I said aloud to myself.

I wasn't pretty, heaven knew, but I could still hold my head up, and that I did! I could make sure she didn't know just how frightened I was. So, my head held high, I pulled open the door to my great-aunt's sitting room.

My first impression was brightness, for at least ten coal-oil lamps in brackets and several beautiful lamps on pedestals and tables illuminated the long room. It seemed to me that they concentrated their yellow rays on a very small, bold, upright figure perched on the very edge of a large, ornate, mahogany settee which sat before a white-marble-faced fireplace. The rays from the flickering flames danced on her white hair and was reflected from two enormous black eyes which turned to look at me out of a small, doll-like face—and seemed to look through me, too. In my imagination, she became a doll-like cat whose basilisk stare told me nothing.

But suddenly she smiled, and her whole expression changed. Now it gave out a feeling of warmth and welcome.

"Come in, my dear Adelia," she said in a light, bright tone of voice that had the lilt of violin music in it—music that smiled as even did her lips and her eyes. She was so tiny with such a small face that she didn't appear to be nearly as old as I knew my great-aunt had to be. Nor was her expression that of an ancient crone, but instead seemed to emanate intense curiosity. "Sit down here, beside me," she added, patting a place on the settee at her side with one slender, beringed first finger.

"Hello, madame," I started to say, and I didn't know if I should kiss her cheek or not. She was a relative, wasn't she?

She appeared to divine my thoughts, for she took my hand and pulled me down to peck my cheek.

"Come and sit down. Call me Aunt Jewel. Let me look at you . . ."

Her light tone warmed me, though it carried a note of authoritative command, too, as if she was certain she would be obeyed. A tiny frown creased a vertical line between her eyes and she shook her head as she examined me, looking sharply at my unfashionable blue gown, my plain face, my brown, mousy hair—at my sensible slippers which were showing signs of wear.

"That," she said abruptly, pointing a slim finger at me, "is a perfectly dreadful garment. It has no chic; isn't right for you at all!"

I felt my face flush and I knew she must see the redness of my cheeks, but I sat bolt erect, my head high, in spite of my inner anger and hurt. "My father believed a woman should not wear pretty things," I said as calmly as I could. "He said such garments were temptations of the devil. He bought my clothing for me," I added, and then hesitated before I went on, for as she examined me, I looked at her exquisite dressing gown and shawl with appreciation and envy. "But your gown, Aunt Jewel, is very beautiful."

It truly was. She did look like a beautiful and expensive doll; the brilliant facets of the crystal pendant at her breast reflected many-colored dancing lights from the fire in the grate in sharp contrast to the black silk dress with the décolleté neckline, which tightly fitted the full breasts and very slim waist. A row of shell buttons glistened from the neckline to the narrow waist. I knew well she must be very old but her appearance denied her years.

She preened a little, and I could tell that she liked my compliment, which I truly meant.

"It came from Paris," she said complacently. She glanced down at the dress, smoothing the skirt over her knees with slender, ringed fingers which moved like the talons of a tiny bird. I saw that on her third finger she wore a large diamond ring below a wide gold wedding band. "I am French, you know, Adelia," she said proudly as she lifted her eyes to look directly into mine. In spite of the light from the bracketed coal-oil lamps, the shadows beneath her cheekbones seemed to make them even higher and more prominent than they truly were, and made her delicate chin appear a trifle sharp.

"I met my husband, John Orne, in Paris, and, instead of shooting myself, like a fool I let my father, to save his business, sell me to him—and let him bring me to this godforsaken country," she said with a trace of sardonic humor in her light voice, which still carried some of the accent of her mother tongue.

I didn't know what to say, so I said nothing, my hands folded primly in my lap, my feet and knees placed close together. As I waited for her to speak again, a sense of unrealness swept over me and I felt as if I was in a dream that was just about to change into a horrible nightmare. I felt a quick chill and despite myself I suddenly trembled, though I knew not what had frightened me.

"What is it, child?" Aunt Jewel asked sharply. "Are you ill?"

"No, madame—Aunt Jewel," I answered quickly.

26

For an instant she said nothing, her big, dark eyes peering at me steadily, and then as if she dismissed whatever thoughts she'd been thinking, she gestured to her left, and following the motion with my eyes, I saw against the far wall near the door that led into my room under the tower a writing desk with a closed, curved top. The dark wood which appeared to be mahogany gleamed from many polishings.

"That writing desk—there is where you will work. It is called a davenport, you know, after the man who made the first one. There are plenty of drawers. . . . Go and look at it," Aunt Jewel ordered, and I rose to walk over to it.

"Slide the top back, and the desk board pulls out," she added, and again I did as she directed. It was a beautiful desk and I knew I would enjoy working at it.

But as I walked back to the settee her mind shifted to my unfashionably plain dress. "We shall have to see that you are better attired," she said with a slight grimace of distaste. "I couldn't bear to have you in the same room with me in that—that costume," she said with a slight curl of her thin lips. But then she apparently repented her words or her tone of voice, for she added, "I don't blame you, dear." Her voice sounded conciliatory. "You shall have some new frocks as soon as possible. You know you can buy fine frocks ready-made now, don't you? They're so clever, they can make dresses by machinery!"

She inspected me more in detail. "The nurse would never come to me if I had to look at you in that awful garment. My dear, you *are* plain, but there's something good in your face—and you do have the Orne bone structure. Your father should have been horsewhipped for making you dress like that." She paused and then asked, "By the way, Adelia, dear, just what exactly did that rascal father of yours do?"

I didn't want to talk about my father, but I told her in as few words as possible. "He didn't love Mamma and he never loved me either," I said as I ended the dreary story.

"You know, don't you," she asked, "that your father came to Orne Hall once before you were born? He claimed to know something about your mother—I haven't any idea

27

what it was—and tried to blackmail my husband. John," she went on, "told him he'd shoot him dead should he ever show his face here again. And that was the last we ever saw of him."

"I didn't know," I protested, startled at the information. So that was why my father so hated the Ornes!

"He was a scoundrel, Adelia," Aunt Jewel said with a nod of her head. "He married your mother just to try to squeeze money from the Orne family—the silly fool." She glanced at me, curiosity showing in her eyes. "Do you think your mother knew about it?"

I shook my head, for I knew my mother would never have been a party to such a thing. "Mamma wouldn't have . . ."

Abruptly, she changed the subject. "Have you eaten this evening?"

Just as quickly I realized that it was because I was so hungry that I felt faint, and I'd had nothing since dawn. I shook my head and said, "Not since early morning, Aunt Jewel!"

Without another glance at me my aunt opened her mouth and what came out had to be called a screech. "Ellen!" she called, so loudly that I nearly jumped from the settee and in my fertile imagination my aunt became like a parrot I'd heard screeching back in Newton in the house of an old retired sea captain.

Almost instantly Ellen opened the door—not the one I'd entered but another in the middle of my aunt's long sitting room.

"Yes, madame?"

Apparently she was used to my aunt's screeches, for she betrayed no great concern for the way she'd been called.

"Take my niece to the kitchen and tell Charity to give her some supper," Aunt Jewel ordered peremptorily, her words clipped and betraying that faint trace of French accent. She turned back to me, the little finger of her right hand raised in an awkward gesture of admonishment. "Then you will come back here," she added. "I will want to talk to you more."

I felt relieved that the conversation was over for a while.

I rose to my feet and smoothed the dark blue skirt down over my hips.

"Yes, Aunt Jewel," I said, and I followed Ellen out of the sitting room, down the long corridor. But instead of turning to her left to go down the wide staircase, she led the way the length of the Great Hall on the balcony following the gallery at the hall's end, and then down another dark corridor to a spiral staircase.

"Don't fall, Miss Adelia," Ellen warned me. "You can trip here if you are not careful."

We stepped out of the staircase into a hugh kitchen, the two walls of which were curved like the walls in my room, and I knew it had to be located under the round turret, too. A huge fireplace followed the curve of the far wall, and I glimpsed heavy iron pot hangers inset into the sides. But there was a big cast-iron stove, too. A large-boned blond woman stood at the range, stirring vigorously something that bubbled and smelled delightful.

"Madame says for you to give Miss Adelia some supper," Ellen said to the cook, her voice sullen and resentful, as if she'd been put upon.

The cook turned away from the stove and I could see that her large eyes were bright blue, but her expression wasn't happy. Something about the sadness in the woman's eyes made me feel for her at once. So this is the butler's wife, I thought to myself as I smiled a greeting. "Hello," I said. "I'm terribly sorry to be a bother. . . ."

"It is no bother," she said with a trace of a Nordic accent. Then she smiled, and her face changed—it was no longer sad, but happy and pleased. She appeared to be taller than even my own five feet six, and she might have been sixty or so years of age.

A girl of about sixteen with a round face of youthful innocence and vacant eyes worked in a chair at a wooden bowl in her lap, stirring with a big wooden spoon. It was the same girl who had helped draw my bath.

"That's Holly," the cook explained. "Holly, say hello to Miss Adelia." The girl nodded and a smile turned up her lips. "Holly isn't very bright," Charity added. "But she's a

29

good girl, and a fine worker." She smiled affectionately at the girl.

"Sit down, Miss Adelia," she said, and pointed to a bench that rested beside a long, heavy worktable whose scarred top showed it must have had years of use—and abuse.

I sat down heavily, and Charity commented, "You look fair tired, Miss Adelia. You must have come a long way."

"Yes, the journey by train was taxing," I answered. "But, please, a cold supper will be enough—"

"You will have a good hot supper, I will see to it," she said firmly. She turned to Ellen, who still stood at the foot of the spiral staircase. "What are you standing there for, gaping? Go about your business," she added sharply.

"I don't have to take orders from you," Ellen said with a toss of her black hair.

"No?" Charity said with a grim expression. She picked up a butcher knife from the chopping block and walked toward Ellen.

Ellen gave a small shriek. "Don't you dare!" she cried, but she disappeared up the spiral staircase with a flurry of skirt and petticoat.

Charity laughed briefly and put down the heavy knife as she shook her head. "She's a bad one," she muttered more to herself than to me. But then she looked at me squarely. "Don't you ever turn your shoulders to her," she warned me. "But now I will get you something to eat." And she did, too, moving with big-boned awkwardness, but still in minutes she placed before me fried eggs, a rasher of bacon, biscuits. . . .

I asked her how long she'd been at Orne Hall.

"Ever since I was a girl. Paul—he's my mister—he's been here longer. I was the upstairs maid when I first come," she explained.

"Were you here when my grandfather, Joshua Orne, still lived here?" I asked, curiosity getting the better of me.

"That I was," Charity answered briefly, in a tone that said clearly she did not care for such questions. So I asked nothing more.

I ate with relish and then, when I could eat no more, I

rose to my feet. "Thank you, Charity," I said, and I really meant it. "I must now return to my great-aunt. Everything tasted wonderful."

She stood at the black stove across the scarred table from me, and I hesitated, for suddenly she no longer smiled.

"Miss Adelia," she said softly, "it isn't my place to say anything, but . . . but you should leave Orne Hall. Go away and don't ever come back, for things . . . it is not good for you." She made a gesture with her two hands, holding her fingers outspread and letting them tremble a moment. "It is cursed, our Hall is!" She took a long sighing breath. "There's death within these walls," she added.

Her words made me feel a quick fear and I felt a shiver travel over my body, for it *was* a strange place.

"What do you mean?" I asked, a tremble appearing in my voice, too. I remembered the motto above the mantel in the Great Hall: DEATH IS THE REWARD FOR ALL WHO ENTER HERE.

"Too many bad things have happened; there is too much hate here. And death, there—there's always death. . . ." Her voice trailed away, and there was only the sound of the soup bubbling in the black pot on the range, and the sound of a door being slammed somewhere in the big house.

"You are trying to frighten me," I said as calmly as I could. "No one has reason to hate me or to harm me," I added, and some confidence returned to me. I did not know why Charity sought to terrify me, but my common sense told me it was foolish for me to be frightened. Still, Charity's words seemed to hang in the quiet of the kitchen, in some strange way harmonizing with the bubbling soup.

"You don't know . . ." Charity started to say, and then she stopped abruptly. "I've said enough," she muttered. "There are things you don't know about." She spoke over her shoulder. "Go back to your great-aunt. She's waiting for you."

At the spiral staircase I hesitated. "I—I'm not sure I know the way back," I said, feeling stupid.

Charity turned and pointed to another doorway with her

big wooden spoon. "Go through that door—it goes to the Great Hall. You can find your way then. . . ."

"Thank you," I said, and went out of the kitchen.

I walked down the corridor and then down three steps into the Great Hall and its multitude of chairs and tables. I could see the wide stairway at the far end and started to walk toward it, not immediately becoming aware of the tall man who stood before the fireplace, his back to the glowing logs, his two hands raising his coattails behind his back, the better to warm himself. A movement of his dark head drew my attention to him as he lifted his face and glanced at me. Then I first became aware of the large black eyes that seemed as if they might be made of polished pieces of coal. I saw the dark hair which curled over his ears, and the strong chin covered with a carefully trimmed beard—and the sardonic smile that now wreathed his lips.

# Chapter III

I'd reached the midpoint of the Great Hall when I suddenly felt impelled to stop in my tracks. My hand rested expectantly on the polished surface of the Duncan Phyfe table as if I were caught midflight by the almost hypnotic effect of the man's very black eyes.

He didn't move. "My dear cousin Adelia," he said, still remaining standing as he had been, warming his body from the glowing coals of the fireplace. "I am John Orne. Permit me to welcome you to Orne Hall, and to hope that your stay here will be a happy one."

I caught my breath at the terribly deep voice which came as a rumble from his broad chest. It seemed somehow cold and uncaring despite the words he had spoken. But there was a sardonic note in his inflections, too, which I felt was directed at me, and I felt a trace of responsive anger.

I stood quietly at the table, my fingers just touching the mahogany, my head held high.

"Good evening, Cousin John," I answered as coolly as I could. "You are very kind!" I was determined that no one was going to suspect how frightened and unsure I felt inside. I spoke with all of the cold dignity I could muster, but at the same time I became aware of something else—of the enormous sensuality and the feeling of latent strength that seemed fairly to emanate from the tall man, as if he could well be the kind of a man who could explode in violent fury—or subside into the intimacy of caressing love. I felt increasingly unsure of myself as I waited for my cousin to speak.

He was in no hurry to break the silence as he examined

33

me. I felt as if I were a prewar slave on the block at a New Orleans auction. I wouldn't have been surprised if he'd asked me to open my mouth so he could count and inspect my teeth.

"Well," he said finally, "come nearer, closer to the fire."

I hesitated, though, for my great-aunt Jewel was waiting for me. Yet, I said nothing, but continued to stand where I was.

"Come closer, that I may see you better," he said gruffly, a note of impatience appearing in that deep voice that seemed even more harsh now than when he'd first spoken. He appeared to be in his middle or late thirties, a man in the prime of his strength and virility, but his tone of impatient authority was in the manner I would have expected from one much older. "Come, girl," he commanded, for still I hadn't moved.

His words and my pride made me walk stiffly around the table toward him, my head held stiffly erect. And as I drew near him before the fireplace I became aware that he was very much taller than he'd first appeared—a head taller than I. The black well-trimmed beard and curled mustache covered and at the same time revealed a strong jawline and even, white teeth. I saw the same shadows below his prominent cheekbones that I'd seen in his grandmother's small face.

Just before him I stopped, staring back into his dark eyes with all the calmness I could command. He looked at me with evident and growing distaste.

"That," he said harshly, "is truly the most horrible garment you are wearing, Cousin Adelia!"

I felt as if he'd slapped me! The careless cruelty of his words and his arrogant, authoritative manner brought tears of anger to the corners of my eyes. I wanted to strike him! Having his grandmother say the dress was terrible had hurt me badly enough, but to be told this by a man was many times worse. "Cousin John," I heard myself retort coldly, "you are most unkind and hardly a gentleman!"

He examined me as if I were an animal he considered for slaughter, his black eyes looking at every part of me, one section at a time, and I felt myself flush angrily. Then,

34

slowly, the corners of his lips turned up in a wry smile. "So I was, wasn't I?" he murmured, his voice rumbling from his broad chest. "Please accept my apologies!" He bowed slightly from the waist, and then he extended a hand toward me. "Welcome to Orne Hall, Cousin Adelia," he said.

I couldn't tell if there was sarcasm in the voice or not, but I held my hand out toward him. He took it in his own, and then with a flourish he raised my hand as he bowed over it and I felt the warmth of his lips touching my fingers; it was a shock which was so strong I was almost frightened. With most unseemly speed I withdrew my fingers from his grip.

His smile did seem sardonic now. "Let me welcome you again to Orne Hall, and to hope your stay will be pleasant."

My knees trembled and I felt weak, but the use of the word *"stay"* jarred me. Was he making it clear I must leave—and perhaps soon? Where would I go, then? He made it sound as if I were a fortnight visitor only. The doubts that came into my mind at that moment made me recognize anew how dreadfully dependent I was upon the whim of this man and others in the Orne household— others I hadn't yet met. But pride made me remain stiffly erect, even though I was aware of his dislike of my blue dress.

"I am sure the stay will be pleasant," I said as calmly as I could. "I must go, for your grandmother wishes me to return to her in her sitting room," I said as steadily as I could. I turned to leave the tall man and the Great Hall of which he was so indisputably the master.

He bowed slightly and said, "By all means, you must do as *Grand'mère* directs. But tell her that you must be furnished with proper clothing if you are to be seen during your visit to Orne Hall."

I heard the sarcasm of his voice and words, and they bit deeply into my feelings as I turned and crossed the Great Hall to the stairway leading to the balcony. I wanted to run, like a child, from his presence, but I forced myself to walk with steady steps, and to climb the wide steps with deliberate decorum.

But as I turned at the landing, I heard a deep, sardonic chuckle from below me, and I felt my face warm with a quick flush. I told myself that my cousin John was a cruel boor and that I already had developed a strong dislike for him, even though I knew it was wrong of me. I had to live here, didn't I? I shouldn't make it worse than it already was by childish hate. Anyway, what difference did it make what he might feel? I stiffly proceeded up from the landing, looking straight ahead. I told myself not to care, but just the same I was all too aware that my blue dress had no proper bustle and that I must truly have appeared woefully unstylish.

I still tingled from the touch of his lips on my fingers, however, and from the masculine vitality that emanated from his strong, virile body. No, I could never like a man as cruel as he—but with sudden feminine intuition, I knew that I could love him. Not that I'd ever get the chance, of course.

At the head of the stairs, my hand resting lightly on the railing, I turned to glance down into the Great Hall, and at the tall man who still stood before the glowing logs burning in the huge fireplace. He stared back at me, his face uplifted, a strong, indomitable figure. The long shadows of the hall, barely illuminated by the wicks of the coal-oil lamps, emphasized the tallness of my cousin, and the breadth of his powerful shoulders, and I had an immediate conviction that he was very much the master of Orne Hall; he was the kind of a man born to be master of all he touched or desired, and I felt a fresh and different fear.

He lifted one hand in a sardonic salute, acknowledging my presence on the balcony. I did not raise my hand in response to the gesture, but turned and walked down the gallery between the heavy framed portraits of strong-faced ancestors. But in my memory I still saw the enormous Great Hall and the dark figure at the fireplace dominating the hall itself and everything in it, as if some great magnifying glass made him larger than any man could actually be in true life.

"Pleasant dreams, cousin," I heard his voice calling after me, his voice echoing briefly in the gallery, bouncing off the high ceiling. I wanted to escape him; I hurried on to my great-aunt's room.

Once at the doorway of my great-aunt's sitting room, I hesitated, for I heard faintly the sound of light laughter through the heavy oak. Someone was with Aunt Jewel, and I wondered if I could bear to meet any more of my relatives that night. I was so weary and my mind in such turmoil from the events of the trip and from my introduction to Orne Hall and its inhabitants that I didn't want to do anything other than go to bed and sleep.

Charity's dark warning still remained at the edge of my thoughts, and Johm Orne's sardonic laughter still seemed to follow me. I was sorely tempted to go on down the hallway to my own room and to retire, but I couldn't ignore my great-aunt's explicit command, could I? The sound of voices was too faint for me to understand the words, except that I thought I did hear my name spoken. I couldn't just stand in the hallway eavesdropping! So I put out my hand and tapped lightly, and, I must add, with great timidity, on the heavy door.

"Come in!" The shriek was like that my aunt had used to call Ellen, and I responded by a quickly drawn, deep breath, and I had a sudden desire to laugh, because it was like a foolish play on the stage where characters all do silly, outrageous things. I pushed the door open and stepped inside.

Aunt Jewel still sat on the settee before the fireplace, and sitting beside her, his arm over her shoulder, holding her close, was a tall man I instantly recognized, for it was the handsome blond man I'd seen on the train, the one whose intensely blue eyes had first discovered, examined, and discarded me as not worthy of notice.

"I'm—I'm sorry," I heard my voice say with a stutter as the man released Aunt Jewel's hand and rose to his feet with a single graceful movement. He was in such great contrast to my cousin John, with his yellow hair and light coloring; he was as tall, but lithe and more slender, with great grace in his movements. He looked at me with frank curiosity showing in his blue eyes, and I felt my face warming again as I saw recognition take place.

37

"Cousin Adelia! The girl on the train!"

Aunt Jewel spoke directly to me. "Adelia, this is Rex Orne, your cousin. His mother is my daughter-in-law Melinda, whom you will meet in the morning." She turned to the slender man, touching his hand with her fingertips. "Rex, welcome your cousin, Adelia Dorsey, to Orne Hall," she finished archly with a slight lift of her small head as she gave her grandson a look of pure adoration out of the great dark eyes. I guessed that this grandson must surely be a favorite of hers—as I believed the tall bearded man with the harsh, deep voice and arrogant manners could not be the favorite of anybody.

Though I still looked at my aunt, I felt Rex's direct blue eyes fixed on me. I turned to face him and I became aware that his lips lifted in a friendly, charming smile. Unlike his brother's, Rex's face was smooth-shaven and I saw that the high, shadowed cheekbones were less prominent and his face had softer, more rounded contours, yet it was still the face of a strong man.

"Dear Cousin Adelia," he said in a voice that filled the room as with soft music. He came toward me as I stood at the doorway. He held out both hands toward me, and then as he reached me, he took my two hands in his own, and before I could even move, he kissed me on the cheek! "Welcome to Orne Hall," he murmured caressingly as he held me a moment longer than necessary, and though I automatically stiffened at his presumption, the feeling was delicious.

"If I'd known you were coming to Orne Hall, I'd have left the train at Pykerie Junction, too, instead of going on to Waterloo and driving back."

When he did release me, he tucked my hand through his arm and led me back to his grandmother. His closeness made me tremble and I couldn't help comparing his affection and seeming sincere greeting with that of Cousin John, which had been so indifferent and so cruel.

Before the settee he turned around and gently seated me. Then he stepped around the back of the settee to stand behind his grandmother, his hands on her narrow shoulders as he looked down at her.

I was struck again by the rounded contours of Rex's smooth cheeks and the fact that the bone structure was so different from that of John and their grandmother. His lips were full instead of being thin and straight—and far less stern. But the touch of his hands and lips had the same power to make me tingle as did John's, and inwardly I wondered if the great magnetism was a characteristic inherited from their grandfather.

"You have eaten supper?" Aunt Jewel asked. "Charity fixed you something tasty?" Her voice had just a touch of sharpness and impatience and it drew me back from my rude gaze at Rex's handsome features and my inward conjectures about Orne men. I'd been so engrossed in examining his smiling lips and eyes that I'd quite forgotten my great-aunt for a few short seconds. Even as I answered, a thought slipped through my mind that my aunt could be a jealous woman.

"Oh, yes, Aunt Jewel," I said breathlessly, perhaps from my fast ascent of the stairs from the Great Hall, but more likely from the remembered touch of Rex's lips on my cheek. "You—you have all been so very kind," I added. I turned again to glance up into Rex's smiling face. "I—I met Cousin John as I returned from the kitchen; he introduced himself." I sat carefully erect on the edge of the settee, my head held high. But as I sat there, I felt my inner defenses beginning to crumble, for suddenly I realized I was among relatives, wasn't I? Blood runs thicker than water, doesn't it? But even as I felt that warmth I knew also that my mind was in an idiotic and pointless turmoil.

Rex's smile broadened as he shifted gracefully to sit on the arm of the settee. "You mean that the old boy bent low enough to say hello to you?" he asked, and laughed lightly, and perhaps a bit ruefully. His voice, light and charming, was so much more pleasant to listen to than the harsh gruffness of John's that I was induced to join him.

"Well, he did say I was welcome, although a bit reluctantly, I think," I murmured.

"John has many things on his mind," Aunt Jewel said with a small touch of admonition in her voice. "Rex, you haven't been very helpful. . . ."

Rex threw up his hands in a gesture of helplessness, and in a way that emphasized the good fit of his handsome jacket. "Grandmamma, you know better! John wouldn't trust me to handle the teats of a dry cow. And anyway, why should I? I live a pleasant life, and he must take charge of everything, and you well know it!" A little resentment seemed briefly to color the tone of his voice. He turned to me, though, still smiling. "I am a butterfly, Cousin Adelia," he said lightly. "I neither spin, nor do I sew. . . ."

"Most butterflies don't, but you haven't the look of one either," I broke in suddenly, and I was delighted with his warm laughter. I'd not felt so accepted or so well treated by any man in my whole life—and I conveniently forgot his dismissal as being unworthy of attention when he'd seen me on the train that afternoon. The brightly burning logs on the cast andirons in the wide fireplace, the glow from the high-turned wicks of many lamps—my aunt's gentle smile—everything made me feel warmed inside—in contrast, I thought to myself, to the coldness of John's harsh voice as he greeted me down in in the Great Hall.

Aunt Jewel laughed, too, but then she struck playfully at Rex's waistcoat as he sat close beside her on the arm of the settee. "You are lazy, Rex," she said. The she turned to me, and her expression became serious.

"John has many worries," she explained. "You mustn't mind his brusqueness and bad manners. The railroads . . ."

Rex laughed and broke in quickly. "*Grand'mère,* don't burden our guest with our problems."

"She isn't a guest, she's a member of our family now," Aunt Jewel told him crisply, and I wanted to kiss her out of my gratitude! "Anyway, Adelia, the fortunes of the Ornes depend on the Erie Canal and the industries in cities beside it. And now the awful railroads are taking away the canal's business. It's dreadful! The government giving the railroads money to build track . . ."

"*Grand'mère,*" Rex broke in gently, "the government's money built the canal." He turned to me and shook his head. "Everything begins—and someday ends, even life itself. The canal's days are numbered—"

"No!" Aunt Jewel interrupted sharply. "John will find a way."

Rex said there wasn't any way, and for several minutes they argued as I listened, hardly following what they said or meant, except that railroads traveled so much faster then the mule-drawn canal boats.

Once I interrupted to ask what seemed to me to be a reasonable question. "Why don't they use steamboats in the canal?" I asked. "Then they'd be as fast as trains. . . ."

"Adelia," Rex said gently, "anything faster than mules makes waves that wash the canal's banks away. It's been tried and it destroys the canal itself. . . ."

Finally Aunt Jewel ended it. "Go away, Rex. We're boring Adelia with business. I want to talk to her," she added with a dark eyebrow lifting over one of the splendid dark eyes.

"Shame on you, you horrible woman, driving me away," Rex said with pretended petulance, even as he winked a blue eye at me and smiled. He got to his feet. "I'll see you tomorrow at breakfast, dear cousin. I'll show you around Orne Hall and the grounds. Good night and pleasant dreams."

I said good night, and after kissing his grandmother's cheek, Rex left the room, making a fine figure of a gentleman in his excellent suit and shirtwaist. Aunt Jewel drew my attention back to her.

"Adelia, if John was rude—and I expect that he was—don't mind. John has many worries."

I said nothing about our meeting, but kept my attention fixed on my aunt as I waited for her to go on. I had the feeling that she hadn't finished what she intended to say.

"You see, Adelia, John runs the family businesses, and those awful trains, they're changing everything on the canal. But Rex is wrong! John will save the business."

"Rex doesn't help his brother?"

Aunt Jewel's lips turned up in a rueful smile. "Rex is charming, but I'm afraid he has no ability in business. John makes all the decisions. But Rex is artistic. He plays the piano beautifully, and his paintings are fine."

Aunt Jewel examined me for a long moment, obviously

preparing to change the subject. "You know, don't you, dear, that there had not been one word passed between your branch of the family and this one? Except for your late father's attempt at blackmail, of course. Not since my husband, John, and his brother, Joshua, your grandfather, quarreled?"

"I know, Aunt Jewel. I—I never knew why. Mamma never told me—she died when I was only ten. I never really knew my grandmother or my grandfather, either. What was the quarrel about, Aunt Jewel?"

It seemed to me that a veil suddenly slipped down over my aunt's dark eyes, and I could read nothing in them as she answered briefly, "It happened long ago, child. It is no concern of yours."

I must have shown my reaction to her quick coldness, for she smiled ruefully and shook her head. "Someday, perhaps, you will learn. It's an old story and not a nice one." She paused a moment, seeming to study me. "You've met the boy, Harlan? He went with Toby to fetch you from Pykerie Junction, didn't he? Did you like him?"

"Oh, yes!" I answered, and nodded. "He's a very nice little boy, though he seemed to be lonely."

"He's Paul and Charity Wiley's grandson," Aunt Jewel explained briefly. "His mother, Alice, was their daughter. She disappeared shortly after Harlan was born."

"Disappeared?"

"One morning she was gone." Aunt Jewel's expression on her small face hardened, and her lips straightened to a thin line. "Harlan is the bastard son of Alice and some unknown man; Alice would never tell who had dishonored her, and ultimately she must have run off with the man."

"Oh, I'm sorry," I murmured inadequately. I could think of nothing else to say.

"She was very beautiful," Aunt Jewel said, her tone suggesting she was remembering, rather than speaking to me. But she brought herself back to the present quickly. "Never mind," she said briskly. "So, you know how to operate a type-writer! Tell me, how did that happen?"

"My father bought one—he always had to have the first one of everything new. He made me learn to use it to help in his newspaper office," I added. "I believe I must have had a natural talent," I said, holding out my hands, fingers outspread.

"You have the Orne hands," Aunt Jewel said softly. "Those long tapering fingers; Adelia, your hands are very beautiful!"

She startled me with her words and I flushed with pleasure. No one had ever called anything about me beautiful—certainly not my hands. I looked at them as if they belonged to somebody else. It occurred to me then that no one had said anything nice to me since Mamma died, and without my wanting it to happen, my eyes filled with tears. I turned my face away so that Aunt Jewel wouldn't take notice of my foolishness. "I am so homely," I murmured.

From the corner of my eyes, though, I saw my aunt stare at me, *her* eyes narrowing. "Who said you were homely?" she asked sharply.

"Everyone," I answered. "Mostly my father after Mamma died. He—he often said that no man would ever look at me more than once—or ever desire me. He said I was doomed to die an old maid without—without ever . . ."

"Hold your hair away from your face," Aunt Jewel broke in to command briskly, and I did so, feeling my face warm under her critical examination. She told me to turn my head to the left and to the right. But all she said was "Humph," as she blinked her large eyes in concentration.

"All right, Adelia," she said abruptly, "the type-writer should arrive this week. Tomorrow morning we will start working on the letters." She gestured at a tall secretary that stood between two windows, its leaded, irregular panes of glass reflecting the fire flames. "The secretary is filled with letters. More are stored in boxes. They must be sorted and arranged. But I know you must be weary from your long trip, and I believe you would like to retire. Do you like your room?"

"Oh, yes, Aunt Jewel," I exclaimed. I made a gesture at the room with outspread arms. "Everything—Orne Hall—I felt it hard to believe! How—how did it happen to be built?"

Aunt Jewel's expression became ruefully grim. "My husband bought it and had it moved here—from France, piece by piece." Her lips curled slightly as she went on. "It was part of the price of buying me."

Her words startled me and she spoke them in such a matter-of-fact way. "Buying you?" I asked incredulously.

"That's right, Adelia. John David Orne bought me from my father." She eyed me with some speculation in the large dark eyes. "Do you know how the Ornes, my husband and your grandfather, made their money?"

"No," I answered. "On the canal?"

"The canal wasn't completed until 1825," Aunt Jewel said. "It was long before that. Importation of slaves was prohibited in 1808; Joshua and John Orne were slavers before and after that. They sailed to Africa and brought back black slaves and sold them at the southern ports."

It startled me to learn the unsavory history of my own ancestors and I felt an odd letdown. Aunt Jewel went on.

"They were rich. They came to France, and had business arrangements with my father. But when my father lost a lot of money and when his business—he bought and sold wine—began to fail, he asked John Orne for a loan. He got it, on condition that I would become John Orne's bride. And John Orne bought this horrible château in France and had it brought here and erected on this awful hill. I bore him three sons, and then I told him I would kill him if he ever came to my bed again. And he never did!"

It shook me to hear my aunt talk thus. I said nothing, almost holding my breath as I waited for her to continue.

"Our firstborn married Melinda Corsairs—and died defending her sullied honor." Her lip curled. "She wasn't worth it!" She twisted the large diamond ring on her third finger, and she seemed to be thinking now of other things. "Horace, our second son, is a physician in Waterloo. Walter, who came late, he—he's nobody." Her lip curled. "You'll meet him at breakfast."

She stopped abruptly, and she seemed to suddenly become old and tired, and lines I hadn't noticed before now became apparent, and I remembered with some surprise that my aunt must surely be in her eighties; her earlier vitality had so thoroughly belied her age.

44

"Go to bed, Adelia," she said. "Ellen will wake you at six. Breakfast at seven, sharp." She paused, and I was astonished to see that her eyes glistened with unshed tears. "I am so glad you came," she said softly, her lips wreathed in a gentle smile. "I—I always wished I'd had a daughter."

"I'm glad, too, that I came, Aunt Jewel, " I said gently, and at that moment I truly was glad. My doubts came later when I learned more of the Ornes who lived in Orne Hall.

"You had to come, finally," Aunt Jewel mused, almost as if she spoke to someone else, rather than to me, someone I couldn't see. I felt a shiver as I leaned down to kiss my aunt's cheek. "You had to come back, didn't you?" she whispered. Her eyes closed as she spoke.

"Go to bed! Sleep well," she murmured.

I straightened, wondering if I should leave her alone thus, nearly asleep. She seemed so tiny now, and so tired— I felt guilt that it was I who had tired her. But she answered my question softly.

"Ring for Ellen, please," she whispered.

I walked to the cord beside the fireplace and gave it a quick pull and I heard very faintly the answering ding of a bell. Almost immediately, even before I had reached the door of my own room, Ellen entered the sitting room.

"Prepare my bed, Ellen," Aunt Jewel said in a small, weary voice. "I am tired. . . ."

I went through the door to my own room, pulling the door shut behind me, careful that it made no noise. Once inside, the warm rays from the fire laid in the grate flowed to me. I removed my clothing, carefully hanging the dress and petticoats in the paneled wardrobe. After I untied the corset ribbons that narrowed my already slim waist, I could breathe easily again. I stepped out of my drawers and for a moment stood before the long mirror. In spite of what my father had said about me, it didn't seem to me my body was so awful. Unbidden, the picture of Rex came into my mind, as though he'd come into the room. I shook my head to banish the vision and I scolded myself for having thoughts no gentlewoman should ever have.

A moment later I turned down the wick of my lamp, and puffed out the flame, cupping my hand over the hot chimney as I did so. The room became dusky as the flickering blaze of the hearth fire threw dancing shadows on the ceiling and on the walls. I snuggled under the covers and felt the light pressure of the bed that I knew must surely have been filled with duck breast feathers. It gave me a warm, safe feeling. Perhaps Orne Hall would truly be a home to me. Aunt Jewel—already I loved her—was like a beautiful doll . . . handsome, warmhearted; and gallant Rex, so different from his brother, John. . . . As I drifted off to sleep, echoes of Charity's warning were engulfed by dreams of Rex.

I dreamed of Rex, looking at me with adoration in his blue eyes. Slowly he lowered his head to mine and kissed me—and I turned into an ugly frog. His expression changed to pity and disgust—and then into anger. He was going to strike me! His arm was raised and it held a sword that glittered in the light! The arm began its downward sweep as he lunged toward me. I threw myself away from him with a cry that stuck in my throat—and suddenly I was awake, lying stiff and unyielding under the covers, my eyes wide open. For only a part of a second I didn't know my whereabouts. Then it came to me I was at Orne Hall— and I heard a faint click.

I turned my head. The fire in the grate had burned down, so that the room was now in deep shadow. What was the sound? Was it the door closing? Had someone been in my room? Fear congealed my muscles and I couldn't move until by utter willpower I forced myself to light the bed lamp with a sulphur match.

There was no one in the room and the doors were shut. I scolded myself for my awful nightmare and got back into bed. But I turned the wick low, and left the light on, but dimly. . . .

Finally I slept again.

# Chapter IV

I dreamed that I was a little girl again, and I heard my beautiful mother say to me that I shouldn't cry, and that it was all her fault. She held me on her lap, my face against the softness of her breasts as she rocked me gently.

"Don't you cry, honey," she whispered. "Everything will be all right soon. I promise. . . ."

Then someone shook my shoulder and I heard Ellen's voice say sharply, "It's six o'clock, Miss Adelia. Madame said I should wake you."

"Oh, thank you, Ellen," I managed to murmur. I rubbed my sleep-filled eyes and stretched under the warm feather comforter.

"Shall I lay out your clothing, Miss Adelia?"

"No, don't bother. But thank you."

"It's what I'm paid for, miss," she said with calm impudence. "Breakfast at seven. . . ."

She left the room and I slid out of bed, reaching quickly for my drawers. Then I put on the hateful corset, drawing the ribons as tightly as I could. The chemise and the red flannel petticoat followed, and then the two additional petticoats, which would give some fullness to my skirt.

I cinched the blue day-skirt over my hips, and then the matching bodice jacket with the tiny white buttons. It occurred to me that I didn't know when in the future I'd have any new dresses. I didn't even know if my Aunt Jewel intended to pay me anything for helping her with the letters. It reminded me that I knew nothing of my future status in this big house. Perhaps I'd be expected to dress in a servant's livery! I completed dressing, washed my face, and went down the corridor, past the framed portraits, down the long balcony above the Great Hall. The wall lamps had been lighted, and I could see well enough in the predawn gloom, but I wondered if I would be able to remember the way to the second-floor family dining room.

I made the circuit above the Great Hall, and I heard voices coming from the corridor down which Ellen had led me the night before, and I saw the yellow line beneath the door that I was sure would lead to the family dining room. I felt shy about going in, but I told myself not to be a foolish ninny, so I pushed open the door and stepped into the brightly lighted room.

First, I saw John's bearded face turned toward me from the head of the long table, his dark eyes staring at me, expressing not even recognition, it seemed to me. But I was wrong, for he rose to his feet and bowed slightly.

"Good morning, Cousin Adelia," he greeted me, his voice deep and heavy, almost a rumble.

"Good morning," I answered, aware of the faces turned toward me.

"Adelia," Aunt Jewel called from the end of the table nearest me. "Come, sit beside me—I have saved you a place." She gestured to a chair at her right.

I walked to her side, hesitating a moment as Aunt Jewel nodded to the woman who would be on my right.

"This is my daughter-in-law Melinda," Aunt Jewel said briefly. "She is the mother of John and Rex."

"Good morning," I said, smiling at the heavy woman whose cheeks and jowls sagged. I saw nothing of the Orne high cheekbones in her face, but then, they weren't in Rex's face either. Instead, Melinda's face was round and heavy with small eyes that seemed like apple seeds stuck in white dough. It passed through my mind that it was a wonder such a woman could bear two handsome men like John and Rex.

She simply said, "Hello," in a flaccid, indifferent voice and began to eat her cooked oatmeal again, ignoring me.

"You've met both John and Rex," Aunt Jewel went on, and I smiled at Rex, who had risen to his feet at her left, and then at John, who still stood at the head of the table.

**48**

"Please do sit down," I said, embarrassed by their having risen to greet me. "And good morning to you both."

Rex said nothing, and I saw less charm in his features in the light of the dining-room lamps than I'd seen the night before. John asked if I'd slept well as he seated himself.

"Yes, Cousin John," I murmured.

"And this is my son Walter," Aunt Jewel said, a dry curtness in her voice as she gestured at a man of perhaps sixty who leaned his narrow face forward and peered at me from his place next to Melinda at my right. His gray eyes had an emptiness that contrasted with the deep tan of his face—that is, to such of his face that I could see above the graying, untrimmed beard.

"Hello," he said in a voice just above a whisper. "Welcome to Orne Hall." It seemed to me his voice whined the words.

"And this is Reverend Homer Whitney and his wife, Clarissa, who are house guests at Orne Hall." Aunt Jewel's voice had a sharp cutting edge and I didn't find her smile, which she bent on the couple, very warm. "Homer and Clarissa, this is my grandniece Adelia, who has come to live with us, and to help me with my memoirs."

I was looking directly at the reverend's round, florid countenance, and it seemed to me that when Aunt Jewel mentioned her memoirs, a pained but speculative expression flit over the preacher's full, smooth-shaven cheeks. Then it was gone and his big voice boomed out a greeting.

"Good morning to you, Miss Adelia."

His wife merely nodded, peeking up at me as if she was afraid she might be struck with something. She bowed her head in a tiny, seated curtsy, and then drew her gray shawl more closely around her thin shoulders.

"Good morning," I responded, with my best smile.

"And this is my granddaughter Felice," Aunt Jewel went on in a level voice from which emotion seemed to have been completely removed. I looked at the very thin-faced woman who sat next to John at the far end of the table. I saw the Orne high cheekbones and the shadows beneath them. Though her eyes were of Orne black, her hair was a horrible drab brown and pulled severely back. She looked about John's age. She said nothing, however, simply leaned her thin face toward me, the better to see me, her thin lips a straight line.

"Hello," I said, trying to put some cheerful greeting in the word. She said nothing.

A young girl of perhaps fifteen or sixteen came out of the spiral staircase which I knew led down to the kitchen. I seated myself just as she put a bowl of cooked cereal before me, and then with her other hand poured coffee into my cup.

"Adelia, this is Georgia Pierce, our downstairs maid," Aunt Jewel said in a kindly voice. "Georgia, this is Miss Adelia, come to live with us."

The girl gave a quick curtsy in response to the introduction.

"Good morning, Georgia," I said, and I smiled to assure her, for she seemed so frightened, her pale blue eyes wide. I saw she had incredibily long lashes that swept her cheeks, and that she was indeed a handsome girl, with yellow hair flowing from under her maid's ruffled cap.

Paul Wiley came up from the stairs and took the coffeepot from Georgia. "That will be all," he said briefly. "You may go down to the kitchen."

Georgia fairly scuttled to the stairs and disappeared. Paul continued around the table, filling coffee cups.

I ate as one famished as the talk flowed around and over me, only Melinda and Felice rarely saying anything.

Aunt Jewel engaged Rex and the Reverend Whitney in a discussion of theology, with Rex asking impertinent questions which were unanswerable, not that the reverend gentleman didn't try with exasperated impatience.

"You, sir, are an unrepentant sinner," he said between bites of pork. He shook the fork at Rex. "Your soul is in extreme danger of eternal damnation."

"Oh, I'm not worried," Rex said with a smile. "After all, I'll be with friends—and relatives." He glanced down the table at his brother. "Won't I, brother John?"

"Won't you what?"

"Be with friends and relatives amongst the brimstones after I am dead and gone?"

50

"Friends, anyway," John answered briefly, and then he turned to his uncle Walter, saying something I couldn't hear.

Ellen and Georgia brought food and cleared plates under Paul Wiley's watchful eyes. I became aware that the darkness beyond the leaded windowpanes had given way to streaks of yellow from the rising sun just as Rex spoke directly to me.

"Adelia, this morning I will give you a conducted tour of the house and the estate. Is it all right, *Grand'mère?* Can you spare her?"

Obviously, anything that Rex wanted, Rex would get from his grandmother without question. "Of course, Rex," she said lightly. She turned to me. "Would you like that, Adelia?"

"I'd like it very much," I responded.

"It's chilly, so wear a cloak."

I thought of my shawl—and that I had no suitable cloak at all—and I must have betrayed my thoughts in my expression, for Aunt Jewel spoke to her daughter-in-law.

"Melinda, you have something suitable for Adelia. The girl brought little with her." Then she spoke directly to me. "Melinda was about your size before she got so fat," she said with a bite to the words.

But after breakfast was over, Melinda did disappear and returned with a scarcely worn jacket. It was no longer fashionable, but it was rich and comfortable and it did fit beautifully.

"Very lovely," Rex murmured, and escorted me down to the Great Hall and out the front door. We walked past the now dry fountain, and circled the mansion, Rex holding my elbow firmly in a pleasant grip that made my arm tingle with pleasure.

"It was built way back before the canal was dug," he said with a wave at the house. "You know Grandfather John bought it in France and had it brought over, piece by piece, stone by stone?"

"Yes, Aunt Jewel told me."

"It's horrible, isn't it?" Rex asked pleasantly. "That was way back before the quarrel between our grandfathers." He

51

laughed and gestured at the red-turreted house. "They believed that all the family would live here and be happy ever after," he added with a wry, sardonic humor in his voice. "It didn't last long."

"What happened?" I asked, for I was terribly curious. "Why did they quarrel?"

Rex looked at me in some surprise. "You don't know, Cousin Adelia?"

"No, I don't," I answered with some sharpness. "How could I? My grandparents were both dead before I was five."

Rex stopped and looked down at me as if to divine if I spoke truly, and then he said, "I'm not the one who's going to tell you, then."

"Why not?" I asked with some asperity. "I want to know!"

"Ask your Aunt Jewel, then," he said briefly, and took my arm again. "She's the one who should tell you."

"All right, I will!" I promised with some emphasis.

Rex said little as he led me out north away from Orne Hall, and then when we reached a bluff a few hundred feet from the house I saw spread out before me the wide expanse of the valley. At the bottom I saw the winding convolutions of what I knew must be the Erie Canal. I saw, too, several canal boats crawling slowly behind teams of mules, with tiny figures poling the barges away from the canal shores.

As we watched, the steam whistle of a train's locomotive echoed between the hills, and then I saw the black line of cars drawn by the smoke-belching engine. Compared to the speed of the barges, the train, with its passengers and freight, fairly flew.

"Oh, see the locomotive and railroad cars," I cried, and felt a trifle foolish as I pointed one finger at the snaking black line.

"I see it, all right," Rex said with a rather glum laugh. "That, dear cousin, is the abominable invention that is going to send us all to the poorhouse."

I glanced at him questioningly, though I thought I knew the answer from the breakfast conversation.

"It takes too long for barges—they can't compete with the train's speed," Rex explained. "And come December the canal will be frozen solid."

"Why does anybody use the barges, then?" I asked. I stood close to him in the cold morning air, shivering a little, liking the casual way he held my gloved hand.

"It's still cheaper," he explained. "But the railroad's rates are going down. And when they get low enough . . ."

He left the rest of the sentence unfinished.

"What will John do, then?" I asked. The vision of John's stubborn jawline and cold, dark eyes didn't fit the idea of a failure in anything. Rex smiled and spoke my thoughts.

"Oh, he'll think of something, no fear, Adelia. Nothing stops John Orne, not ever." His tone, despite its lightness, and the small laugh that followed, still carried a trace of bitterness, and I felt constrained to ask him why, but I did not, for who was I to ask personal questions?

"They were pirates, you know," Rex said suddenly. "They traded in human misery."

"Yes," I said, "I know. Aunt Jewel told me. But how did John and Joshua come to be here?" I gestured at the country so far away from the ocean.

"They'd made their ill-gotten fortunes. They wanted to buy respectability. But they couldn't resist a good thing." He gestured at the valley. "Millions of tons of materials have traveled the Erie Canal since it was completed fifty-one years ago—in 1825. It cost nearly ten million dollars to build its three hundred sixty-odd miles of waterways, locks, and bridges. God only knows how many immigrants traveled west, hunting for a promised land." He paused a moment before he went on. "And our grandfathers, like a couple of evil giants, straddled that strip of water you see down there, and made millions in rotten, corrupt ways; they should have been hung, rather than die in their beds! Nor has the plunder stopped. In the past ten years crooks have stolen nine million dollars from the canal."

Rex's voice had become filled with bitterness—enough so that I drew away from him. He turned back, immediately contrite. "Sorry, Adelia. That was long ago. We have to live now, don't we?"

53

"But—but John wouldn't . . ." I didn't finish the sentence.

Rex smiled grimly. "Not John," he said. "He's so honest that—well, he's not much beloved by the politicians in Albany. He's a thorn pricking them." He shrugged with a gesture of exasperation. "Come on, Adelia. I don't like heights!"

He turned us around so that we looked back at Orne Hall. Only a few trees dotted the estate that surrounded the big red-turreted building, and now they stood as separated sentinels, their uplifted branches bare of leaves. Even in the brightness of the morning sun, the bleakness of the landscape and the stark, unrelieved gray of the stone walls of the building, the high-pitched roofs and the scarlet turrets, stood in sullen anger, ready to repel invaders—or perhaps to repel me.

We began to walk back to the house, and neither of us spoke as we approached its rear. But as we passed through the gate and toward the west wing, Rex's hand tightened on mine.

"I hate it," he said almost savagely. "I've always hated it!"

"What do you mean?" I asked quickly, startled by the vehemence with which he spoke.

"That godforsaken imported castle!" he said harshly. "It should never have been brought to this country—it doesn't belong here."

"No," I said thoughtfully. "It really doesn't belong here, does it?"

An odd expression came onto his face. "What would you do with it, if it was yours to decide? Would you tear it down?"

"Would it burn?" I asked lightly.

"The inside would," he answered. "It'd make a lovely fire, now wouldn't it, Adelia?"

We walked up to the wide double doors at the end of the west wing, and I saw, as Rex opened the door, that it was a conservatory, filled with flowers and potted plants.

We went inside; a small fountain, now dry, stood at the

center of the large room; another statue of Diana perched on one foot at the fountain's center.

"I wouldn't want to burn the flowers, though," I murmured as I walked from plant to plant, touching lovely leaves, admiring blossoms.

"We'd move them out first," Rex agreed. "Are you ready to examine the inside of the place now?"

"Yes," I answered, for I was curious.

"We'll get rid of our wraps first," Rex commented.

We did as he suggested and then for an hour we walked from room to room, and I marveled at the size of the building and at the many rooms.

The Great Hall separated the two sections; the family's bedrooms and sitting rooms were in the west wing. Rex's bedroom and John's were on the first floor, as was John's office and the music room, where Rex showed off playing beautifully on the new piano he'd bought at the Centennial exposition held in Philadelphia that summer. To my untrained ear he seemed terribly talented.

Melinda's room was on the second floor, beside Aunt Jewel's bedroom. Rex's mother was in her room, lying stretched out on a chaise longue, a box of sugared candies beside her and a popular novel in her hands.

"Mother, may I show Adelia your room?" Rex asked politely. There was little warmth in his voice. It was a bright, cheerful room, however, except it seemed to me it was overcrowded with tables and chairs, and small trinkets scattered everywhere on every piece of furniture. I thought to myself that Melinda did seem to be quite the most unhappy person I'd yet met in Orne Hall.

I discovered, too, that next to my room was a large guest room, which shared my bath—but there was no one staying at the time.

"We used to have lots of guests years ago," Rex murmured. "But no more. . . ."

The salon which opened onto the Great Hall was filled with pieces of Empire furniture, all of them perfect and lovely, but the room had the feeling that no one lived there. The somber patterned settees seemed to be placed just so and had been there for years.

Rex led the way to a spiral staircase I'd not seen before. "Now we'll look at the dungeon, and we'll need a light," he said. He got a lamp and ultimately we did reach a cellar beneath the east wing. "There's none under the hall or the west wing," he explained. "Nobody comes down here—I haven't in years."

It *was* a gloomy room, with high ceilings. I saw that one wall was filled with racks of dust-covered wine bottles and kegs. I shivered at the dark, dank gloom. There were no windows, so I surmised the cellar must have been dug very deeply.

Rex stopped at one end of a large, single room. I saw his hand reach out to touch a big rusty padlock which was open but which held the clasp of a heavy wooden door. "This is where the pirates hid their gold," Rex said with mock seriousness. "The key's been long lost; anybody locked in there would never get out—not ever." He lifted the padlock and swung the door open. Several steps led down to a small round room.

"How horrible," I murmured. I didn't like it down there and I wanted to leave. "May we go now, Rex?"

"All right. All that's left is to look at the ancestors," he said lightly.

"Oh, I have some more ancestors?" I cried. "I'd love to see them."

"Then see them you will."

He led me to the balcony above the Great Hall. "We'll look at some of my ancestors first," he announced.

So we walked slowly the length of the gallery, and with a quick and light sarcastic tongue, Rex fully characterized each of the people whose portraits hung in heavy, dark frames at eye level.

"That one," he said as we stood before the portrait of an elderly gentleman whose painted piercing black eyes viewed us sternly; he sat bolt upright on the edge of a chair, his military chest puffed out, his white hair carefully groomed. "That one is an imposter," Rex asserted. "His picture came with the house and he's no relation—he's a fake, like all the Ornes, because they're fakes, too." He paused and added lightly, "He looks like he's been sucking a lemon for these many years."

I laughed, because what he said was true.

"Imagine kissing a mouth like that?" I asked, meaning it as a joke.

Rex turned me toward him, and before I had time to protest, he planted a light kiss on my lips and I nearly fainted. I pushed him away, of course, protesting, even as my heart pounded.

"Cousin Rex! How could you?"

"Easily," he said with a smile. "You suggested it, you know."

"I did not!" I protested. "Shame on you, taking advantage of me." But a smile quirked my lips in spite of my determination not to let it happen. "You may kiss your many young ladies, if you choose, but leave me alone."

He winked at me as if to say he certainly had kissed many young ladies and many times.

"You do have your young ladies, don't you?" I asked; an archness crept into my voice.

"Multitudes," he said amiably. "Come, we have lots of ancestors to look at. And cubbyholes to explore."

And so we did. We peered into closets, examined strange rooms, climbed into the tiny attics in each conical turret, and ultimately walked through Charity's kitchen, where she busily prepared noon dinner. She offered us steaming cups of coffee, which we accepted, and as we sat on the backless bench, our elbows on the scarred table. Rex and Charity sparred with each other, exercising good-humored wit, although it seemed to me there was more in the air than simple joking—almost as if they spoke to each other on two levels. The words, I could understand. The feelings, I could not. I studied my cousin as he told Charity she was a terrible cook. Were they truly joking?

At that moment the boy Harlan came into the kitchen from the door leading outside, his high cheekbones shiny and rosy as if he'd scrubbed them, his tow head all awry. He saw me and a smile lit up the young face that someday young ladies might swoon over. "Miss Adelia! We got a

57

baby up at the barn!" He turned to Rex. "Lady Blue foaled this morning!"

Harlan was so excited the words tumbled out, but finally he ran down and Rex asked what he was going to do now.

"Play pirates," Harlan answered promptly. "I'll be Captain Kidd."

Rex laughed and grabbed the boy by the shoulders. "Captain Kidd got hanged, Harlan. You don't want to hang, do you?"

"Aw, I'd just be playing," Harlan protested. He looked at me. "Will you play with me, Miss Adelia?"

"Who could I be?" I asked archly. "I don't think I would make a good pirate."

"You could be the princess I'm holding for ransom," Harlan answered firmly. "You was on a Spanish galleon, and I capture you, and I'm gonna hold you until the King of Spain pays a lot of money, only even then I wouldn't let you go."

Rex put his hand to Harlan's head and ruffled up his already unkempt hair. "Boy," he said with a laugh, "you have too much imagination." He put an arm over my shoulder protectively. "And you can't capture Adelia, Harlan. She belongs to me!"

Ellen came into the kitchen from the spiral stairwell, and I glanced up just in time to see the expression that came over her face at Rex's joking words, and at his placing his arm over my shoulder—an expression of spite and anger brought bright glints to her dark eyes.

"Madame sent me to tell you to come to her sitting room at once," she said sharply to me. "She says there's work to be done, if you're going to earn your keep!"

It was like a sudden splash of cold water thrown on me, though Rex still held me close. I struggled to free myself. "Your grandmother wants me," I said as firmly as I could.

"Very well," Rex said with apparent resignation, but I intercepted the glance he gave Ellen—and I saw her pale when she saw it, too. "However, I will go and face *Grand'mère* with you, to see she doesn't eat you up."

I thanked Charity for the coffee and rose from the bench. Rex rose, too, and as we left the kitchen I could

58

almost feel the weight of Ellen's angry eyes on my back. I couldn't help but wonder why she felt so great an animosity toward me, and then it occurred to me that it might be because of Rex's attention and of his arm over my shoulder. But I shrugged the thought away. Rex was only being kind to me; she had no reason to be jealous, if indeed she was.

However, the thought of Rex and Ellen—that there might be something between them—made me feel a foolish pain. I liked my cousin, and perhaps I might someday unwisely permit myself to fall in love with him. However, with my plainness I was doomed to spinsterhood; a handsome man like Rex would never fall in love with the likes of Adelia Dorsey—this I knew. But at the same time, from down deep inside of me, came my own jealousy; I'd trade places with Ellen in a minute, had I the chance.

We entered the Great Hall just as John strode in from the front entrance, a riding crop in his hand which he tapped in the other hand impatiently. He scowled even before he saw us, nor did his expression change when he did turn in our direction.

"Good morning," he said in his heavy, gruff voice. He directed his dark, brooding eyes on his brother. "Rex, I want to talk to you," he said abruptly in a voice of command. His manner was that of one who would never brook any kind of resistance. He was an imposing figure in his riding boots and breeches, his sheepskin-lined jacket fitting well his broad shoulders. In my foolish imagination I suddenly saw him as if he were on the bridge of a sailing ship over which flapped the infamous skull and crossbones. Was he a pirate, too, as were his grandfather and my grandfather? That is, if Rex was telling me the truth about our ancestors. . . .

"Dear John," Rex retorted calmly, "I am going with Adelia to *Grand'mère's* sitting room. Whatever it is which you have to say to me can wait, can it not, old boy?"

"Adelia can find her own way," John said sharply.

"However, I have no intention that she should," Rex retorted. He took my arm. "Come, Adelia," he murmured, and guided me to the wide staircase leading to the balcony.

"I *can* find my own way," I protested. "If your brother . . ."

"He can wait," Rex said firmly.

"Very well," John called from behind us. "Rex, don't be long. . . ."

My aunt Jewel sat in the settee before the fire as I'd seen her last evening, but now she wore a pearl-gray morning gown and a white paisley shawl which she'd drawn tightly over her shoulders. Her enormous dark eyes seemed cold and preoccupied as she looked up at us and she seemed older in the light of the morning sun.

"Oh, Aunt Jewel, I hope I didn't keep you waiting. . . ."

"Rex," Aunt Jewel said, breaking in on my words, "John must see you at once. Go to him!"

"Grandmamma, I just came to explain why we were gone so long . . ." Rex started to say.

"I know why you were gone so long," Aunt Jewel said shortly. "Now, go to your brother."

She turned to me, dismissing her grandson. I saw his face quickly flush, but he left the room as Aunt Jewel addressed me directly.

"The first thing that we must do for you is to find you something suitable to wear. That skirt and jacket offend me." Her nostrils twitched as if I might smell badly. "You're about Ellen's size—or Georgia's. Perhaps . . ." Her voice trailed off and with a feeling of dismay I discerned that she contemplated that I should wear the severe gown, cap and apron of a servant. Inwardly I forced myself to quietness, because though I was no servant, what choice did I have if this was my great-aunt's wish?

"No," she answered her own questions abruptly. "That won't do. Felice—she is too thin; you'd never be able to button one of her jackets, though you have a narrow waist. Perhaps something of Melinda's . . ."

She caught the expression on my face and laughed. "Not like she is now—she was very slender once—just about your shape. She had gowns she's kept from before the time she let her body get so fat." She said the words in a way that let me know she didn't like her daughter-in-law's grossness.

She seemed to become aware suddenly of the sharpness of her tone and she shook her head as if to admonish herself for it. "That woman," she muttered, and then glanced directly at me. "Melinda was beautiful once; could you believe that, seeing her now as she is—like a sow heavy with unborn piglets?"

It was hard to believe that those bloated cheeks could once have been so lovely, but I said nothing, waiting for whatever my great-aunt might wish for me.

"My son John should never have married her; she came from a village where her father ran a tavern; my son raised her above her station. And he died for it," she added quietly.

Suddenly she opened her mouth and again came that screech, "Ellen!"

The maid must have been right at the door, for she came in instantly. "Madame?" she said, and waited just inside the doorway.

"Take my niece to Melinda—tell my daughter-in-law to see if she has some stored clothing suitable for Adelia to wear," Aunt Jewel said crisply. Her glance shifted back to me. "You return as soon as you find something, and can change into it." Her large eyes flickered over me. "And then give that rag to Ellen to burn!"

I flushed, for though it wasn't fashionable, my blue skirt, with white apron overskirt and bodice jacket, was scarcely a rag! It angered me for her to call it one. "It isn't that bad . . ." I started to protest, but she cut me off curtly.

"It's horrible. Go with Ellen," she commanded, "and don't argue with me!" She turned away with a single quick gesture of dismissal.

"Yes, Aunt Jewel," I said, and I hated myself for being so weak and submissive. But I did follow Ellen through the doorway and out into the hallway.

Melinda's bedroom was next to Aunt Jewel's, so it was just a few steps to the woman's door. Ellen tapped on the door and I heard Melinda's voice telling us to come on in.

Though it was midmorning, Melinda's bed was still unmade, and her room was truly a mess. Dressed in an unbecoming dressing gown, she half sat and half lay on a velvet chaise longue, a novel held in her thick fingers, her light brown hair in full disarray, falling down over her fat cheeks so she seemed to be peering out at us from a cave. She looked up as we entered, her eyes glazed with absentmindedness, the corners of her full lips turned down petulantly.

"Madame says you are to find Miss Adelia something to wear—something you wore before you got fat." Ellen added the last words with frank insolence.

Melinda didn't seem to notice or to care. She heaved herself up into a sitting position. But I was quite wrong in thinking she hadn't noticed, for without any change in her round countenance, she addressed the servant sharply.

"Ellen, you speak to me once more in that tone and I will see that you are sent back to the Rochester whorehouse you came from. Now, get out of my room!" she finished inelegantly.

"Certainly," Ellen answered, her sullen lips stretching in what I suppose she considered a smile, "but, Miss Melinda, maybe you better think about it real hard, 'fore you do." With that she turned abruptly and disappeared, closing the door with a slam behind her.

Melinda said a foul word and then stared up at me morosely. "You poor, silly fool," she muttered. "If you'd had the sense to pound sand in a rathole, you'd never have come to this godforsaken place."

For some reason I felt an unexpected sympathy for the fat woman. She seemed so dreadfully unhappy. I knew she must be at least in her late fifties, but she seemed even older—and yet younger, too, at the same time, and somehow vulnerable.

"I—I had no choice," I answered. "There wasn't any other place for me to go."

"A bawdy house might have been better," Melinda muttered, again startling me with her coarse words. Of course I knew well enough what a bawdy house was.

For some reason, I laughed briefly and explained to Melinda why. "A man once told me that all I could do would be to scrub floors in a—a whorehouse. That I—I wouldn't be good for anything else."

She laughed hoarsely, her jowls swinging, and just as

quickly she stopped. "You don't look like that kind of gentlewoman now, do you?"

She heaved herself to her feet. "I guess I couldn't even scrub floors—I couldn't get up if I once went down on my knees." She took a deep breath and drew the robe about her tightly, her heavy breasts lifting and falling with the effort. "But I was beautiful once. Could you ever guess that, Adelia? That I had men who wanted me desperately." She glanced down at her prominent stomach and broad hips. "I had nice limbs. And look at me now. I am a great big fat cow!"

She didn't sound as if she was sorry for herself; her mouth quirked into a smile even as she spoke, and her blue eyes had a merry glint in them. "I eat all the time because what else is there to do in this awful place?"

"Why—why don't you leave, then?" I asked. I couldn't help thinking that I'd give anything to be as beautiful as she must have once been—and I'd never have permitted myself to get fat like that.

She turned her blue eyes on me, and for a moment they became vacant and empty, and then she suddenly answered my question with one of her own. "Why did you come?" she asked. "Because you didn't have any choice! Well, I didn't either. Where would I go? What would I do?" She made a gesture with one fat arm as if to stop the conversation, or at least to change the subject.

"We're about the same height; I have gowns that will fit you, but they won't be fashionable. I wore them with one of my crinolines, but they'll look all right without the wire frames. They're in the storage room."

She picked up a lamp and removed the chimney so she might touch a sulphur match to the wick. "We'll need a light," she explained, and led the way through the door into the dark corridor. She stopped at the doorway just opposite to the one to Aunt Jewel's sitting room, and pushed it open. It was dark, and the yellow rays of the lamp hardly reached the corners; I saw that the room had no windows.

Many garments hung on racks, protected by wrapping

paper from the dust—it seemed to me that there must be hundreds.

"I used to like clothes," Melinda explained with a wry smile, "before John Orne got himself killed in that silly duel." She began to fumble through the skirts. "Here, you hold the lamp," she commanded, and I took it from her. "He was my husband, you know. The duel was over me," she added with complacency in her voice.

She pulled out a skirt and held it up to the light, it was a day dress of cream alpaca, with spots of mauve and brown. "This will do to begin with," she muttered, and laid it over her arm. I liked it very much. Then she picked out several petticoats and a high-waisted bodice of white. Because it was so out of style, there was no overskirt.

"It's lovely," I murmured.

"It'll go well with your complexion," Melinda commented. "I think it will do until we can get to Waterloo to buy you some day gowns of your own. You'll need everything new. Here," she added, and thrust the armful of garments into my arms. "Let's go and you try them on."

Once back in Melinda's bedroom I felt some embarrassment undressing before her, but she showed impatience as I hesitated.

"Take it off," she commanded, and I began to unbutton the front jacket quickly.

I stepped out of the skirt and lifted off the bodice jacket; my petticoats followed. I reached for the red flannel petticoat that Melinda held out toward me, but she interrupted. "Wait a moment," she commanded, and looked at me, one fat finger held to her full lips. "That corset isn't . . . doesn't fit your body," she said sharply. "Your waist is slim and your bust is good, only that corset makes you look like a log rolled up in a carpet. Take it off!"

"It's all right," I protested. What difference did it make what kind of a corset I wore? I was still plain, wasn't I? And of course if I removed the corset, I'd be wearing only my bloomers, and the thought horrified me to be so nearly naked before a woman I hardly knew.

"Take it off," she repeated, and reached for me, her fat fingers starting to untie the lacing, and then she impatiently

64

withdrew it from my body. She stepped back, surveying me. "Those drawers are awful." She sighed. "You might as well start from the inside out. Take them off!"

She turned to the highboy chest and began to rummage, and after a moment's hesitation I stepped out of my drawers, because what difference could it make now? A sharp knock sounded on the door! I gave a little scream, but Melinda just called, "Go away! We're busy!"

Rex's voice answered. "Is Adelia with you?"

"She is. She's dressing, so go away."

"Can't I come in?" he asked plaintively, and I felt my whole body get hot.

"You may not!" Melinda answered. "Be a good boy, Rex, and go away!"

I heard his light laugh as he left, and I found I'd been holding my breath! I gave a deep gasp, and Melinda gave me a small smile.

"Here, put these on," she commanded, and handed me a pair of drawers and a very small-waisted corset.

I did so, and I felt my face flush with embarrassment and because of the way Melinda drew the lacings up so tightly that I could hardly breathe. The molded form of the corset pressed up my rather full breasts in a most unseemly way. A thought flit through my mind that my father would have died if he ever saw me thus, and then the sobering realization hit me again that he was already dead, and that he could never again force me to dress in such drab garments—and I relished the sight of my rounded bosom pressed up by the corset's tight form.

"Turn around," Melinda commanded, and, as I did so, I felt her draw the lacings still tighter.

"I can't breathe," I whispered.

"Who wants to breathe," Melinda asked, "if she's got a tiny waist like yours?" She turned me around as if I was a huge doll and stepped back to look at me from a greater distance. Her eyes no longer made me think of apple seeds in dough, for they were now alight with interest. "Adelia, we're going to make a new woman to replace the dowdy one who came in. That is what you and I are going to do."

"You can't give me a new face," I said tartly, "even if you can squeeze me into a new shape!"

"One thing at a time," Melinda muttered, her blue eyes critical as she surveyed me head to toe. "Put on the other petticoats—with that skirt you must wear four; it was made for a crinoline frame, you know."

I knew that back in the fifties ladies wore skirts over the wire crinoline frame, but that was years before—even before the bustle and apron overskirt became fashionable.

I did as she commanded, lifting the petticoats over my head and sliding them down until they were snug at my waist.

"We forgot the chemise!" Melinda said suddenly. She went to her chest of drawers and brought back a fine silk garment. "You'll have to tuck it under the petticoats," she muttered, and helped me do just that.

The bodice jacket was the last garment, and instead of having buttons it was laced tightly. Once the ribbon was tied in a little bow Melinda stepped back and surveyed me.

"Now," she murmured. "Your hair, it should be loose." She came to me, turned me around, and freed my hair from the pins so it fell in loose curls around my shoulders, soft and caressingly.

"Now, look at yourself," she commanded, and turned me to the full-length mirror.

Melinda was right, I was a different woman! Even my plain face seemed a little less plain, and the full skirt and the tight, body-fitting bodice gave me a figure I couldn't believe was my own. "It's lovely," I whispered, almost overcome. Never in my life had I dreamed that I might wear such garments—or that I might look like the young gentlewoman who stared back at me from the mirror.

"Shoes," Melinda said abruptly. She rummaged at the bottom of the wardrobe and came back with a pair of shiny patent-leather slippers. I sat down, the skirts billowing, and unbuttoned my own shoes and then slipped my feet into the ones she handed to me. They did fit, too, and as I slipped the buttonhook through the eyelets and shaped the round black buttons through, I knew they were quite the nicest slippers I ever dreamed of wearing.

"There," Melinda muttered as I rose to my feet, "you're a new woman—you're a lady!"

I was surprised to see that her blue eyes had misted with unshed tears. She brushed them away angrily. "I looked like you once," she murmured. "But after John died, I—I didn't care. . . ."

"You loved him very much," I said softly.

She stared at me, wide-eyed. "I hated him!" Melinda answered angrily. "I was sold to him, like a female slave! He bought me, he used me!"

Her tone and coarse words startled me; she was a woman of many contradictions. I blinked and waited as her mouth curved up in a vicious smile, her fat lips parting to show small, white teeth. Suddenly, I remembered that Aunt Jewel had said she'd been bought by her husband, too, and I wondered what kind of menfolk the Ornes must have been.

"But I got even with him! I paid him in full for what he did to me!"

I suppose my expression showed my astonishment, and my curiosity, too, because her expression closed down, and she shook her broad face slowly from side to side. "I will not tell you," she said, and gave a short burst of sardonic laughter. "You'll learn someday, but not from me! Not from me! Now go to your precious aunt Jewel. Let her see you." Her smile widened. "Go on now," she added, and gestured to the door. "Go and let my mother-in-law see you!"

She made the words harsh and unforgiving as she pushed me out of the room. I tried to thank her, but she just shook her head. "Go," she said again, and closed the door behind me. But I heard raucous laughter coming from her, muted by the heavy door.

I tapped on my great-aunt's door and I heard the light voice of Aunt Jewel bidding me enter.

I'd thought that Aunt Jewel would be pleased with the transformation, but I hardly expected the reaction I perceived as soon as I entered the room. She sat still, as she had when I'd left, on the settee before the fireplace. I saw her large eyes turned toward me, and then I saw her face flush and spots of red anger appear on her high cheek-bones. For a moment she was unable to speak, and then practically hissed. "That woman!" she whispered in fury. Her big eyes took on a hard glitter.

"What—what's wrong, Aunt Jewel?" I asked in a tone that faltered. "Don't—don't you like it?"

For a moment she just stared at me, and then she made a visible effort to control her obvious anger. I saw her breathe deeply, and gradually the glitter left her eyes, though the red spots remained on those prominent cheek-bones. "Of course I like it," she said softly. "It's just that that garment . . . never mind, Adelia. Yes, the dress fits you perfectly. She gave you a corset, too, did she not? You have a lovely, gentlewoman's body."

"Aunt Jewel, why are you angry with Melinda?"

"Never mind," my aunt answered. "Someday you'll know, I suppose, but there's no reason to tell you now."

"Is it the gown? Does it remind you of something?" I persisted, my curiosity getting the better of me.

"Yes, it reminds me of something that is no concern of yours," Aunt Jewel answered briefly. But then she went on and told me anyway. "She wore it the day my oldest son died—in a duel. We will talk no more about it, Adelia." She pointed to the secretary against the west wall. "Bring that cardboard box to me, Adelia," she commanded. "You may as well get started on earning your keep," she added.

I didn't know the meaning of the small, rather compla-cent smile which touched her thin lips but which touched the enormous dark eyes not at all.

"Yes, Aunt Jewel." I rose and went to the secretary and picked up the box, which was tied with a blue ribbon. I carried it back to my great-aunt, and placed it in her out-stretched hands.

She held it a moment, her eyes fixed on the carefully tied bow. It seemed to me that her small mouth turned up in a grim, sardonic smile.

"Adelia," she said softly, "there are letters in this box which some very important people would pay a fortune to read—or destroy. Maybe both." She glanced up at me out of those large eyes and I saw in them a hard glint. "People

68

all up and down the canal would kill to get some of them away from me. People as far away as Buffalo and Albany."

"Why?" I asked, feeling considerable curiosity, and some fear, too. After all, I had no liking for the idea that I might be killed by someone who sought to get the letters. However, I did assume she was exaggerating.

"You are too curious," Aunt Jewel said in a sharp tone of admonishment. Then she relented a little. "Adelia," she said, "people think that the Erie Canal has water between its seventy-foot-wide banks. It isn't water, niece, it is blood; the canal will run red forever!"

Perhaps my expression showed my astonishment, for Aunt Jewel gave a laugh that was more of a snort. "Your grandfather and my husband were brigands. But there were many others—and the letters in that box name them—and they know it. There are rich and eminently important families whose names will be well tarred when the letters are published—and they deserve it!"

Aunt Jewel went on to explain that a Boston publisher had come to Orne Hall and suggested that she write the memoirs. "I suspect they will make a considerable amount of money," she finished with a touch of pride in her voice. "Now, these letters must be each removed from its envelope, the date recorded, and the letters then filed in the order of the dates on which they had been written. Do you understand?"

I nodded that I did and she went on.

"You will file them in that file case beside the desk. But don't bother to read them. Not now." A sly smile touched her lips. "All right, Adelia, you can work on the davenport," she commanded as she pointed to the writing desk with the curved lid.

She handed me the box and I rose to carry it to the davenport. "Are these all of the letters, Aunt Jewel?" I asked.

She drew up her hands and shook her head violently. "Heavens, no, child! There are boxes and boxes of them! Now, it is time you started."

# Chapter V

That was the beginning of my life at Orne Hall. During all that remained of the morning I took letters from the box, removed them from their envelopes, and sorted them into neat piles according to the dates on which they had been written. I saw that many had no date other than one recorded in the spidery hand of my great-aunt. Many of the envelopes were yellowed with age and, according to the dates, written long before I was born—at a time when Aunt Jewel became the reluctant bride of John Orne I. Many of them must have been hand-carried and delivered in person, for the envelopes showed no evidence of having gone by post. A few letters carried return addresses of places in France with strange names. But I couldn't help noticing that a great share of the letters were addressed to John Orne, and not Jewel.

I had a great curiosity about the contents of the letters, but Aunt Jewel had taken up a needlepoint stretcher and watched me intermittently between stitches, so I didn't try to satisfy my interest. Anyway, I'd know soon enough, wouldn't I?

The same people gathered around the table in the family dining room for the noon dinner—except John.

"He's gone to Waterloo," Rex explained casually.

Everyone commented on the skirt and bodice which Melinda had loaned to me, and Aunt Jewel's daughter-in-law claimed full credit, just as if I hadn't even furnished the body! She made remarks which caused Aunt Jewel's small face to flush an angry red but which sounded innocuous enough to me. Still, I sensed again the antagonism between the two women, and since I sat between them, it enveloped me almost like a fog. Yet I was also well aware of the glimmer of interest in Rex's bold eyes, and as we left the table he possessively took my arm and escorted me back to Aunt Jewel's sitting room. I saw my aunt's eyes upon us and it seemed to me her expression was approving.

Later in the afternoon, at a time my shoulders were beginning to ache from bending so continuously to the letters, Rex strode into his grandmother's sitting room and asked me if I had ever ridden. I responded that I was hardly an experienced horsewoman, though of course I had been on a horse.

"Good," he said emphatically. "This afternoon we will ride," he added. "Won't we, *Grand'mère?*"

"I—I can't," I protested. "I—I haven't any riding garments. I could hardly ride in this skirt," I added, gesturing down at its fullness.

"Mother used to ride a lot, didn't she, *Grand'mère?*" Rex asked. "If that garment fits you—and it really does, you know—she'll have riding clothes, too."

"Oh, but the letters . . ."

Aunt Jewel said there was plenty of time for letters. "They have been in the box for generations," she said lightly. "Go with Rex—Melinda will see that you are properly dressed."

Who could fail to want to go riding with a man as handsome as Rex Orne, with his bold blue eyes and quick smile? Even though I reminded myself of my plainness, still, why not enjoy the pleasure of his company when I could? There would be plenty of other women who would seek his favors at other times.

Melinda did have clothing for me, and an hour later, seated demurely sidesaddle on a lovely gray mare, I cantered beside Rex as he followed the lane that led northward toward the bluffs. For a moment we hesitated, and I luxuriated in the view of the valley before me, with its winding Erie Canal as it reflected the blue of the sky and the white scurrying clouds. I thought then that it hardly looked blood red, but quiet and placid—and as leisurely-moving as the canal boats that moved so slowly.

We were lower than the hilltop level of Orne Hall, and

when I turned and looked back up the slope to the gray-stone building with the central hall and the two wings, it looked smaller and less important and forbidding.

"Remember," Rex said lightly, his gaze following mine, "someday we're going to burn it down!"

"It looks so much smaller from here," I protested. "At least, it doesn't appear important enough to burn."

"It's important enough," Rex murmured. "It deserves burning." He kneed his mount and moved down the path which followed the ledge of a bluff high above the valley and I urged the mare to follow. He swung around to point down at the valley. "At one time nearly every third barge was one which bore the Orne name," he said with some pride. "We carried grain, hides, all kinds of raw materials east to Albany, and then to New York City. And they carried back plows, machinery, bolts of cotton cloth—and years ago they carried thousands of immigrants going west in search of land."

It seemed like a long way down, but ultimately we reached the valley, and for a time rode beside the slow-moving waters of the canal. We passed barges drawn steadily by teams of patient mules. Often a lad of tender years would walk ahead of the teams, yanking impatiently on a lead rope; others followed the teams with whips which they cracked over the backs of the dogged creatures. The clumsy, often unpainted, blunt-nosed barges frequently had small, low shanty houses built on them. On some we could see women, their shirtwaist sleeves rolled up, working at washing clothes in zinc tubs or doing some other such household chore.

Some of the boats were completely covered, with many windows, but others were open, with tarpaulins covering the cargoes which were piled high.

"There used to be packets carrying a hundred or more passengers," Rex told me. "But they stopped using them when I was a boy about ten; there hasn't been a passenger packet on the canal since fifty-one." He smiled ruefully. "I had several trips in them. They were awful."

"I—I read about them," I confessed, "in a book by Dickens. He hated them, too."

"He did, indeed, and I don't blame him!" Rex said, nodding his head for emphasis. "They smelled terribly; they were so crowded." He pointed at a low bridge up ahead. "They are all that low, and there are hundreds of them; men and women had to duck every time the boat went under one or get swept into the canal!"

For an hour as we rode slowly along the towpath Rex regaled me with stories of the early years of the canal. "The towns grew up and lived off the canallers; they were wild, with crowds of loose women waiting at each tie-up point and lots of drinking." He shook his head at the idea, but his bold eyes laughed at me. "Many canal towns are still unsafe for a good woman alone," he said solemnly.

"Oh, dear," I murmured in mock dismay. "You are frightening me!"

"I will protect you," he promised. But then he talked again of the canal. "If it hadn't been for that seventy feet of water, the states and territories out west—Illinois, Michigan—would still be a wilderness." He gestured at the canal. "It brought the people that settled the west. Only now the locomotive's steam whistle is sounding its death knell."

Rex was so attentive, such a skillful conversationalist, I felt drawn to him. For the first time in my life I basked in the attentions of a fine gentleman. Of course, I knew that he was simply being nice to a plain cousin, but even that I appreciated. If I dreamed foolish dreams that someday handsome Rex would see me as more than just a distant relative, that was my concern, wasn't it?

As the shadows began to lengthen in the late afternoon, we turned back and made our slow way up the long, steep climb to the hilltop and Orne Hall. As we rode up to the stables, which were located just north of the hall, a grinning Toby and the boy named Aaron came out to meet us. As the lad reached for the bridle to steady the gray, I was aware of his bold and confident gaze. Rex dismounted and then lifted me to the ground with careless ease. He told Toby and Aaron to see that the mare and gelding had a good rubdown.

"Yes, Mr. Rex," Toby responded, with an obsequious dipping of his head.

That evening, when we gathered in the dining room for supper, I wore still another gown which Melinda had found in the storeroom and insisted that I put on. It had a bright red astrakhan-lined corselet quilted with white silk that I wore over the bodice of yellow and an overskirt of white fringed with red braid. It was a garment not so far out of fashion, for it had affixed to it a small bustle and a velvet sash of red.

"I am never going to wear them again," Melinda said, regret in her voice. "So why shouldn't you?"

My aunt and our house guests, the Reverend and Mrs. Whitney, had not arrived in the family dining room when John strode in. He ignored everyone, including me, but demanded of Rex an explanation of where he'd been that afternoon. "I told you that I wanted you to stay here," he said coldly.

"John," Rex reported lightly, though I saw hard glints in his bold blue eyes and a bit of color on his cheeks. "You don't need me or anybody else, and you know it! I took Cousin Adelia riding."

Only then did John deign to look at me. I saw him blink twice before he greeted me.

"My apologies for my rudeness," he said in his gruff, deep voice. "May I compliment you on your gown?"

"Thank you, John," I answered quietly, "but you should compliment your mother. It is her gown, which she kindly let me wear."

He nodded with a small smile. "You wear it well, Adelia," he said, and then turned to Rex, again obviously dismissing me from his mind. "We will talk after supper."

"As you will," Rex said carelessly.

At that moment Aunt Jewel entered the dining room, followed by a flushed and obviously angry Reverend Whitney—and he in turn was followed by his pallid wife, whose pasty face seemed frightened, and whose clasped hands trembled.

"Please, everyone, sit down," Aunt Jewel said at once. She turned to the minister. "You and your good wife, please take your regular places," she commanded. Her voice sounded sharp and unfriendly.

"Yes, Madame Orne," the Reverend Whitney said.

Rex held the chair for his grandmother at the end of the table, and we all sat down at the same time. The butler, Paul, his white hair neatly combed and wearing his usual dark livery, began to serve supper. The Reverend Whitney addressed John directly.

"You, sir! I appeal to you. Can you not persuade Madame Orne not to use those letters she has kept for these many years? Surely she can write memoirs that will—ah—titillate the readers without using any of the missives she read to me this afternoon. They will do an incalculable harm to innocent people."

The corners of John's lips lifted in a grim smile. "Sir," he answered, "I cannot persuade my grandmother to do anything—and I don't think anyone can either."

"Do you want scandal spread the length of the canal? Do you want dead people defamed when they cannot respond or defend themselves? Do you want simple people damned beyond repair in the eyes of their families—their neighbors?"

Rex broke in, his voice light but biting in tone. "You mean, sir, that those corrupt people who killed and robbed and pillaged the length of the canal should go free?"

Aunt Jewel broke in, her voice clear and sharp. "Reverend Whitney, you may be sure of one thing: I shall tell the truth!"

Rex's laugh was infectious, as if it were a great joke. "*Grand'mère*, that is precisely what the good reverend is deathly afraid that you will do."

"I just know that some very influential people asked me to intercede in their behalf."

"Such as Colonel Carter?" John asked grimly.

"Tell your influential people to go drown themselves in the canal," Aunt Jewel said lightly, though her high cheekbones were bright with color and glints of anger still shone in her large, dark eyes. "Now, no more talk. We will eat the food that Charity has prepared for us. . . ."

So for the next half hour there was little said as we consumed the excellent supper Charity had prepared and that Paul, with the help of Ellen and Georgia, served us. But when we had finished our dessert of bread pudding and thick country cream topped with brown sugar, John spoke directly to his mother, Melinda.

"Tomorrow morning, Mother," he said briefly but with a voice of authority which brooked no dispute, "you will go into Waterloo with Adelia, and you will purchase her suitable clothing." He quickly glanced at me. "I am sure Cousin Adelia would prefer her own clothing; that gown you are wearing is very attractive, but it is hopelessly out of fashion. There is a store, Job's Clothing, which has ready-to-wear female clothing of good quality."

"An excellent idea," Rex cried. He too glanced at me and added, "You will return a ravishing beauty."

"You are too kind," I said to Rex. "And hardly honest."

There was a brief lull in the conversation at the table, and then Felice, who'd scarcely said a word to me, spoke up, looking directly out of the dark eyes and thin face.

"Adelia," she said, bitterness in her voice, "men are never honest. Never, never!"

Aunt Jewel shook her head at her granddaughter. "But we have to have them, Felice," she said with a small smile. Then she turned to me. "Felice is bitter because a man jilted her," she said with calm cruelty. "Pay her no mind, Adelia."

"*Grand'mère,*" John said in a tone of rebuke, "you are being unkind."

Again a pause, broken by the reverend's clearing of his throat.

"John," Aunt Jewel said to her grandson at the opposite end of the table, "*I* will go with Adelia."

But John's voice brooked no interference. "No, *Grand'mère,* you will not," he said. Then his voice softened. "You are not well enough for a trip, and it may be cold."

Aunt Jewel's dark eyes flared wide open, and then, curiously subdued it seemed to me, as she lowered her glance, apparently contrite.

"Very well, John," she murmured.

These people of the Orne family seemed to me to be filled with inconsistencies. Why would Aunt Jewel be so quickly subdued by John's commands? It had seemed to me that she was indomitable, but suddenly she appeared almost to cower. I couldn't understand it. Still, I was aware that Melinda smiled at her mother-in-law in a way that was distinctly pleased.

"We will leave early and spend the entire day," Melinda said with some complacency, much as if she'd won a game.

"Rex, you will accompany Mother and Adelia," John said directly to his brother. Then he turned to address me. "We have a good carriage and a fine team. I think you will find it a pleasant trip."

Then, to Rex, he said, "Tomorrow I will meet with General Court and Martin Hespick."

John's voice seemed filled with a queer portent, as if the words should carry a special meaning, though Rex just nodded negligently and said nothing. But if the significance of the reference to the two gentlemen meant nothing to me, it was obvious it meant a great deal to all of the others, including, it seemed to me, the Reverend Whitney and his wife.

Nothing more was said, and after we'd eaten our dessert and drunk our coffee, Aunt Jewel said she was tired and now would go to her room. "I will go to bed early, I think," she said. She addressed me directly. "Adelia, I will see you in the morning before you leave." She cast a quick glance at Melinda on my right, but when she went on she again spoke to me. "You will need advice as to the type of garments that will be suitable for your future life in Orne Hall."

"Yes, Aunt Jewel," I murmured. "Shall I go with you to your apartment?"

"No, Ellen will take care of me," she said, and rose to her feet. Ellen came immediately to her side to assist her.

The gentlemen rose in concert and remained standing until the thin old lady had left the table, her arm tucked through Ellen's.

At the door she turned and spoke to the Reverend Whitney. "I hope you have a pleasant trip home. I am sorry that your time has been wasted. It is too bad your trip to Orne Hall has turned out to be fruitless."

"I am sorry, too, madame," the reverend gentleman responded. "My wife and I will leave at dawn's first light, for it is a long trip home."

"John, have Toby harness the reverend's team before dawn," Aunt Jewel said, uselessly, it seemed to me, because John would scarcely let a guest harness his own team. It seemed to me, too, that a hard glint appeared in John's eyes for a second, to be replaced by a note of merriment.

"Madame," the Reverend Whitney said to Aunt Jewel, "let me plead with you once more. I beg of you, do not use those letters! Only tragedy can come from your willfulness—tragedy that may touch you and yours as well as others whom you have no reason or excuse to harm."

"I will do as I please," Aunt Jewel said petulantly.

"Madame Orne, I promise you that you will forever regret . . ."

"Sir," John broke in from the head of the table, standing there imposingly tall and strong. "Do you threaten Madame Orne?" he asked in a harsh, angry voice. "If you do, you may not realize that you are treading on dangerous ground. We Ornes do not take threats idly."

I noticed that Rex, also, faced the minister, a dark scowl on his lips, his blue eyes hard and angry. I sensed that suddenly the two Orne brothers were on the same side of this quarrel—and for the first time since I'd met the two of them.

"I mean no threat," the Reverend Whitney weakly said. "I am a minister of God. . . ."

"Your cloth, sir," Rex said steadily, "will not save you."

"Please, good sirs, I meant no harm. . . ." The minister was obviously frightened and I observed he appeared to wish to be any other place than this.

"That is well," Rex said, this time lightly, except his voice still carried the vibrant quality which suggested a quick readiness to do battle for the Orne name. "As my brother has suggested, we Ornes do not take threats lightly. We suggest you return to your principals and inform them of the same fact."

But the Reverend Whitney was not a total coward. He stretched to his full, impressive height. "I beg of you to

**78**

recall that my principals, as you refer to them, are wealthy and powerful people who are not without influence in Albany. You may well regret . . ."

"I'll wager they have no influence with Governor Tilden," Rex broke in.

"I didn't say . . ."

John broke in coldly. "Your team will be ready at dawn. Cook will have a hot breakfast ready to sustain you on your journey. Perhaps your good wife and yourself would prefer to retire to your apartment now? We will see that a fire is laid in the hearth that you may be comfortable during the chill of the night." His tone was one of dismissal, and it acknowledged no resistance.

"Very well. Wife, we will leave."

His wife did rise, and followed him past Aunt Jewel and Ellen, who still stood at the door. "Good night, madame," the Reverend Whitney said to Aunt Jewel as he disappeared. His wife merely bobbed her head and scurried past.

Aunt Jewel shook a jeweled finger at me. "Remember, I wish to see you before you leave!"

"Yes, Aunt Jewel," I promised.

The two disappeared and John spoke directly to Rex. "Come into the hall. I wish to talk to you."

"Very well," Rex responded, and he winked at me knowingly.

Uncle Walter also left without a word to anyone, and Melinda told me again to be ready early. "Ellen will wake you," she promised. Then she, too, left, and only Felice and I were left at the big table. Paul and Georgia carried the last of the dishes and disappeared down the spiral staircase. Felice looked at me, and for some reason my heart went out to her, for she seemed on the verge of tears.

"He did jilt me, you know," she said in a voice that trembled. I saw her mouth twitch at the corner. "I loved him," she added.

"I'm sorry," I said. "Was it long ago?"

"I was twenty-two then. I'm thirty-two now," she said. She peered at me, her brows lowered a little, and I saw that her mouth pursed. "I was very pretty—even prettier than Melinda," she said.

Her black hair, drawn so tightly away from her temples, made her face seem overly thin, but then as I looked I realized that her features were good, very good, and were hurt primarily by her bitter expression. There was a similarity between her high cheekbones and those of John and his grandmother.

"I think you are very pretty now. Why do you draw your lovely hair back that way, so tightly?" I asked.

"I don't want to be pretty," she said abruptly. "Do you read books?"

"Of course," I answered.

"I read a lot. I have many novels. Perhaps you'd like to see them sometime. They are in the library, and in my room."

"I would love that," I assured her, "and thank you, Felice."

Then she said, not following her conversation at all, "I wish I could fall in love again. . . ."

I told her that she surely would, and I went to my own room, confident that now I wouldn't get lost because I was sure of my way. As I crossed the Great Hall on the balcony, I saw that John and Rex, down below, talked earnestly before the wide fireplace, and they seemed to be arguing with some heat. Rex saw me, however, and waved genially.

"Good night, Adelia," he called.

"Good night, Rex . . . and John," I responded, and walked on, my hand trailing the smooth, darkly stained railing, awed again at the size of the room I glanced down into again. At the wide stairs I paused, turning back to look up into the darkness of the height of the ceiling, which was but little touched by the seeming weakness of the kerosene lamps, and it seemed to me I could see dark figures that moved noiselessly though I knew them to be only shadows cast by the hearth fire. Yet the heavy weight of the darkness rested on my shoulders as if it were something real, something alive, something that menaced me.

Reluctantly, I walked on down the hallway, turned, and finally reached the door to my own room. I pushed it open, and quickly closed it behind me as if to shut out the darkness. Though it was still early for bedtime, the fire burned cheerfully in the hearth, and two lamps gave me a warmness that seemed to be welcoming.

For a time I read the latest novel by Mark Twain, entitled *The Gilded Age*, but my eyes soon tired, and finally I undressed and slipped into bed, my body caressed by the sheets and quilts over me.

I was just going to sleep when a fearful, though distant scream brought me bolt upright in my four-poster bed, my heart in my throat, the blankets falling away from my breasts.

A terrible fear, engendered by the agonized cry, held me in a cold grip so that for a moment I couldn't move!

# Chapter VI

The scream ended abruptly, as though the sound had been cut with a knife. The cry had been one filled with terror; who had screamed?

I reached for a robe and drew it over my bare shoulders, and turned up the wick on the bed lamp, so that the yellow rays illuminated the room. I thought I heard the sound of footsteps in the hallway outside my room. I picked up the lamp and tiptoed to the door. I opened it so I might see the length of the hall. There was no one there—but just at that moment a dark figure came into the hallway from the door to the guest room beside my own—the room Ellen had said was unoccupied. I gasped, and then I recognized that it was John who stood there, looking at me, the lamp's light reflecting in his dark eyes.

"Oh," I said, my voice trembling, "I heard a scream. . . ."

"It was nothing, Adelia. It is no concern of yours. Please return to your room and get some sleep." He actually smiled with his lips, though not with his eyes. "You'll be rising early for your drive to Waterloo."

I wanted to ask who had screamed, but his cold eyes intimidated me, and all I was able to say was "Yes, John."

He gently escorted me back into my room.

"Sleep well, cousin," he said quietly, and closed the door.

I was too frightened and nervous to sleep. For a time I sat in the Phyfe chair, trying to read. Finally, I gave up, and instead sat with the closed book on my lap, trying to think. This was only my second night in Orne Hall, yet it seemed as if I'd been there for a long, long time. I thought of the strange people who lived here, and of the tensions that seemed to arise from everywhere and to touch every living soul. I had the foolish idea that the sins of Joshua and John, the slavers of long ago, were truly being visited on the children of at least three generations. I realized that Rex had spent much time with me and he'd been charming, yet I felt I knew him so little—as if he was a chameleon who might change his colors at any time. But John—I'd spoken very few words with him, and he'd been so cold, treating me as if I barely existed, yet for some reason I could not fathom, it seemed to me that I knew John better than I knew Rex.

I lay back on my pillow and still tried to puzzle out my feelings, and I'd nearly drifted off to sleep when I heard sounds that I couldn't identify. I tiptoed to the bathroom— the sounds were coming from the guest room. And it was at the door of that room that I'd met John.

One of the voices was heavy—the other was more like the voice of a woman; she might be crying. I stood there, listening, until I knew that to eavesdrop was unforgivable. It was no affair of mine, anyway.

I returned to my bed, and held my fingers over my ears, and ultimately I went to sleep.

No light had yet penetrated the room when Ellen awakened me.

"Miss Adelia, it is six o'clock," she said insistently.

"Oh, Ellen," I said as I awakened. "Is it morning already?"

"Yes, Miss Adelia. Miss Melinda told me to tell you to wear again the gown you wore to supper. May I help you dress?"

For the first time I looked directly at her, and I saw that one of her dark eyes had been heavily blackened, and that there was a big bruise on a cheekbone.

"Ellen! What on earth happened to you?" I asked before I remembered the scream.

"I fell in the dark," Ellen answered briefly. "Miss Melinda said I was to help you get dressed," she added with a trace of stubbornness.

It occurred to me that perhaps I would need help with

that corset. "Very well," I said as I slid out from under the covers.

Everyone was at the table when I entered the dining room—except the Reverend Whitney and his pallid wife and Felice. I said good morning, and seated myself beside Aunt Jewel.

Immediately Georgia and Paul began to serve us.

"You are late, Adelia," Aunt Jewel said severely. "We breakfast precisely at seven."

"I'm sorry," I murmured, distressed that I'd brought on the rebuke.

Rex spoke up for me, quickly. "*Grand'mère*, don't be difficult," he said. "She was only a trifle late. . . ."

And there ensued an acrimonious debate between Rex and his grandmother about the virtue of promptness, but I felt neither meant the sharp words they interchanged.

Melinda had found for me a fur-lined cloak to keep me warm on the trip, and soon after breakfast we went out the front entrance to where Toby waited in the high seat of the handsome four-in-hand carriage harnessed to four spirited blacks which stamped impatiently in the cold dark of dawn.

Rex opened the door that his mother and I might enter, and then climbed in himself. Aaron, a shadowy figure, closed the door, and with a call to the team by Toby, we were off, snug and warm inside the cab.

"It's quite the nicest carriage I have been in," I told Rex and Melinda.

"Just pretentious show," Rex said negligently. "It's obsolete. We'd have done better going to Pykerie Junction and taking the morning train."

"I like this better," I told him, snuggling down beside Melinda.

"So do I," she agreed.

The journey was pleasant and Rex and his mother told me much lore of the Erie Canal, how the canallers and their women lived, almost like tribes of gypsies, about the hard drinkers and bawdy women; strange and sometimes hilarious stories of events of long ago.

"For every dollar spent on the canal," Rex said once,

"another dollar was stolen. Nothing was ever more corrupt than the building and maintaining of the Erie Canal. And," he added with a smile, "our respective grandfathers were the worst of the lot."

"I wish somebody would tell me why they fought," I said with pretended petulance. "Is it a secret?"

"Over a woman," Rex said. "What else is worth fighting over?" His grin teased me, but I had to be satisfied with his answer.

It was a lovely day, and the Ornes cared little about what things cost. The day was spent trying on one garment after another. Melinda chose for me day dresses, riding habits, walking dresses, dinner gowns that I couldn't imagine myself wearing, a dozen corsets, bustles, stockings . . .

She shamed me, too, by telling me that Ellen had informed her that I wore nothing to bed. "Today fine ladies sleep in nightgowns," she explained firmly. "It isn't decent to sleep without anything on."

I'd heard of the rich people sleeping in a garment called a nightgown, but I'd never had one—now Melinda saw to it that I would have six!

Of course Rex went on about his own affairs, though he met us at dinner in the Maryland Hotel's dining room at twelve o'clock. And that the Ornes were important in Waterloo was very evident, for the waiters gave us every attention. We dined on trout and roast beef, both of which were delicious—and of course Rex selected a fine dry wine from the long wine list.

"What have you been doing?" I asked Rex with some impudence.

"He's been gambling," Melinda said with a short laugh. "It's in his blood. He never wins."

Rex smiled at me and took out a wallet; from it he removed a sheaf of money bills. "Mother, take this and buy yourself something," he said with one eyebrow cocking, his blue eyes dancing with his triumph.

"So you did," Melinda said. "Did you cheat?"

"An Orne cheat? Never!"

"Who better!" Melinda turned to me. "All the Orne men

cheat," she said. "Particularly with women. Watch out for them."

It was good-natured banter, but I thought I saw a glint in Rex's eyes which indicated he disliked what his mother had said.

As we finished our dessert, which consisted of apple pie and whipped cream, Rex announced that we were going visiting in the late afternoon. "There are Ornes you've never heard of. My uncle, Horace Orne—he's a doctor—and his wife. They have a son—my first cousin, Robert, who's a lawyer." He glanced at his mother. "What does that make Robert to Adelia?" he asked.

"Third cousin, I guess. Or fourth—I don't know."

We did meet Dr. Horace Orne, a hearty, bluff type of a man, and his lovely wife, Rose. We had tea with them and they treated me very nicely. As we left, Dr. Orne admonished me to stay well. "I don't want you for a patient," he said, and I promised I'd do my best.

We started home, knowing that we would arrive late, and I found myself nodding, my head resting on Melinda's shoulder. I was aware of the boxes and boxes of lovely garments that were safely tied in the carriage boot. All of the earlier fears I'd had at Orne Hall had disappeared. I felt happier than I'd felt in a long time as I dozed. Once I was aware that Rex's hands were gently and carefully tucking the lap robe more closely about me and I liked the touch.

Once back at Orne Hall and out of our cloaks, we went to the kitchen, where Charity got us a night supper. Somehow we felt so carefree—we joked and laughed, and Rex drank a glass of ale.

Charity and the girl I knew to be called Holly served us. Again I was interested in the round face of the girl, and the strangely empty eyes, though she served us well enough.

Then Melinda and I went to the other wing and up the wide stairs. In the hall, I, on a quick impulse, kissed Melinda's cheek.

"Thank you," I whispered.

"Go to bed—and wear a nightgown," she answered, and gave me a little push.

The boxes had all been brought to my room and carefully stacked. I'd no sooner closed the door than Ellen tapped and entered when I bid her to.

"Can I help you undress, Miss Adelia?" she asked. Her voice seemed small, not as strident as it had been, and it seemed to me that she could well have been crying.

"I'd like to have you help me," I said in a kindly tone. "You can help me put things away."

She did so, and as we opened the boxes, she made many comments of pleasure at the softness and the richness of the goods and the smart fashions in which they were sewed. Somehow a little warmth entered into our conversation; though she was older than I by a few years, we seemed more like two girls, and our conversation became punctuated with giggles and light laughter.

Then, when all was put away, and she helped me unlace my corset, she said suddenly, "I wish I might have nice things like these—but I never will."

Her voice had a plaintive note that tugged at my heartstrings. "Someday you may," I answered. "Why, only a few days ago I had nothing and now"—I made a gesture at the things we'd put away—"now I have all this."

She said nothing. I couldn't see her face, for she was behind me, but suddenly I remembered the black eye and the bruised cheek. "Ellen," I said suddenly, "I heard someone scream last night. Was it you? Did someone strike you?"

I turned that I might face her and I was surprised to see tears forming in her eyes even at the time that her mouth was turning down. "I fell," she said stubbornly.

"Did you scream?" I asked, and she nodded.

"I was afraid," she said.

But the words lacked the ring of truth. As I looked at her, she failed to look me in the eye, instead turning her head away so that I saw her face only in profile. I was struck again that she was a very pretty girl, and that the dark eyes and hair were in vivid contrast to the lightness of her skin.

"Ellen," I said impulsively, "you're such a pretty woman. Someday you will have nice things, too."

Her expression changed and the warmth we'd felt before

was gone. Her lips curled and she wiped her eyes with the back of her hand. "You are a fool," she practically hissed. "You don't know anything about the Ornes! You don't deserve those dresses—they should have been mine!"

The change was so quick and so startling that I took a step backward, momentarily frightened at the pure vindictiveness of her words and her tone of voice, so that I nearly fell.

"I know I don't deserve them," I agreed when I caught my balance. "But I don't know that you do, either." My mind began to work, tugging at the meaning of her words. "Or do you? Tell me, Ellen, why do you think you should have them?"

"I won't tell you," she said sullenly, and again her mood changed so quickly I was unable to follow her thoughts. Suddenly she smiled weakly. "I didn't mean anything, only I—I'm jealous, I think."

This I could understand, so I nodded. "Thank you for helping me, Ellen. You may go now. I am going to get into bed."

She hesitated and then said good night. I watched her go out the door, and then I removed the corset and the drawers. I slipped one of the new nightgowns over my head, and turned down the wick. In a few minutes I was dreamlessly asleep.

At six Ellen awakened me and laid a fire in the grate. At seven I joined the family at breakfast, and Melinda and I told of our experiences in Waterloo. After breakfast Aunt Jewel insisted on seeing every garment that we had purchased, and that I dress in some of them for her critical eye. Some she liked very much, and others she disapproved of, but in the end she very graciously told Melinda that she'd done well.

"You turned a crow into a peacock," she said, and I felt a touch of anger mixed with hurt, for what girl likes to be called a crow?

It was midmorning before I returned to the task of sorting the letters. Aunt Jewel took me to the storage room, where we selected more boxes for me to work on. But when I began the second box Aunt Jewel told me that I should read the letters as I removed them from the envelopes. "Pin the pages of each letter together so none will become lost."

Most of the letters were addressed to John Orne, and I began slowly to understand why the Reverend Whitney's principals, whoever they might be, were upset, for the pattern of the letters made it clear that John Orne had been involved in much corruption related to the building of the Erie Canal and the letters revealed the names of many corrupted. The letters began to read like a novel—a very bad novel with a villain instead of a hero.

Aunt Jewel was at times capricious, difficult to get along with, and at other times tender and gentle—and affectionate. The days went by so quickly. There were times when the menfolk were both gone; there were other times when Rex, with seeming abrupt impulse, sought me out to ride with him, and Aunt Jewel always appeared delighted.

Although Rex was delightful to be with, his brother John remained the same distant, reserved, and seemingly harsh person he had been on the day of my arrival at Orne Hall. Always his words carried the authority of the master of the Hall, and it seemed to me he gave of himself to no one, but one afternoon while Aunt Jewel rested, about two weeks after my arrival at Orne Hall, I happened to take a walk, for it was a lovely day, unseasonably warm. Properly accoutered with a warm jacket and shawl, I set out past the stable to walk to the ledge that overhung the valley. But at the corner of the stable I heard voices. I recognized the childish treble of Harlan immediately, but it took a moment for me to identify the deep voice of John. I had no intention of eavesdropping, but I did hesitate a moment when I heard Harlan's delighted laughter as he cried out that he'd won!

"So you did, so you did," John's deep rumble agreed with a chuckle. "Now it's my turn."

His voice sounded utterly different from the cold commanding tones he usually used, and when I turned the corner I discovered that John and Harlan were down on their knees and that they were playing mumblety-peg with a jackknife, facing each other in deep concentration as John prepared to throw the blade.

He did so, and the knife failed to stick into the ground.

"Shucks," John muttered, much as a boy might. "Let's see if you can do better!"

Then they both saw me and Harlan's face lit up with his recognition in an expression of delight; but John's face became an immobile mask, the only face he'd ever let me see.

"Good afternoon," I said a little primly. "Don't let me interrupt your game. I was just going for a walk."

"Can you play mumblety-peg?" Harlan asked eagerly.

"I used to, when I was a little girl," I answered with a smile at his happy face. He glanced at John and I couldn't help observing the adoration his eager young face reflected. I saw that Harlan truly loved the big man.

"You play a game with us," Harlan begged, getting to his feet. He came over and tugged at my arm. "Please!"

Some impulse led me to permit myself to be drawn toward John.

"Are you any good at it?" John asked soberly, and there was just a hint of laughter in his dark eyes, contradicting the sternness.

"I was pretty good," I confessed, "when I was Harlan's age. Perhaps my hand has lost its cunning."

"I bet I can beat you," John asserted suddenly. His face still remained set, but the expression in his eyes still contained restrained laughter.

"You're on," I responded. "What will the stakes be?"

"That if you lose, you go riding with me," John said positively.

I was startled that he would want to go riding. I'd never seen any hint that he ever did anything for the pleasure of its doing.

"And if you lose?" I asked, and some archness crept into my voice as I lifted one eyebrow at him quizzically.

"Then I go riding with you," he said promptly.

"Can I go, too?" Harlan asked eagerly.

"Of course," John said, and his deep voice expressed affection, as did his big hand, with which he ruffled up Harlan's tow head of hair.

"Your turn first," Harlan said to me, and handed me the big blade.

We played for several minutes, our banter on the level of Harlan's eight years, and I was astonished at the way John fell in with Harlan's and my chatter! His stern expression gradually eased.

I lost, of course—but so did John. Then Harlan announced we two would have to ride with *him!* "'Cause I won!"

John's call brought both Toby and Aaron on the run. "Saddle up the mares and the gelding," he commanded in his usual tone, which brooked no hesitation.

"At once, Mr. John," Toby responded, bobbing his head and reddened nose obsequiously. But I saw that Aaron's glance at me was overbold and calculating—and so did John, for I saw flecks of anger appear in his eyes as they widened dangerously. But he said nothing as Aaron turned away.

We rode down the slope toward the ledge and then turned to follow the path leading east, through a grove of oaks whose winter-brown leaves still clung to the heavy twigs.

Harlan wanted to race, and he kneed his mount into a gallop; but John and I followed a more sedate pace.

"How is the work with *Grand'mère* going?" John asked politely.

"Well, and interesting," I responded. "Your grandfather—he was really a buccaneer, wasn't he?"

John smiled and nodded. "Of course, he tried later to buy respectability," he said. "Before he died he became a stained pillar of society of the whole area from Buffalo to Albany." He laughed shortly. "He even tried to buy immortality; in his will he wrote that no one but one of his direct blood descendants could ever inherit. When my grandmother dies, Uncle Walter, Uncle Horace, Rex, and I will be the heirs."

It seemed to me a little strange that John should tell me this; though he spoke casually, it seemed to me I could detect beneath the casual demeanor a purposefulness. "You didn't mention Felice," I observed.

"Felice was adopted," John explained. "She is the granddaughter of Grandmother's sister; she was brought from France when she was just a small child. My mother and father adopted her legally, but she can't inherit because she's not of the family blood."

Suddenly he changed the subject. "Are you happy at Orne Hall?" he asked.

"Yes," I answered, "though I guess I don't like the Hall itself. I like my room, but the Great Hall is so gloomy."

"I don't like it either," John murmured. "Neither Rex nor I have any affection for it."

"Why do you stay, then?" I asked.

John shrugged. "*Grand'mère* would never leave it, even though she hates it, too."

I was looking down the slope to where Harlan raced the mare and I said, "His mother must have been very beautiful—and he is going to be an uncommonly handsome man."

"Yes, she was beautiful," John said, and I detected a softness in his heavy voice. He sat the big gelding erect and strong, but his face showed a pensiveness. "She was a headstrong, lovable, beautiful girl, and then, woman."

"And she just disappeared? Just like that?"

"Just like that," he answered. "One morning she was gone; nor did she take anything with her—not even clothing."

"She didn't pack a bag? She just walked out the door?"

"Someone must have been waiting for her," John said. "Her lover, Harlan's father, perhaps."

"Why hasn't he come forward and claimed his son? Wouldn't a gentleman have done that?"

"Perhaps he wasn't a gentleman," John said grimly. "Perhaps she ran away to *escape* Harlan's father."

"But no one has seen her since?"

"She's been gone seven years; I passed the word up and down the canal, but no one ever said he'd seen her; of course, she might have taken a train, but no conductor said she'd got aboard at Pykerie Junction." He shook his head. "She disappeared completely, and Charity and Paul undertook to raise the boy." He glanced at Harlan ahead on the path. "When he's old enough I'll take him into the business. . . ."

He fell silent and I watched his face furtively; it seemed to me that his way of telling the story sounded false, though I couldn't put my finger on why. And anyway, why should he lie to me? In any event, I tucked the idea away in my memory that John Orne III knew more about the disappearance of Alice than he'd expressed to me. For one thing, Orne Hall was too distant from other dwellings for a farmhand to make the surreptitious trip to see Alice very often without discovery. And that almost certainly meant that the father of Harlan must be one who had stayed at Orne Hall, at least for a period of time.

I nearly gasped aloud when it suddenly occurred to me that John could have been Alice's lover. Or Rex! If it was John, it would well explain my intuitive feeling that he lied as he talked to me.

"I must return," I said suddenly. "Aunt Jewel will have awakened by now, and she may be cross with me!"

"I'll tell her I abducted you," John said grimly, though the grimness was belied by the hint of laughter in his dark eyes. He raised his voice to a shout. "Harlan! We're riding back. Come along!"

But Aunt Jewel still napped and John had no reason to defend me. And as I worked the afternoon hours away, sorting and filing the letters, I thought of John and how different he'd been with the boy. He's got a soft side after all, I told myself, and I discovered I was liking him more than I'd thought possible. Certainly he wasn't a gay companion like his brother Rex, but I could tell that he was truly fond of Harlan.

Often Orne Hall had guests who frequently would stay for several days. When that happened Aunt Jewel's sitting room would become a salon for conversation and laughter. Norris Peters and his wife spent three days at Orne Hall; Mr. Peters, who was a selectman, and Aunt Jewel had many a sharp interchange on the politics of the day. Mrs. Peters, a homely, roly-poly type of a woman, said little, but would work her needlepoint continuously. On those days I tried to work, and many times the guests would quiz me, to seek the contents of the letters that I read and sorted. But I laughed at them and told them nothing.

As the day of Thanksgiving neared, Aunt Jewel decided to have a ball, and to ask important people from up and down the canal. For days the preparations were furious, for there were many things to be done. Aunt Jewel began to lean on me heavily to see that her orders were carried out. Invitations had to be sent, new gowns for Felice, Aunt Jewel, and myself, arrangements for food and drink—oh, there were enough tasks to keep me hurrying.

A number of the guests would be staying overnight, of course, since they would be coming from a distance, so the guest rooms had be be aired and prepared for occupancy.

John himself drove Felice, Aunt Jewel, and me to Waterloo, where we sought suitable formal gowns for the great occasion. But Melinda refused to buy a new gown. "I will still be fat," she complained, "so what's the use?" Aunt Jewel selected for me a beautiful gown of blue and white —with a form-fitting bodice jacket that fit my body beautifully. Her own selection was in the highest fashion, and, as she preened in it, she seemed a perfectly beautiful doll. But Felice's unhappy expression made each dress she tried on seem wrong for her, and in the end she selected a brown silk that none of us liked very well.

"Well, Felice, you are the one who must wear it," Aunt Jewel said.

When the grand night came, Rex escorted the daughter of the Waterloo mayor, Jeannette Topley, and I felt a twinge of jealousy, for she was very beautiful and an accomplished dancer.

As for me, I had some nice compliments on my dress, but no one but Harlan said I was even a little pretty. "I like you best," he said, and I hugged him for it.

The servants, Ellen and Georgia, wore new servant's dresses, but I saw that Ellen's expression betrayed the envy that I knew she felt. She wished that she was a guest, not a servant serving others, and the thought occurred to me that she was so much more beautiful than I that it was I who should be the servant.

But the music was intoxicating, as was the wine, and when Rex invited me to dance with him, I was delighted. The manly scent of his cologne and the nearness of him were more warming to me than the small glass of port that I'd sipped. He was tall, but so graceful; his blue eyes, which crinkled at the corners as he smiled, were enough to make my heart thud against my ribs.

"You dance very well, Cousin Adelia," he murmured.

"Because I am dancing with such a fine gentleman," I said archly.

And he did cut a figure of a fine gentleman with his formal evening dress coat of black superfine and waistcoat with wide satin lapels, contrasting so with his light hair and bold blue eyes. But it was the expression in his eyes and the smile on his lips that pleased me most, for he seemed to be so enjoying himself. But still I, as always, held myself somewhat aloof, for I knew he danced with me from a sense of proper duty, and he would soon return to his lady-love, the mayor's daughter. I still clung with inward strength to the determination never to be involved with any man.

"I think," Rex said as we danced, "that you have a hard rock for a heart. Won't you please smile?"

"Of course," I said coolly, and I did. "Is that satisfactory, Cousin Rex?"

"Your heart wasn't in it," he responded.

But when the dance was over and we parted, he returned to the mayor's daughter. I saw them talking and laughing, and later I saw them disappear into the conservatory.

That night, when the house was quiet and all were supposed to be in bed, I heard sounds from the guest room— sounds of giggles and laughter, lightly muffled by the partitions—and I felt hurt, for no one sought me out and no man ever would.

That night I slept badly, and my dreams were peopled with beautiful men who ignored me as if they could see through me. I awakened, and I realized that each of those beautiful men was Rex.

You're falling in love with him! I told myself angrily.

You are being foolish. But another part of my mind said plaintively: But distant cousins may marry!

In spite of myself, tears filled my eyes; in a way it seemed it would have been better never to have come to Orne Hall, never to have known Rex at all. My girlish attraction to him was foolish—and in the night I admitted to myself I was becoming infatuated. And I became even more determined never to let anyone know—and to drive the foolish feelings right out of my heart.

That is why, when the gay days and nights were over, I maintained a cool and dispassionate exterior when chance brought Rex to me. Nor did I accept any more of his invitations to ride, begging that the duties to Aunt Jewel's memoirs were too important.

Only toward Harlan did I betray my affection, and at my suggestion he began to spend the time with me, learning his numbers and letters. He was a quick pupil, and there were times when I watched him I saw in his eager face an expression that seemed vaguely familiar. Then it was gone, and though I puzzled my mind with it for a while, I became determined to forget the idea.

Still, it did return to puzzle me, and suddenly one day at supper I saw Rex turn his head so that I saw it in profile, and it struck me that it was the profile of Harlan's youthful nose, mouth, and brow. It came almost as a sledgehammer blow and I felt as if I'd been struck in the middle; Rex was Harlan's father! My mind told me that it was foolish—others would have observed the likeness if it was there. I had to be wrong—but my womanly intuition refused to agree.

Rex turned to glance at me casually as I looked at him, and I saw a quizzical expression crinkle up the corners of his blue eyes. "Adelia, this is Rex. You know me, don't you?"

"Yes, Rex, I know you," I responded, and perhaps I put more meaning into my words than I intended, for a redness suffused my cheeks, though he laughed.

"*Touché*, Adelia," he said gaily.

Aunt Jewel's glance moved from me to Rex and back again, and in her expression I saw a hint of doubt and speculation. But she said nothing except to tell me to eat my supper.

Two days later Rex accosted me in the gallery as I walked to breakfast.

"Adelia," he said, taking my arm and holding me from going further, "you have been acting as if you hated me. What have I done? You won't ride with me, or talk with me."

"I have other things that are better than that to do," I responded. "Please let go my arm, Rex. It is breakfast time and you know your grandmother dislikes us to be late."

"Not unless you tell me why you are so cold and distant." He responded as if he truly meant it.

I don't know why I spoke as I did, or where I got the courage, but my tongue and lips betrayed me, for I asked the question that had been troubling me.

"Are you Harlan's father?"

He stared at me, his blue eyes becoming cold and wide, nor did his lips curve in a smile.

"What has made you ask that question?"

"There are times when—when he looks like you," I faltered, wishing I'd not spoken, for it was none of my business.

"So that is what's bothered you? Why you have been so cold." Now Rex did smile. "Cousin, you have an evil imagination. Harlan is not my son! Nor could he be." He continued to hold my arm. "Now, do you believe me?"

His expression warmed as he looked down at me. "Adelia," he said softly, "I do want you to think well of me." No longer did I see cold fury in his eyes. "It is terribly important that you do."

A feeling of thankfulness swept over me, for it wasn't true! I'd not realized the emotions which had become bottled up within my bosom. I gave a quick, deep breath. "Yes, I believe you, Rex," I murmured. "Forgive me for thinking . . ."

"You're forgiven," he said lightly. "Providing you will ride with me this morning."

"Oh, I must work on the letters. . . ."

"No! I will tell *Grand'mère* that you need fresh air. And we will ride."

At breakfast he did just that, and his grandmother granted permission as she gave me a coy glance. "Of course, Rex. That is, if Adelia wants to ride with you."

What could I say but that I would be delighted.

For two hours we rode, and Rex was charming, gay, and attentive. He told me more of the lore of the canal, which fascinated me—and stories about his grandfather which astonished me.

We stopped and dismounted for a time under a grove of pines to let the horses rest a moment, and then as we walked on the pine-laden forest floor, he held my arm. My foot caught a root and I stumbled, almost falling forward, but his arm holding mine swung me toward him and brought me close. I looked up into his bold blue eyes and before I could divine his intention, he lowered his lips to mine, kissing me in a way I'd never dreamed. A feeling like fire swept through me, but I pushed him away.

"Why did you do that?" I asked, almost close to tears. "Why did you spoil everything? It has been such a lovely day."

He was instantly contrite. "I didn't mean to, but all at once, you were in my arms, and it—well, it just happened."

I pushed out of his arms and turned back to the horses. "I must go back to the Hall," I said primly, aware that my face must be crimson, and that my heart pounded far too fast.

"No, Adelia," Rex said, and caught my arm. "Not until you say you forgive me."

"You promise you won't kiss me again?"

"No, I won't promise you that. But I promise I won't kiss you against your will."

"Then you will never kiss me again, and I forgive you," I said with a light laugh, my anger dissipating quickly. He was so contrite, and in my secret heart I knew I'd wanted him to kiss me, so why should I not forgive him?

Riding back to the Hall, he asked me how my letter sorting and reading was going.

"Slowly. Aunt Jewel is going to start writing the memoirs next week, and I shall be using the type-writer."

"Have you learned anything about your grandfather and mine?" he asked.

"Nothing except that John must have hated Joshua very, very much." I glanced at him. "I know they fought over a woman, but there's never been a mention in the letters. Do you know who they fought over? Was it Aunt Jewel?"

Rex laughed with boisterous glee. *"Grand'mère* taking up with a weakling like Joshua? Never! If she ever had a lover, it would be a strong man, not a puking coward!"

I bristled at this description of my own grandfather. "But Aunt Jewel had hated her husband," I said. "She told me that."

"Most people did," Rex agreed. "He wasn't the kind of a man that people loved."

We returned to the hall, and later in the day I heard him playing the piano beautifully in the music room. I crept down to sit outside the door and listen awhile. He never knew that I listened, and later when I went to bed it was with the tingle of Rex's kiss on my lips.

The next morning I awoke with a start, and I discovered that the tall clock's face read six-fifteen. Ellen had not yet awakened me. I rose and dressed quickly, and when I left my room I met John in the hall just at Aunt Jewel's door, his hand on the knob.

"Ellen is dead," he said without preface. "She threw herself out of the window of her room."

"Oh, John," I whispered. "How terrible!"

"I must tell Grandmamma," he went on.

I didn't know how my great-aunt would take the terrible news, but her large, dark eyes betrayed no emotion. "Those who live by the sword, die by the sword," she murmured.

"Nonsense," John said sharply. "The girl is dead. Speak no ill of her now."

"No, I shan't," Aunt Jewel murmured. She glanced at me in the doorway. "Get my shawl, Adelia. I must go down. . . ."

There was no breakfast that morning, and the next days were most unhappy. Even Charity, who had fought with

Ellen, cried most of the day. Paul's face was a frozen mask, betraying nothing. Both Georgia, the second maid, and Holly, the scullery maid who helped Charity, walked around with pale faces and wide, staring eyes.

It was Charity who laid Ellen out, and it was John who made the arrangements for the funeral. No one of the family wore mourning of course, for it would be scarcely suitable, but the funeral was held in the Great Hall, and the Reverend Hacket came from Waterloo to say the words. Ellen had no family that anyone knew about, so it was only the Ornes and the servants at Orne Hall who attended the service, and who talked behind the board coffin to the newly dug grave under a large oak tree north of the Hall.

Aunt Jewel tossed a handful of dirt on the lowered coffin. Toby and Aaron stayed to fill the grave.

"We'll get her a stone," John said, and Rex nodded his agreement.

Then it was over. We went to our rooms and I lay back on the bed, thinking of the lovely girl and I wondered what tortured thoughts had driven her to take her life.

I recalled the one long conversation we'd had soon after I'd come to Orne Hall when we'd unpacked my new garments, and I remembered her vanity. It seemed so strange to me that she would take her life and permit everyone who might, see her naked body. She had such a fierce pride; would she let others see her thus, her body broken and sprawled in such a fashion? It seemed incredible to me. I could not believe it, yet it had happened.

Unless someone threw her from her window! I rejected the thought, and then brought it back into my mind again. Was it possible? Many times that night and in the days that followed I went from one thought to the other, unable to accept either. Who would want Ellen dead? Rex? I thought of that resemblance between Harlan and Rex—had he lied to me? Could Rex's bold eyes have failed to observe Alice's beauty—or Ellen's?

Then I thought of the way she died and I walked to the window of my room, which was on the same level as hers in the other wing. It didn't seem so far down that one would certainly be killed by the small distance, and how would one know she would not simply be maimed for life?

Then one day when Aunt Jewel was napping in her room and I was alone in her sitting room, John came in to speak to his grandmother.

"She's asleep, John," I said. "Shall I awaken her?"

"No, no need," he responded. He turned to go, but hesitated at the door. "It was of no importance." Again he paused. "Adelia, would you care to ride with me this afternoon?"

"No, thank you," I answered primly. "There is much to do. Your grandmother is becoming impatient to begin writing the memoirs."

"Is Georgia doing well as the upstairs maid?" he asked. "Is her work satisfactory?"

"Certainly. She is a pleasant and hard-working girl."

"It was a tragedy—Ellen's suicide."

This was an opening for me to speak the thought that had been troubling me. "John, was it a suicide?" I asked quietly.

I saw one dark eye quirk up as he looked at me with what appeared to be surprise. "What do you mean?" he asked in a low, rumbling voice. "Why do you ask a question like that?"

"You found her, John. How did you happen to be out beside the east wing that morning—it wasn't light yet, was it? John, Ellen was a vain, pretty girl. Why did she destroy herself and leave her naked body for discovery?"

My hands trembled at my boldness, and I knew that I was being foolish, yet I wanted to know.

"John," I asked again, "did Ellen kill herself, throwing herself out the window?"

"I don't know," he answered heavily, though his dark eyes expressed some anger. "Cousin Adelia, you are thinking dangerous thoughts. You are implying that if Ellen did not kill herself, she was murdered!"

I felt my face grow cold at the harshness of his words, and I regretted terribly that I'd said anything.

"Do you believe that I threw Ellen out of her window, her body bare to the cold?"

And suddenly I couldn't believe it. I thought of the John

I'd seen briefly who cared for the boy, Harlan, and who was gentle with his grandmother. Surely he couldn't . . . but then I suddenly thought that if Harlan was his son, naturally John would feel that affection. Was it John who had sired Harlan? Was it John who might have visited Ellen's room in the night?

"I don't know, John," I answered, though my heart had jumped into my throat. "Did you, John?"

"I did not," he answered, and that cold fury came back into his dark eyes again. I saw that the fingers of one hand curled to a fist, and the skin over the knuckles whitened. "I am not a murderer!"

"Are you Harlan's father?" I asked in a tight voice, well aware that I meddled in affairs that were none of my business.

"No, I am not," John answered. "Adelia . . ."

Words apparently failed him, for he went out of the room, closing the door with a slight bang behind him.

I was left trembling at my own temerity that I should ask such questions. I turned to my work, finding it difficult to concentrate on the work I sought to do.

But to my astonishment, at noon dinner, John told Aunt Jewel that he and I would ride that afternoon.

Rex broke in with a light laugh. "John, you're getting weak, taking a female riding during working hours."

John ignored his brother's jeering words. "I will meet you at the stables at two-thirty," he said with quiet authority, and his grandmother said nothing at all.

At two-thirty I presented myself at the stables, properly dressed for riding in a split skirt, shawl, and heavy wool jacket, for though the sun shone, the wind was out of the north, and cold.

John awaited me, and as I neared, Aaron and Toby led forth the black stallion and mare. John's manner was cold and reserved as he assisted me in mounting. Soon we were cantering away from the stable and Orne Hall. The stallion was fractious, but John's strong hand quickly brought the beast under control. "I let no one else ride him," he explained. "The animal might kill another rider."

John said nothing, nor did I, until we had reached the

canal and had stopped for a moment as the horses nibbled at the dry grass of the meadow.

"Ellen was murdered," John said suddenly, without any introductory remarks. "She was dead before she was thrown from the window. I have known it from that day."

I was astonished and I felt quickly ill.

"Murdered! How could you know?"

"How did you know?" he countered. His tone accused me as his eyes narrowed.

"I truly didn't, I just suspected," I said. "But you act as if you know."

"I do know. She had been clubbed, hit over the head, in a way that made a wound the fall could never have caused. My evidence is physical, and yours merely a surmise."

"But you told no one? The constable?"

"No. In the Orne family we take care of our own."

His cold words and manner frightened me as did the glare from his coal-black eyes.

"Who did kill her?"

"I don't know," he answered.

With a quick divination I said rather than asked, "You believe it was Rex!"

"I suspect no one. A woman might have done it, as well as a man."

I gasped at the implication of his words and I felt a quick anger. "You suspect me?"

"Is there any way you could prove that it was not you?" he asked pointedly.

"No more than you can prove that you aren't the one," I retorted.

Suddenly he smiled, and his face was transformed, though the somberness did not totally leave the dark eyes. "I don't believe that you could murder anyway, Adelia," he said softly in his still deep, but somehow gentle voice. "I think you are too good a woman to hurt anyone."

"Thank you," I murmured, and lowered my glance, disturbed and pleased at the same time at the quality of his words, and by the way he'd spoken them.

But he shocked me again.

"Are you in love with Rex?" he asked in the same quiet voice.

I looked up, startled. "I—I don't know, John," I faltered. "No, I am not in love with Rex, nor will I ever be. The likes of me will never love or be loved."

"Why do you say that?" he asked quietly.

"You know why I said that!" I flared, looking directly at him. "Look at my plain face! What man will ever want to look at that face each morning of his life?"

"I would, Adelia," John said softly. "It is a nice face."

"It is an ugly face! Why do you tease me and lie to me!"

For a long moment he looked down at me from his great height, his black eyes sober and perhaps a little angry.

"Beauty is in the eye of the person who looks," he said finally.

Now I did become angry, for who could know better than I the untruth of what he said! I turned quickly to my mount. "I wish to return," I said coldly.

"Because you were hurt once, you have become a coward," John said, without moving to assist me.

Anger turned to fury, for I was no coward! I whirled around and flared at him.

"How dare you say that to me? What do you know about—about what happened in my life? What do you know about what a woman feels! All you think about is your business. . . ."

"I know more about you than you know," John broke in. "Don't flare up at me, Adelia." His eyes had turned cold with his own anger.

But my fury mounted and I glared back at him, giving him as good as he gave.

"At least Rex, your brother, has the manners of a gentleman. Which you do not! Are you going to assist me in mounting the mare?"

Suddenly his expression changed to one of good humor.

"Of course, Adelia," he said, and stepped up beside me. But instead of giving me the kind of assistance a lady expects when she mounts, his big hands grasped my waist and he lifted me bodily and placed me firmly in the saddle.

"There, you little spitfire," he said amiably. He handed

me the reins, and then he gave the mare a smart slap on the rump, and all at once she jumped and was off at a run. My quick fear disappeared at once because I held my seat and the wind through my hair and against my face exhilarated me, and before I had ridden a hundred yards I heard the pounding hooves of John's stallion behind me.

"Race you to the stables," he called.

"You're on!" I cried with a burst of delighted laughter. I dug my heel into the mare's flanks.

The stallion drew up beside the flying mare, and held there, and although I did win, I suspected John had deliberately let me.

"I won," I cried.

"So you did," John answered as Toby and Aaron came running from the stone stables.

He dismounted and then lifted me from the saddle, and as my hands touched his strong shoulders, I was aware that my heart thudded not only because of the excitement of the race, but because of his nearness, too.

"Take good care of the horses," John said to Toby and Aaron, and then he took my arm in a familiar gesture. "You're a fine horsewoman," he said to me as we started for the Hall. "You seat your mount very well."

"Thank you, sir," I rejoined.


But when we gathered for supper that night, John's expression had become somber, and cold. He paid no heed of me as I entered with Aunt Jewel, but immediately addressed his grandmother.

"I have received a letter from Governor Tilden in Albany," he said. "He has appointed me chairman of a commission to investigate the corruption of the canal's maintenance contracts."

Aunt Jewel's enormous eyes stared into his dark ones, and for a moment said nothing.

"You will accept?" she asked finally.

John nodded briefly.

Rex exploded into laughter.

"Sending a fox to guard the chickens!" he chortled.

"Rex!" John thundered, and rose to his feet. "That is enough!"

Rex's raucous, derisive laughter subsided immediately, but he stared back at his older brother out of blue eyes grown icy.

"John," he said in a mild tone that belied his expression, "mind your manners."

Aunt Jewel shook her head at me, as I stared from one brother to the other, confused by the angry interchange.

"Don't mind them, Adelia," she said. "Their quarreling doesn't mean anything."

Uncle Walter, whose wizened, narrow face had been turned to watch John as he still stood at the head of the table, suddenly spoke out. "The sins of the fathers visited unto their children. . . ."

"That's enough, Uncle Walter," John said sharply, glancing down at the little man.

The violence of the quarrel had startled me and made my heart pound, but its sudden disappearance surprised me. For a moment it appeared that physical violence was threatened, and then, just as quickly, it was gone. John returned to his chair, and Paul and Georgia began to serve the viands of our supper, which, as usual, were delicious.

A moment later Rex glanced across the table at me, his bold blue eyes speculative. "Cousin," he said, "I have written a song for you, and after supper I would like to sing it for you."

Naturally I was flattered, but suspicious, too, for why would he write a song for me?

"You are joking," I said. "But I'll listen, anyway."

"Rex composes nice songs," Aunt Jewel assured me. Then she glanced archly at her grandson. "But may I come, too?" she asked.

"You think we should be chaperoned?" Rex asked with a teasing smile.

"I certainly do," Aunt Jewel answered.

The talk became general, but when we had finished the peach pie which Charity had baked and which was still hot when it was served to us, and when we'd drunk our coffee,

Rex escorted Aunt Jewel and me to the music room. His grandmother and I seated ourselves on the settee, and then Rex sang a lovely little song about a brown-haired girl who didn't know her own mind.

I inwardly squirmed a little at the words, but when he had finished I joined Aunt Jewel in applause.

That night I dreamed of the brothers—both of them—and the dream was not unhappy.

# Chapter VII

I woke early, long before the first rays of the sun would enter my room. The fire in the hearth had turned to ashes, but I was warm and comfortable under the soft duck's-down featherbed. I stretched in the soft flannel nightgown, feeling cozy and safe. My eyes adjusted to the darkness of the room, barely discerning the faintly lightening sky through the window. As I lay there, my thoughts turned back to my ride with John the previous day—and to the quarrel between Rex and his brother at supper.

"Beauty is in the eye of the person who looks," John had said. Had he meant that he saw me as one who was beautiful? I shook my head with a touch of anger, for my mirror gave back the bitter fact that I was plain, and plain I would be in anyone's eyes! Still, John must have meant something, otherwise why should he have said it? I moved restlessly, remembering the strength of his two hands about my waist as he lifted me into the saddle, and the warmth of his dark eyes when he laughed. But I remembered, too, his fury at his uncle's words, "The sins of the fathers . . ." That had to be a reference to their grandfather, for surely he had been a great sinner—he and my grandfather, his brother.

Again, I wondered idly, what could that quarrel have been about, except it was over a woman? From what I'd heard about the two men, a quarrel seemed unlikely, for one was weak and the other strong. Again, my mind shifted, remembering that John had announced his appointment to be the chairman of a commission by no other than the new governor of the state. I remembered that in the campaign candidate Tilden had sworn to correct the corruption surrounding the canal. It was surely a great honor for John to receive the appointment. But then Rex had said something about a fox sent to protect the chickens, and I was hardly so stupid that I could fail to discern Rex's implications. But I couldn't believe that John was corrupt, could I?

I dozed awhile and then Georgia touched my shoulder.

"Miss Adelia, it is six o'clock."

"Oh, thank you, Georgia," I murmured.

She had already kindled and lit the fire in the grate, so a warmth pervaded my room. She left, then, to attend to Aunt Jewel and for a moment I stayed under the warm featherbed cover, reluctant to get up and face the day. I wondered what it would bring me, but nothing in my imagination prepared me for what that day would be like.

Breakfast was quiet that morning. John told his grandmother that he would be gone for two days, and he instructed Rex to attend to a mare that appeared lame and might need shoeing.

After breakfast, I accompanied Aunt Jewel to her sitting room, and I began to work on the letters. It was midmorning when I came to one in a pink, scented envelope. I slid out the single pink sheet, prepared to read and file it as I did with each letter. It was addressed simply to "M" in an angular, difficult-to-read script. It spoke of a night's bliss, and of the promise of more nights. But it also spoke of the necessary care that must be taken lest the lovers be exposed. It was signed simply "P."

It was so different from the other letters I had been reading and sorting that I wondered if it should truly be with them. On an impulse I carried the pink sheet to Aunt Jewel as she sat on the settee with her needlepoint before the fireplace.

"Aunt Jewel," I said with some hesitation, "do you wish this letter to be filed with the others?"

I handed it to her. She put down her needlepoint and pushed her spectacles more firmly onto the bridge of her nose. She read the letter, her dark eyes intent. She finished the short missive, her lips moving as she read, and then for a moment she stared at nothing, the letter in her lap. She drew a long, deep breath, and then looked up at me. "Burn it in the fireplace," she said crisply. "It is a foolish letter from long ago."

"Yes, Aunt Jewel," I murmured, and did as she directed.

When the pink paper had been reduced to curling, black ashes, Aunt Jewel said slowly, "Let the dead bury its own." Then she gestured at me to return to my work.

As I continued my task, my mind kept returning to the pink letter. It was old—the note had a date of 1841, and that meant thirty-five years had passed since it was written. The only "M" that I knew in the Orne household was Melinda, John and Rex's mother. But of course there could have been many another "M" come and gone at Orne Hall. In any event, it was none of my business. Still, I was curious about how Aunt Jewel would have become the possessor of such an intimate letter.

Yet when I finally blurted out the question that had formed in my mind, I rather surprised myself. As we prepared to leave my aunt's sitting room for noon dinner, I asked her with pretended idle curiosity how old John was.

"Let me remember," Aunt Jewel murmured, her eyes narrowed in thought. "He was born in 1840, so he is thirty-six. Rex is two years younger."

I felt my heart beating in my throat as I remembered the date on the pink letter—1841. We walked along the balcony overlooking the Great Hall, and as we did so, I told myself to stop being concerned with what was none of my business.

Later in the afternoon Orne Hall had an unexpected visitor in the person of the mayor of Waterloo, a potbellied, bustling little man with bright, hard blue eyes.

The first I saw of him, he was escorted by Paul Wiley to Aunt Jewel's sitting room. He entered and bowed low to Aunt Jewel, and then he inquired as to my aunt's health.

"I am quite well. To what do we owe this unexpected visit, Mr. Mayor?" Aunt Jewel asked coldly while raising her hand to greet him.

"I have a matter of greatest importance which I believe we should discuss in private," he said with a glance at me, hard at work at the davenport.

"Adelia," Aunt Jewel called, "leave us alone for a while,

please. You've been working so hard you need a rest, anyway."

"Yes, Aunt Jewel," I murmured as I rose from my chair. I went through the door at the end of the sitting room, into my own bedroom. I sat down in the comfortable chair before the fire and picked up the novel by Mark Twain I had been reading. I'd just reached the place in the novel where Laura, after meeting Colonel Selby, whom she desperately loves, follows him to Washington, where she shoots and kills him in his hotel room, but my eyes grew heavy and I nodded. I put the book down on my lap and leaned back, my eyes closed.

But I found my attention drawn to the angry voice of my aunt and the raised voice of the mayor in what must have been a very serious argument. It was not long before I heard the tinkle of the small bell which Aunt Jewel used to summon me.

So I re-entered the sitting room to discover the mayor still standing in virtually the same position I'd last seen him, his florid face bright red, the veins of his skinny neck standing out like thin ropes.

"Very well, madame," the man said as I closed the door behind me. "Believe me, you will regret your decision."

"I doubt it," Aunt Jewel answered in cold, even tones. She glanced at me as I approached. "Adelia, please escort this very unpleasant little man to the front door—and out."

"Yes, Aunt Jewel," I murmured. I gestured with my hand at the mayor. "This way, sir," I said.

He turned on his heel and strode on short legs out of the sitting room.

He spoke not a word to me, and, leaving the house, he mounted and rode off at a canter. I returned to my aunt's sitting room.

"Adelia," Aunt Jewel said, weariness in her voice, "he is a most unpleasant man."

"I heard you arguing," I said. "I could hardly help it."

"He, like many others, is afraid of the letters you are sorting—afraid of what they may do to him. And well he should be afraid!" Her last words were spoken with great

**111**

anger, but then she laughed, yet not as if it was humorous. "He is a pig," she said. "He needs to be slaughtered."

Then Aunt Jewel changed the subject quickly. "Has Rex returned? Did you see him in the hall?"

"No, I didn't," I answered. "I don't know."

"Ring for Paul, please."

I went to the cord and pulled it. In only minutes Paul Wiley tapped and entered. "Yes, madame?"

"Find Rex and tell him that I must see him at once," Aunt Jewel commanded.

"Immediately, madame," Paul answered, and disappeared, the door closing softly behind him.

Aunt Jewel turned to me, impatiently. "Get on with your work, Adelia. But when Rex comes, you skedaddle, understand? And don't eavesdrop!"

"Of course, Aunt Jewel. You know I wouldn't. . . ."

"I don't know anything of the kind," she broke in grumpily. "That little man put me in a bad mood," she added. She glanced up at me from her dark eyes, one brow raised sardonically. "You have a big bump of curiosity, Adelia. Don't pretend you don't!"

"Don't you, Aunt Jewel?" I asked sweetly.

She smiled ruefully and nodded. "It's the lot of women to be curious because there's so many things their stupid menfolk don't tell them. We have to be curious, don't we, Adelia?"

I nodded and laughed.

In less than an hour Rex entered, and I immediately rose to leave the sitting room as my aunt had directed. But Rex called after me. "Wait, Adelia! I want to see you, too."

"I sent her away," Aunt Jewel broke in. "I want to talk to you!"

So I closed my door and returned to my novel. The voices of my aunt and Rex rose to levels I could hear, but I could not discern the words. Again, my aunt's voice sounded sharp, and Rex's an angry rumble. I tried hard not to listen, to read my book, and in any event I couldn't understand any of the words, except that once it seemed to me I heard my own name spoken. I could hardly pretend I didn't become interested then, but I could understand nothing.

When Aunt Jewel summoned me back to her sitting room, I asked quietly if she and Rex had quarreled.

"He has many things on his mind," she said evasively. "It is nearly six and time for supper. Help me up, please."

In the ensuing days Rex became a different man, for he paid great attention to me, and it was apparent that Aunt Jewel greatly encouraged it. My work suffered, but Aunt Jewel turned my comments away with airy gesture.

"There is plenty of time for work. You are young," she added archly. "You must enjoy life while you can."

I must admit that I did enjoy Rex's extravagant attention. When Edwin Booth came to Waterloo with a touring Shakespearean troupe, Rex took me to see the great actor play *Hamlet*, and I enjoyed it very much. Rex explained that Mr. Booth had gone bankrupt in 1873 and had been forced to go on tour.

We stayed overnight with Horace Orne and his family, and there was much gaiety and laughter, and then on the next morn, when we traveled home, Rex told me that it was one of the most pleasant interludes of his life, and I was much flattered and touched.

Christmas came, and with it a lovely brooch from Rex, and a delightful music box from John. We had a great Christmas dinner with guests from Waterloo, and for the second time since I had arrived, we dined in the formal dining room in the east wing, three steps up from the hall. Later, everyone danced, and several gentlemen drank too much, but it was a truly joyous occasion, and I realized that part of my pleasure came from the attentions of John as well as Rex. I'd seen little of John in the previous weeks, for he was often gone, attending to the affairs of the commission to which he had been appointed chairman by Governor Tilden.

There was mistletoe of course, and I was kissed soundly by several gentlemen, including John and Rex. In spite of my awareness of my plain face, I felt quite the belle of the ball.

Yet, when I returned in the small hours of the morning,

113

and lay abed under the warmth of the soft feathered comforter, my head spinning from the wine, I had a strange uneasiness that it was all like Cinderella's ball, and that none of it was real. Only I had no fairy godmother to turn me from plain Adelia into beautiful Adelia.

Nearly asleep, I wondered if I was truly falling in love with Rex, and if he truly cared for me.

Orne Hall became crowded a week later with another party on New Year's Eve and at the moment of midnight Rex kissed me and whispered he had to see me alone.

I let him lead me to the music room, which was empty at the moment. He turned me to face him, his hands on my shoulders. He looked down at me out of his bold blue eyes, which seemed somehow to be sad, and he said in a gentle voice, "Adelia, will you marry me?"

"We're cousins . . ." I protested.

"Remotely, and it is of no matter. Will you marry me?"

A tiny voice somewhere in my astonished mind begged him to say he loved me. For I loved him, did I not?

"I don't know," I murmured. "Rex, you don't love me."

"I care for you very much, Adelia," he protested. "I want you to be my wife. Would I want that if I didn't love you?" His grip on my shoulders lightened, and I confess I wanted to say yes, for my future would then be forever secure, would it not? But still, I remembered my plainness and I hesitated, for how could he love me—and if he didn't love me, why did he wish to marry me?

"I have to have some time to think about your proposal, Rex," I answered. "You've surprised me."

"You are surprised? We've been together almost every day. Surely, you must have known."

"My mind is fuddled, Rex. I've drunk too much wine to make a serious decision like this. Let me think about it?"

"Why do you have to think about it? Either you love me or you don't, Adelia."

His grip tightened, and the expression in his blue eyes became colder.

"You're hurting me, Rex," I protested, and struggled to escape his grip.

"I'm sorry," he murmured, instantly contrite. "Will you

think about it, Adelia?" he asked. "I want to marry you soon."

"Rex, I'll think about it," I answered. "Thank you, for asking me." It sounded weak and inadequate. This wasn't the way I thought a proposal should go, and I was ashamed of myself and my foolish feeling. I did love Rex, didn't I? I would think about it and I would tell him that, yes, I would marry him, and then everything would be perfect forever!

We went back to the hall, where I danced, flirted, and then, finally, went to bed, my head spinning from the wine, and my heart and mind hopelessly confused by my feelings. But my last thought as I slipped into dreamless slumber was that tomorrow I would tell Rex that I would marry him.

But when I woke, I was no longer sure. In the predawn light, I remembered Ellen's broken, naked body sprawled on the ground below her window, and I heard again John's savage words, "She was murdered," and yet nothing had been done. Why was Rex so anxious to marry me? Affection might be in his heart, but never love; I'd seen the beautiful mayor's daughter and I knew he could not desire me above her.

Georgia came to wake me, for even after a ball, Aunt Jewel would insist that we breakfast at seven. I was already awake, and as I slipped from the covers to dress, my head began to spin. I closed my eyes and morosely decided I'd never again forget that I was merely a poor relative taken in by kindly people.

No, I would never marry Rex. I was resolved as I entered my aunt's sitting room to join her in the walk to the dining room.

In the cruel light of coming day, my aunt's complexion seemed splotchy, and her large eyes weary and depressed; her expression matched my mood, and my smile betrayed me, for Aunt Jewel stared at me sharply.

"Too much wine?" she asked tartly. "Adelia, you look . . ."

"Plain? Aunt Jewel, I was plain last night, too," I retorted.

"Did Rex ask you to marry him? He informed me that he was going to propose to you."

"Yes, Aunt Jewel," I answered.

"What did you answer?" I caught a touch of eagerness in her voice.

"I said I would have to think it over," I said calmly. "However, today I will tell him my answer."

"What will it be?" Aunt Jewel pressed, her eagerness little hidden.

"It isn't a concern of yours, Aunt Jewel," I said tartly.

She smiled ruefully and nodded. "Forgive me for a meddling old woman," she murmured. But the expression in her dark eyes gave little evidence she felt truly contrite. "Shall we go to breakfast?"

We said nothing as we walked along the balcony above the hall. The debris of the ball remained scattered about the hugh room. I supposed our guests still slept, for, though Aunt Jewel required that the family breakfast at seven, she did not rule that the guests must do likewise.

Everyone in the family was present in the upstairs dining room, waiting for Aunt Jewel and me. After the chorus of good-mornings, and after the grace had been said by John and Paul had begun to serve us our cooked oatmeal and hot coffee, Rex broke into the general conversation.

"Everyone," he said loudly, "I need your help. I have asked Adelia to marry me, and will you plead my cause for me?"

He smiled across the table to me and then glanced at his grandmother. "*Grand'mère*, tell her she should marry me. . . ."

But it was John's voice that broke in on Rex's plea.

"Rex," he said sharply, "you have embarrassed your cousin. Enough of this! Adelia, I apologize for my brother's indelicacy."

I drew a long breath. I was offended by Rex's importuning at breakfast. It seemed the wrong time, and should he truly want me to be his wife, if he truly loved me, would he speak in this manner? I doubted it. My pride was hurt, too, by his words in the presence of the others.

"I will give you my answer now, Rex," I said firmly. "I

thank you for the honor, but no, I will not marry you, for you don't love me, nor do I love you."

My words brought a silence to the room. I kept my gaze on Rex across from me, and I saw the change in his expression. First I saw anger, and then wry humor took over and he made gesture as if he said: So be it.

From behind me I heard the low voice of Georgia whispering, "Do you wish a hot coffee, Miss Adelia?"

"I do," I answered.

And for a time no one said anything.

As breakfast ended Aunt Jewel told me a little sharply that there was much work to be done, so I excused myself and started back to the sitting room, aware that Rex had pushed back his chair, too, as I rose. I knew that he followed me, but I walked without hurrying to the balcony above the Great Hall, and it was only when we reached the midpoint that I felt his fingers on my arm. He drew me to a stop, and I waited, a little frightened, though I didn't know why.

"Cousin Adelia," Rex said softly, "you're going to be very sorry!"

I turned quickly, to look at him directly. "What do you mean?" I demanded.

His bold eyes crinkled at the corners. "I am a good catch," he said.

# Chapter VIII

I withdrew my arm from his clasp.

"Yes, I suppose you are, Rex, and I wish you every success. Now I must go to work. . . ."

His smile lifted the corners of his lips and wrinkled the corners of his eyes, but it seemed to me that the bold blueness smiled not at all, and I felt a chill. Without another word I hurried on, my head held stiffly erect. Yet inside I felt as if perhaps Rex would be right, and that I would be very, very sorry that I refused him.

The day passed quickly with little of special interest, other than the reading and sorting of various letters dealing with the business interests of the Orne brothers.

Later, in the evening after I'd retire to my room, I read more of a foolish novel about lovers who were kept apart by such a stupid misunderstanding that I longed to tell them to stop being idiotic; still, the novel held me and when I glanced at the big clock, I saw it was approaching eleven, which was much past the time I would normally be asleep—though I knew that there were often others of the household awake very late at night.

I felt the pangs of hunger, and I decided that I would go to the kitchen and make myself a sandwich of the delicious ham Charity had cooked for our supper. I'd not undressed, but I put a warm dressing gown over my shoulders, took the small lamp from the bed table, opened my door, and walked down the dark hallway.

When I reached the balcony, I saw that two wall lamps still burned, one at each end, though the wicks had been turned low. I felt just a moment of fear, but I knew that was foolish, for no one in the household had reason to hurt me, and I had no reason to fear; the sardonic thought crossed my mind that there *were* certain advantages to being so plain, weren't there?

The usual night sounds attended my ear—the creaking of an old building in the wind, the banging of a shutter, as I crossed to the far side of the gallery, and then descended the spiral staircase to the kitchen.

A clump of coals still glowed in the wide, curving fireplace. I found a fresh loaf of bread and the large section of smoked ham saved from supper. Of course I knew where the carving knives were kept, and in minutes I was eating a delicious sandwich and sipping from a large glass of milk. I had seated myself on one of the backless benches, my elbows resting on the scarred tabletop. I thought I was totally alone when suddenly I heard a deep voice from behind me.

"Cousin Adelia, what are you doing here?"

I turned to look up at John's bearded face, his dark, piercing eyes reflecting the yellow rays of my lamp. He wore a greatcoat as if he'd just come in from the outside. As he looked at me, he tugged off his gloves and then he slipped out of his coat.

"You couldn't guess, could you, John?" I asked impishly.

"It looks good," he murmured. "I'm thinking I will have a ham sandwich, too."

"Let me," I said quickly. "I'll fix one for you; I'm very good at it!"

"You're very good at many things, Adelia," John murmured. "However, I believe I prefer lager to milk."

He went to fetch a draft of lager as I sliced more ham and bread. When he returned, the sandwich was ready and waiting.

For a moment we munched our sandwiches without speaking. Then John asked me why I had refused Rex's offer of marriage. "As far as I know, there isn't an unmarried maiden in the country who could ever refuse him anything," he said with a chuckle. "Or even married maidens, either, if there is such a thing."

"Because he has no love for me, and I don't know why he made the proposal," I responded with a little heat. "He did embarrass me at breakfast."

He seemed to accept my explanation. I stared at him, thinking that there would be few unmarried maidens who would refuse him, should he choose to marry.

"John, why have *you* never married?"

"I was waiting for you, Adelia," he said with false gallantry.

"You didn't even know I was alive," I retorted. "You barely know it, even now. So, speak the truth, John. Why have you never married?"

He took a long sip of his lager, and then drew a deep breath. "There have been several times when I considered it, Adelia," he said. His brows drew together as if he was puzzled. "I honestly don't know why I never have."

"Who will take care of Orne business, if you leave no heirs?" I asked. "If neither you nor Rex leave heirs."

"Perhaps Horace's son, Robert. He's a lawyer, you know. And anyway, there may be no Orne business to be taken care of, if the railroads destroy the canal business."

"Why won't you let Rex do things for the business? Surely he . . ."

"He has no mind for it, or for numbers," John broke in somberly. "He's strange, not like the rest of the Ornes."

Suddenly I thought of the letter addressed to "M" which had been written just less than a year before Rex's birth— and the great difference between John and his brother. Perhaps they were half brothers, and no one knew it! I felt the guilty knowledge of the pink letter I'd seen destroyed in the sitting-room fireplace bear down on me. But I said nothing.

The wintry wind howled about Orne Hall, and vagrant drafts made the lamp flicker. John finished his sandwich; I had already eaten mine.

"It is time you were in bed," he said finally. "Adelia, perhaps you should never have come here."

"I had no other place to go," I protested.

"That is too bad," he said heavily. "Go to bed, Adelia." He rose, lit another lamp, and then handed me mine.

"Good night, John," I said as I started up the winding, curcular stairs.

He said nothing, and my last glimpse of him was that of

a tall, immobile, strong man standing by the table, the yellow lamp light illuminating his bearded face and glinting in his dark eyes.

Once at the top of the steps, I walked quietly down the hallway to the gallery above the Great Hall, and then with one hand trailing on the surface of the broad, polished railing, I walked toward the west wing and my own room.

The two lamps with turned-down wicks still weakly illuminated the balcony and the wide stairs. As I reached the top of the steps I hesitated, my attention caught by a sound behind me. I turned around but I saw no one, though a chill penetrated my bones from the cold drafts that swept the huge hall.

For a moment I leaned on the railing, looking down at the darkness so little affected by the small lamp I carried. I set the lamp on the wide banister and leaned forward to peer down into the Great Hall.

There was no warning. Suddenly strong hands grasped me around the waist. I felt myself being thrown over the railing, and one hand clung with desperate strength to the newel post at the top of the stair. I recall I screamed, and then my body was tumbling down the wide steps to the landing. My head hit something very hard, and I knew no more. . . .

Bright lights shone in my eyes as I opened them. I stared up into John's dark eyes, which reflected the dancing flames of several lamps held above me. I saw Paul Wiley and Charity leaning over me, too, and behind them, I saw Georgia's frightened face.

"Thank God, she's alive," Charity cried, and came down on her knees beside me, her blue eyes frightened under her frilled sleeping cap.

Suddenly Rex's face appeared, too. "What has happened?" he asked quickly.

"Adelia fell down the stairs," John said soberly. Then he spoke directly to me, his dark eyes fixed on mine. "Do you remember exactly what happened, Adelia?"

Yes, I did remember, for it all came flooding back to me; I remembered the strong hands at my waist—hands as strong as those which had once lifted me into the mare's saddle—hands that threw me over the railing. I remembered clinging to the newel post, my body bouncing over the banister and falling. But some caution which came from the fear that filled me made me shake my head at John.

"I don't know," I whispered. "I don't remember." Did I see relief in his eyes at my words? "I—I must have tripped and fallen."

"Can you move?" Rex asked. "Do you hurt terribly?"

I tried to move arms and legs, and I discovered that I could, though there were many bruises on my body, and my head hurt.

"Oh," Charity cried suddenly, "she's bleeding on the head!"

Suddenly John scooped me up in his two arms. "I will carry her to her room," he said firmly. "Rex, saddle the black gelding and ride into Waterloo for Horace."

At that moment Aunt Jewel appeared at the head of the stairs.

"What's happened?" she called down, her voice shrill.

My body stiffened in John's arms as he answered, "Adelia fell down the stairs. Her head is hurt; I'm taking her to her room. Charity," he called over his shoulder, "bring a basin of water and some cloths."

Aunt Jewel stepped aside as John reached the top of the stairs. Only seconds later John lowered me onto my bed. "You'll be all right, Adelia," he said softly.

When Charity brought the basin of water, and Georgia trailed her with white cloths in her arms, it was John who personally bathed the wound at the back of my head, and who ultimately bound bandages so that my head was nearly encased.

Aunt Jewel brought a bottle of medicine, and poured out a tablespoon of it for me to take. "Laudanum," she explained. "It will make you sleep; it will be hours before Horace and Rex can return."

In only minutes everything grew hazy and indistinct, and I did close my eyes as I slipped into a heavy, dreamless sleep.

When I woke because of the sharp pain in my head, it was still dark; the lamp at my bedside had been turned low and the flame still cast shadows about the bedroom. I turned my head and a small sound of pain escaped my lips. Instantly a chair creaked and I recognized John's bearded face as he bent over me. "I'm right here, Adelia," he said softly. "Are you in pain?"

"Yes," I whispered, but the only emotion I felt was fear. I relived again the feeling of those two hands at my waist and the feeling as if I'd been swung out into space. I recalled my desperate fingers gripping the newel, and then I was in the air—and falling.

He gave me what he said was more laudanum, though I wanted to fight against him. He wouldn't poison me, would he? Again I slipped into a dreamless sleep.

The next time I awakened, Dr. Horace Orne leaned over me. No one else was in the room except Aunt Jewel, who stood on the other side of the bed.

"How do you feel?" Uncle Horace asked, his dark eyes enlarged by his spectacles as he peered at me.

"My head hurts," I said honestly.

"I must examine the wound, Adelia. It may hurt more. Can you stand it?"

I could and I did. He examined my limbs and arms, too, but nothing seemed broken. However, I discovered that I wore my nightgown and I looked up at Aunt Jewel. "Who undressed me?" I asked.

"Charity," Aunt Jewel explained. "With Georgia's help."

I breathed a deep sigh of relief. "Where is John?" I asked.

"He is in his study," Aunt Jewel answered. "Do you wish to see him?"

"No," I cried. I never wanted to see him again. Why had he tried to kill me?

Dr. Horace left some medicine and said that he would be out to see me again in a day or so. "You'll mend all right," he assured me. "You have a strong, young constitution."

Charity brought me some gruel, which she insisted that I

eat. Then I took the medicine, which must have had something very strong in it, too, for again I slept.

Evening shadows were long when the pain of my head wound again awakened me. I discovered that Rex sat in the chair watching me.

"What time is it?" I croaked, for my mouth and throat were dry.

"It's after five," Rex said. He rose and came to the side of the bed. "Is there anything I can get for you?"

"May I have a drink of water?" I asked.

"Of course," he answered. I watched him as he poured a small glass from the pitcher. Then he raised me gently, his arm under my shoulders, so that I might sip. The cool liquid wet my lips and my throat. My voice was less of a croak when I thanked him.

He pulled up the chair, and sat down close to the bed. He touched one of my hands with his fingers. "Adelia, what on earth happened? How did you happen to be out and about the hall that time of night?"

"I don't remember," I lied, for I was afraid to mention that John and I had been in the kitchen together; for it was obvious that John had said nothing about it to Rex. Otherwise, Rex would have had no need to ask.

"Did you trip?" Rex asked, his voice insistent. "What happened to the lamp that you surely must have been carrying?"

I hadn't thought of that, and now I tried to remember. Had I set the lamp down on the broad railing? What had I done with it? If it had been in my hand when I fell, there would surely have been a terrible fire.

"I don't know," I answered Rex.

"Adelia, you could have been killed! Try to remember what happened."

Perhaps if I'd been wider awake, and if my mind had been alert, I would not have said what I did.

"Rex, someone tried to kill me!"

I saw his eyes widen in disbelief. "No one would try to kill you, Adelia! No one would have any reason."

"Someone threw me over the railing," I insisted. "I

**124**

caught the newel post and I tumbled down the stairs and it was the last thing I remember."

"But why were you there?" he asked insistently. "It was late at night."

"I was hungry. I went down to the kitchen and made myself a sandwich, and I drank a glass of milk."

"Did you see anyone?" he asked.

"No," I lied again, some instinct telling me that I was safer if no one knew. I closed my eyes and I resolved that as soon as I could walk I would leave Orne Hall, never to return.

Later, after Rex had left and I was alone for a while, I tried to think clearly. I recognized that my fear of John was mixed with a terrible hurt that he would do something like this to me. There had been those few times when I'd felt close to him. I remembered his gentleness with Harlan. Why did he try to kill me? I asked myself.

Then, of course, doubts began to creep in; how did I know for certain that it *had* been John? Yes, he knew I was still up and about, but I'd left him in the kitchen. How could he have reached the balcony so quickly and so quietly? Yet, who else could it have been? Though those two hands had been so strong, Rex's arms and hands were probably equally strong. Paul Wiley surely had sufficient strength. I thought, too, of Toby, but it could hardly have been him. Then I remembered the stableboy, Aaron, really no boy at all, and I remembered his muscular arms. Yes, Aaron could well have done it. But why? Why did anyone wish me ill?

Melinda visited me for a time. "I slept through it all," she explained. "I am such a heavy sleeper," she added plaintively. "How do you feel, Adelia?"

"All right," I answered, but I kept looking at those heavy arms of Melinda. Was she strong enough? But she surely had no reason to try to kill me.

The next morning I became deathly ill, vomiting terribly. Charity held my head, and Georgia's frightened face hovered in the background.

"It was that bump on the head," Charity said a few minutes later as I lay back, exhausted by the violence of my vomiting.

"It does that."

I said nothing, lying with my eyes closed, my arms at my sides, but I didn't believe it, not for one minute! Someone still sought to kill me! Someone had put some poison in my food. I thoroughly believed it, and I even looked at Charity through a fog of suspicion.

That evening Rex came to my room. He seemed to be purposeful, and right away he proposed to me again.

"Adelia, I said things so very badly. Of course I love you, but I found it hard to say the words." He leaned over me, and with one gentle hand he brushed my hair away from my forehead. "Let me take care of you, darling," he said softly. "Marry me, because I do love you."

I looked up into his blue eyes, and I saw from their expression he appeared troubled, and it came to my mind that he certainly would not want to marry me if he'd been the one who tried to kill me, would he? The two ideas failed to mix. I was so frightened and I felt so terribly alone, and under the influence of my own fear I said directly to Rex, "I didn't fall, someone tried to kill me. And someone tried to poison me!"

"No!" He seemed astonished. "No one would have reason to kill you, Adelia. You're imagining things."

"I am not," I cried. "I—I'm afraid, Rex. I know someone is trying to kill me. I know it!"

He gathered me up into his arms and held me close, and I clung to him as I began to cry, for my relief was so great.

Finally, he laid me back down on the pillow again and he gently wiped my eyes.

"No more tears, Adelia," he said softly. "We'll be married at once. No one will dare try to hurt you once you are my wife."

"All right," I whispered. He'd said he loved me, hadn't he? Everything would be all right. "Can we go away from here?" I asked. My mind was still muddled and unclear.

"Of course," he said. "We'll go to New York City for our honeymoon."

126

As he talked of the wonders of the great city, some of my fears began to leave me. And it wasn't until he left my bedside that I began to think more clearly. Rex didn't seem to be particularly interested in really trying to find out who had wanted to take my life. It didn't seem natural, somehow. Lying in the darkness, I remembered that I was a nobody and I could bring no dowry. I was honest with myself, too, asking if I truly loved Rex, or had I turned to him because of my fear?

In the morning I told Rex that I'd acted foolishly. "Rex, if you still want to marry me when spring comes, I'll marry you. But not now—not so fast."

Did I detect a touch of relief in his manner, or was it that I just sought for it? I found it so difficult to believe that he could ever love a woman like me.

"Very well, Adelia," he said quietly. "However, I shall never be far from your side. I will protect you."

"Thank you, Rex," I whispered, and after I'd closed my eyes, I felt his lips touch mine lightly and I thought to myself: I do love him, very much.

But after he'd left and I was alone, the old feelings kept flooding back. Why did I delude myself? No man would ever love me, and should I be foolish enough to believe so, only hurt would be the result. Yet, I asked myself why I must doubt. Why couldn't I believe that Rex truly desired me? Why did I believe I saw some tiny relief in his blue eyes when I told him I would not marry him at once?

I never saw John again until the day that I rose from my bed and felt well enough to join the family at dinner. I'd been bedridden for nearly a week, seeing only Rex, Charity, and Aunt Jewel, and sometimes Georgia would come to spend some time with me.

Rex came to assist me, and we walked together down the hallway to the balcony. There, at the head of the stairs, I stopped a moment and looked down to where I'd fallen. Idly I caressed the highly polished newel post, and suddenly I was aware that it was slightly loose. It had never been before. But more than that, I saw four faint scratch marks and I knew they were caused by my nails as I had desperately clung to it. I felt a strange affection for it;

had it not saved my life? If I had gone over the rail, down to the oaken floor . . .

"Come," Rex said gently. "The others are waiting."

And so they were. It was pleasurable to have them greet me with affection—and even John seemed pleased. He rose to his feet as we entered, and it was he who hurried around and held the chair for me. Then, when he'd returned to his place, and we bowed our heads as he said grace, he added a word of gratefulness that I had recovered from the fall.

As I lifted my head to look at him, he glanced directly at me, and I told myself that I was an idiot, for no man could try to kill me and then pray gratefulness that I survived.

Melinda, on my right, touched my cheek with a fat finger, and said she was so glad I could be up and around.

"Adelia," she added, "you are the one person this family needs to have around all the time."

Felice called to me from down the table. "Adelia, don't ever do that again, because we miss you so much."

I felt warmed by their words, and when Aunt Jewel leaned over to kiss my cheek, I felt it flush with pleasure. For the first time I felt as if they were my family, and for a while I let myself believe that none of these could wish me harm, could they? I was a member of the family, I felt my gratitude toward each and all of them.

"Thank you, everyone," I said, my throat tight with emotion, and tears filled my eyes. "You're all so wonderful."

The very next day I began work with the letters, and in the evening our table had a guest I had not met before, Colonel Carter, a tall, white-haired man with an angular face and angry eyes. He spoke with a faint southern accent and he was very attentive to Aunt Jewel, but eyed me with only careless and indifferent curiosity.

After we'd finished our dessert and coffee, John made a strange request. "Adelia, will you do something for me? I will be talking to Colonel Carter, and I would like to have you take notes of the conversation. You have had experience taking notes, I know."

"I—I'd be pleased to, if you think I am capable," I said.

"An excellent idea," Aunt Jewel said. She turned to

Colonel Carter with a smile that seemed to carry a special meaning.

"You will find Adelia very capable."

It was easy to discern that Colonel Carter was little pleased with the prospect.

So, after we'd finished, John came around the table to remove my chair. He took my arm gently, and nodded to Colonel Carter. "I think we can be excused and get about the business, Colonel," he said.

Although I'd never been there, I knew that John had an office directly under Aunt Jewel's sitting room in the west wing. We walked around the balcony of the Great Hall, descended the stairs where I'd fallen—or rather been thrown—and then down the hallway to the office.

We entered the large room, and I was astonished to discover that its walls were completely lined with books. John's large desk was set near one end, and comfortable chairs surrounded the fireplace.

"Sit where you'll be comfortable," John told the colonel, and then he suggested I take a tablet from his desk. "There are pencils there, too."

A moment later I was seated in a chair between the colonel and John, pencil in hand, and the tablet on my knee.

"Colonel," John said in an even voice, "why don't you tell me why you have come?" He asked the question in a low, even tone, his manner neither friendly nor unfriendly.

The colonel was obviously ill at ease. "It's about that confounded book of memoirs your grandmother is supposed to be writing, and about that commission of Governor Tilden. And you know it! Why are you having her write things down?"

"So we will have a record of the conversation," John said mildly. "In the first place, I have no control over what my grandmother may or may not write or publish. In the second place, if it has a little to do with the commission, or my being chairman of it, I want a record."

"I want no record of this conversation," the colonel flared angrily.

John simply looked at the tall man for a long moment.

"Then there won't be any conversation, will there? What are you afraid of, Colonel?"

"Nothing! I have nothing to be afraid of. Listen to me, Orne, you know very well I've done nothing that your own grandfather didn't do! So don't you go trying to be holier-than-thou on me!"

John seemed to deliberately talk slowly, with long pauses, so I had no difficulty in keeping up with the words.

"I know it," John said mildly. "The big difference is this: the Ornes are no longer doing it, and you still are."

"You try sinking me, and I'll sink you with me!"

"How?" John asked, his voice very quiet, but expressing a bit of humor at the same time.

"I'll wreck your barge company. . . ."

"That's a threat," John said. "No, Colonel Carter, you'll do nothing that you can't do behind bars. Because"—John's voice suddenly came hard and angry—"I am going to see that you are put behind bars! You and your company are completely corrupt, and you've been stealing from the canal for years—and you're still doing it. And I am going to prove it!"

"How? With your grandmother's letters?" the colonel said with a sneer.

"No, Colonel, though they may help."

The colonel glanced at me.

"Stop writing," he commanded. I glanced at John, who smiled and nodded permission. The colonel turned to John. "I'll pay you a quarter of a million dollars to whitewash the commission's investigation. You know you can't change anything. It's been that way since before the canal was even completed. Nothing is going to change it—and it's been good for the country! Sure, we made some money, but millions of tons of materials have moved on that stretch of water! What will you gain by it?"

John laughed shortly and shook his head. "In the first place, Carter, I don't need your money, and in the second, I wouldn't take it. All right, you've made your offer. We'll put you up for the night, and in the morning you can go about your business."

"I'll go tonight," the colonel said angrily. "You're an ig-

130

norant fool, Orne, if you think you can get away with it! I'll break you! I'll have your barges dumped; nobody will ship anything, and you'll go under."

"Colonel," John said softly, "I no longer own the barge company—instead, I own a good share of the railroad!"

The expression on the colonel's face was laughable at first, as his eyes bulged and his fury made his mouth tremble.

But John's voice changed now. "However, Colonel Carter, if anything happens to anyone in my family, or to any of my business connections, I'll ask no questions. I will simply kill you!"

The last words were spoken with such great menace that the colonel simply turned gray as he rose to his feet.

"I'll have your horse saddled," John said, "and you can be on your way." He turned to me. "Will you take your notes up to your type-writer and copy them? I will escort the colonel out of the house."

I did as he directed, and for several minutes I carefully typed the conversation precisely as I had written it down, while Aunt Jewel watched with interest. When I finished I took it from the cranky machine and handed it to my aunt to read. She did so, her brows drawn together in concentration. "Remarkable," she murmured. "Adelia, you are so clever."

Later, John came to the sitting room to take the page of typed words. He read it with satisfaction, and then folded it and carefully tucked it into the inner pocket of his jacket.

"Splendid," he said, and gave me a warm smile, and again I felt somehow ashamed that I'd thought that he could have pushed me. Yet, who could it have been, if not John?

"*Grand'mère*," John said to my great-aunt in a very serious tone, "Colonel Carter is a vicious man, and I want everyone in the house to be on guard. If you see any suspicious persons anywhere on our grounds, tell me or Rex at once. From now on," he added with careful emphasis, "one of us will be on the premises all the time."

"Oh, he wouldn't do us any harm," Aunt Jewel protested, peering up at him out of her small face. "He isn't insane, is he?"

John's deep, rumbling laugh came from his chest. "Probably not, Grandmamma, but we should be careful." He paused before he continued. "You are still determined to write your memoirs and to publish the contents of those letters my grandfather received—and some that he wrote?"

"I am," his grandmother said with spirit. "I want to see those horrible people squirm."

"*Grand'mère,* you are a vicious woman," he said with a smile that took away the sting of the words.

For the following days everyone did keep one eye open for strangers. John gave Aaron orders to ride around the estate several times a day, and particularly just after dawn and before dark. "You can't tell what he might flush," he explained as he told us of his instructions.

But no one was seen, though Rex brought back from Waterloo the story of some hard characters who had been seen at the Bouncing Bull Tavern, a drinking place for canallers and the like.

"Probably has nothing to do with Orne Hall," he said as he told us. "But we'd better keep a hard watch, for the colonel might be crazy enough to try something."

As the days went by, each of us busy with our tasks, we gradually became less vigilant.

Each day I worked on the notes and took down the words which Aunt Jewel wished me to type and then I'd carefully work the machine. The book of memoirs gradually began to take shape, and with it a detailed and true story of the sorry amount of corruption which had attended the building and operation of the canal.

One Monday evening I felt a trifle indisposed, as if I might be coming down with a cold, so I told Aunt Jewel I proposed to retire early.

"I'll send Charity up with some sassafras tea," Aunt Jewel promised. "It will end your cold in a hurry."

I rather doubted that it would, but nonetheless, when Charity brought it to my room, as well as a hot warming pan, I permitted myself to be cared for. She sent Georgia down with instructions that Aaron should bring up more kindling for the hearth, lest I get cold in the night.

Finally, Charity had left and Aaron had stoked up the fire until I was as warm as toast. So I read for a time, feeling much better, and I must have fallen asleep in bed, the book falling down on the covers over my breast. I didn't know how long I'd slept, but suddenly I was awakened by some sound and I lay a moment with my eyes wide open. Then I heard it again—a sound like a weak cry. The nature of it made me tremble with fear and my heart seemed to leap into my throat. The sound came from the door to Aunt Jewel's sitting room.

Without giving thought to my actions, I slid from under the covers and went to the connecting door, which I opened cautiously. The sitting room was dark, but I saw a faint light under the door at the far end of the room which led to Aunt Jewel's bedroom and I heard the sound again. It came from my aunt's bedroom!

Throwing the door wide, I raced across the sitting room, which was barely lit from the light in my own bedroom. Even as I did so, the light I had seen under the doorway disappeared. I reached for the door handle of the bedroom door, but it pushed against me suddenly, and I was knocked off my feet, my head hitting the floor with an awful thud. A dark, heavily shrouded figure ran past me and out of the sitting room into the hall, and in the darkness it had been just that—an unrecognizable blob. I got to my feet as quickly as I could and ran to my aunt's room.

It was dark but I could see the bed and the white form lying on it. I ran to it and leaned down, crying Aunt Jewel's name. I put my ear to her breast and I could just barely hear its beat. She was alive!

I ran back to the sitting room and then to the door to the hall, and I screamed at the top of my voice, "John! Rex! Help!" Then I grabbed the signal cord and summoned Paul and Charity with hard pulls which I knew would jangle in the kitchen and in their apartment.

John and Rex arrived at the same time, each bare above the waist, wearing only their trousers.

"Your grandmother!" I screamed. "Somebody tried to kill her!"

"Get a light," John ordered, and I ran back to my room to pick up the already lighted bed lamp.

John and Rex were already in Aunt Jewel's bedroom when I arrived with the light. "Somebody tried to smother her with a pillow," John said grimly. "She's breathing, but she's unconscious."

He turned to me.

"What do you know?" he asked in steady, harsh tones.

"I was asleep—something awakened me. I heard what seemed like a muffled cry, and I opened the sitting-room door. I saw the light under the door, then it went out. When I reached the door, it was flung open. I was knocked down and somebody big and heavy went by me. I went to your grandmother and I heard her heart was beating. Then I called you."

Paul and Charity arrived, followed by the rest of the household. They all gathered in the sitting room, wide-eyed, frightened, asking questions. Melinda, in her flowing gown, seemed near hysterics.

"We'll all be killed in our beds," she cried.

Charity, Paul, and John and his brother worked over Aunt Jewel. Then Rex appeared in the doorway and addressed Aaron directly.

"Ride in and get Dr. Horace, and get him fast!" Then he gestured to me. "You help Charity; do whatever she asks. John and I will go out to search the grounds."

"Yes, Rex," I murmured, and I did as he said, though there was little that we could do but keep Aunt Jewel warm, and pray that she would be all right. She did not regain consciousness as we watched and waited. It was near dawn when Aaron and Dr. Horace arrived. His clothes were wet and muddy, for it had rained in the night. He ordered all of us from the room except Charity.

I suggested that since there was nothing we could do, everyone should dress.

"Georgia and Holly," I said directly to the girls, "I guess the three of us can get breakfast properly, can't we?"

They both nodded, though their wide, staring eyes attested to their fear and disquiet.

We did so, and when I sent Aaron to summon the others, it was near our usual time of seven o'clock. By chance Rex and John returned to the house at the same time and joined us in the family dining room.

"Did you find anything?" I had to ask.

They both shook their heads as they placed their game guns in the corner and shed their cloaks.

"How is *Grand'mère*?" Rex asked.

"Dr. Horace and Charity are still with her," I explained. "I don't know."

"I'm going up," John said grimly. "I'll be down. Georgia, pour my coffee."

Little was said as we ate our first meal of the day. John came back, shaking his head in response to the question in the eyes of all of us. "She hasn't regained consciousness," he said. "Dr. Horace said we must pray; there is little he can do and little else we can do."

I closed my eyes and I did pray, and it wasn't until then I realized how dear the tiny old lady had become to me, how much I loved her. I felt the tears filling my closed eyes and spilling down my cheeks as I sat there, my hands gripped in my lap.

John's deep voice murmured an amen, and we lifted our heads. I wasn't surprised to see tears in the eyes of the others, and even those of Georgia and Holly showed wetness as they served us.

"I'm going to kill him!" Rex burst out, the muscles of his jaw tightening, and his blue eyes taking on an insane look of anger.

"No, Rex," John said grimly. "We have no evidence that Carter was involved. It may be another."

Suddenly I thought of something—that I should have thought of at once.

"Excuse me," I said hurriedly, and I ran back to the sitting room and to my desk, and to the file. The dawn's light was enough so that I could see, and I knew instantly that someone had been through the file—and that some of the letters were certainly missing!

135

At once I hurried back to the dining room.

"Whoever tried to kill your grandmother was interested in the letters, for many are missing," I said to John and Rex.

"There," Rex said in almost a shout. "Now we know. . . ."

"No, we don't know it was Carter," John broke in harshly. "Rex, don't go off half-cocked. There are others, many others who had an interest in those letters." John turned to me. "Can you tell which letters have been taken?"

"I can tell some, but not all," I answered. "They were taken from the file-case drawers, so they were letters I have read and sorted. If they took others, there is no way I could know."

"Later, try to make a list," John said in even tones. "Now, finish your breakfasts."

Aunt Jewel never recovered consciousness. Sometime near noon, when most of us were gathered in the sitting room and waiting, Dr. Horace appeared in the doorway. We could hear Charity crying.

"It's over," he said heavily. "She is dead. God has taken her soul to his breast."

I felt the erupting tears choking me and with a wail I ran to my room and closed the door. I threw myself down on my bed and began to sob in a way I hadn't cried since my mother died so many years before. I cried so hard my chest pained me and I thought I would choke.

The door opened and I felt a hand touch me, and I whirled over. John stood beside the bed, looking down at me. "You loved her very much, didn't you?"

I nodded, unable to speak.

"She loved you, too, you know," he said, and paused. "Adelia, what would she want you to do—what would she tell you to do, if she could return and talk to you?"

I knew what he meant instantly, for I knew what my great-aunt would say.

"Yes, John," I murmured, and I sat up. I began to wipe my eyes with my apron, and then I got to my feet. John looked at me, saying nothing as I nodded. "I'll do what I can," I murmured.

Aunt Jewel would never let go; her indomitable spirit would never give up, and nor should I. The household would now need a strong, firm woman's hand. I knew that Melinda wasn't capable of taking over, nor was Felice. It was up to me. I rose to my feet and went into the sitting room.

So it fell to my lot in the awful days that followed to lay out my great-aunt; though the tears fought to be released, I wouldn't let them. I did those things that each day my aunt had always done. Yet, when we seated ourselves for our meals, Aunt Jewel's chair remained empty, and there were never completely dry eyes around the table.

Harlan came to me the afternoon that Aunt Jewel died, and asked me if it was true, and I explained that it was true. He sniffled and rubbed his eyes, and only began to cry when he ran into my arms and I knelt to receive him.

The funeral was attended by hundreds of people who came from many miles. Aunt Jewel was laid to rest in the family plot in a grove of pines. I stood beside the grave between Uncle Walter and Felice, my fingers tucked through the arm of each. Afterward, there was much food spread out on tables in the Great Hall, where people congregated and talked about Jewel Avigny Orne, who had come from faraway France so many years before. I had little time to myself, for it fell to me to see that everything was as it should be.

Then, when it was all over, everyone was gone, and we had cleaned up the Great Hall, I sent Georgia and Holly to their bedchambers. Both John and Rex had retired to their rooms, too. For a while I walked from one room to another, and Aunt Jewel's presence was in every one.

Yet she hated this place, I thought. But her presence would be there forever.

I returned to the sitting room where I'd spent so many hours with my great-aunt. I stood in the middle of the room, and her presence was so strong that I spoke her name, "Aunt Jewel?"

It was almost as if I might hear her answer in her light

voice. I could almost see those enormous black eyes, and I could hear her screech as she used to summon Ellen.

What now? I wondered. It was all over. I had done what I could, but now my usefulness was finished. In the morning should I pack and leave? To go where?

I heard a step in the hall and the door opened. John came into the room, towering in the doorway. "I thought I would find you here," he said in a deep voice. I saw that his eyes were reddened by his personal grief.

"Yes," I said quietly, "I am here."

"Tomorrow will you try to make a list of the letters you can identify as being missing? I will want them."

"I will try," I said.

"Will you finish the book? You've talked to Grandmamma so much you must know what she wanted to do. Could you continue her work?"

"I—I don't think so, John," I answered. What could I do without Aunt Jewel directing me? Would she want it? I didn't know.

"We'll talk about it later, Adelia. Go to bed now."

"Yes, John," I said wearily, and turned to the door that led to my bedroom.

"Adelia," John called after me, "I don't know what Rex and I would have done without you. We are grateful."

"I did what I could, only it wasn't enough," I murmured, and I turned to him, tears filling my eyes again. "If only I'd awakened a little earlier," I whispered in anguish. "If only . . ."

With three long strides John was before me, his hands on my shoulders. "Don't talk that way," he said sharply. "Don't blame yourself."

"I can't help it," I whispered. I closed my eyes and leaned against him for a moment, my forehead pressed against his chest. Then I straightened and looked up at him. "I hope you find whoever did it, John."

"We will," John said grimly, his heavy voice harsh. "Now, go to bed. I will see you in the morning."

He turned and left, and I went on to my room so weary that I was asleep almost at once.

The following afternoon there was a conference of the

family held in John's office. John had summoned them all, and they stood around his desk as he spoke to them. Even Dr. Horace had come.

"You all should have a say in this. *Grand'mère* had saved many letters, and she was writing her memoirs. Whoever killed her did so to stop the memoirs from being printed, and to obtain certain letters that Adelia is attempting to list now. The question," he said grimly, "is simply this. Do you want the letters to be published, anyway? Or do you want the letters burned, and everything forgotten.

"So, speak up, each of you."

For a moment no one spoke and then Dr. Horace said in his heavy voice, "I never believed that the letters should be published. What good would it have done? I say burn them!"

Felice cried out her opposition. "Somebody killed her to stop her. We must finish what she started!"

Each spoke up and it was apparent that most of the family believed the letters should be published.

"All right," John said. "Adelia is going to continue with the work. She will sort, edit, and select letters to be published. I've contacted the publisher by telegraph, and he has indicated they want very much to publish them. It's decided, then?" He turned to me. "Adelia, there's your mandate. Will you do it?"

"Of course I will," I responded. "I—I can't do it as Aunt Jewel might have done it, but I'll do the best I can."

"Nobody can ask more," John said, and indicated that the meeting was over.

# Chapter IX

Habits are hard to break, and when someone as wonderfully vital as my great-aunt should leave this world, there is, naturally, a terrible hurt and emptiness which is left. Probably that was why, during the days which followed, Charity came each morning to the sitting room to discover what should be served for dinner and supper that day. The first time she came, I sent her to Melinda, but in a few moments she was back.

"Miss Melinda said she doesn't care, Miss Adelia. She won't talk to me! What should I cook for dinner?"

"What do you suggest, Charity?" I asked.

"We have a nice pork loin in the storeroom, Miss Adelia," she answered.

I said that would be fine, and so it went in the days that followed. Charity made suggestions which I told her were excellent. In this manner and in a way that I never intended, I gradually took over the housekeeper tasks which Great-aunt Jewel had always attended to so meticulously.

So it was with Paul Wiley, too, with respect to his duties and those of the girls. I felt a reluctance to do so, but it quickly became apparent that Melinda, who might well assume the responsibilities of the house, had no intention of taking over anything. She grew even fatter, and her only interest seemed to be the trashy novels she chose to read, and her overweening interest in Rex, her youngest son.

I gathered from conversations between John and Rex that they still sought evidence that Colonel Carter had been in back of the break-in and the death of Aunt Jewel. However, none was ever found, and John restrained Rex from taking any action without evidence.

John did consult with the county sheriff, and the man spent one day at the Hall asking questions. However, as Rex said in disgust, the sheriff couldn't have found a live rat in a paper sack without help. So nothing was done and Aaron still made his way around the estate at intervals every day, watching for intruders.

As the days passed, I went systematically through one box of letters after another, carefully noting dates and contents, and developing an elaborate system of filing them, making copious notes of the subjects covered in the letters. Apparently, Aunt Jewel never destroyed anything, and certainly she and her husband had been prolific letter writers, considering all of the answers she received, as her violent husband had.

Gradually, I began to get a picture of those early days before the Erie Canal was even commenced. They must have been licentious and immoral people, all except Aunt Jewel. Certainly the evidence became clear that both John Orne and his brother, my grandfather, Joshua, were unrepentant womanizers who recognized no impropriety in seducing the wives of other men. Frequently I was startled and aghast at the gross references to escapades, particularly those of John, Aunt Jewel's husband. The view became even more dominant when I discovered, one morning, an old diary which my Aunt Jewel had kept for several years. Its yellowed pages told of the anguish my aunt went through when, as a stranger in a foreign country, she was forced to recognize the nature of the man to whom her father had literally sold her. I saw that she arrived a slip of a girl, not a woman, and that she was forced to undergo the terrors of a rough frontier society of a kind she could scarcely have dreamed—and in spite of the elegance of the transported Orne Hall.

The day I discovered that old diary and began to read it was certainly one of the most important days of my life, for in learning something about my great-aunt's secret thoughts, I began to learn something of myself. The indignities, the shattering experiences and difficulties which she faced were enough to destroy any woman—but they didn't destroy her!

For several hours I read steadily, leaving the diary only for noon dinner and supper, so engrossed I became. It was in the evening when I came to the telling of a day when John Orne had come home with a group of rough, drunken canallers and, in his cups, had offered her to his guests.

There were tear stains on the pages, but a resoluteness in the way the words were formed, too.

"I escaped to my room, and took the gun from the pegs on the wall. I loaded it, and I sat in my chair facing the door. I was ready when the door opened and the man who had drawn lots and won appeared. I aimed the big gun straight at his face and I told him I would blow his head from his shoulders should he come one step nearer. At first he thought I wouldn't have the courage, but then, fortunately, he changed his mind and retreated.

"When the men had left the next day and my husband had slept off the liquor he had drunk, I went to his room with the gun. I pressed it against his throat hard enough to wake him.

"When sleep had cleared from his eyes, I told him that I would kill him if ever again he did such a thing, or if he ever again came to my room!

"So far he hasn't, but each night I keep the loaded shotgun beside me."

My great-aunt had never become a big woman physically, but she had grown in inner stature, anyway. As I'd traced the story through her own words, I'd seen her change from the bewildered girl alone in a strange land to a woman of great strength.

I sat with the diary in my lap, my eyes wide open but seeing nothing as I thought about my great-aunt and about myself. I was plain and that was my cross—so plain no man would wish to marry me or could desire me—and I'd let that drive me from living, for I feared that I would be hurt. I'd acted the part of a coward, while Aunt Jewel had never so acted—then I realized it wasn't true. Aunt Jewel had *gained* courage from the horrible events of her life.

If she could do it, why couldn't I? I asked myself, and I resolved that I would *not* be afraid. I would not play the part of an arrant coward, afraid to live!

142

Then, on a sudden impulse, I took the diary and went to the first floor and tapped on the door to John's office. I heard him bid me enter, and I did.

Wearing a black silk smoking jacket, he sat in a large comfortable chair, his feet up on a stool, the *Waterloo Weekly* in his hand, a pipe clenched between his teeth.

He looked up and took the pipe from his mouth.

"Adelia! This is a pleasant surprise."

"John," I said, a little breathless, "I have found a diary your grandmother kept for years, long before you were born. It—it tells about what her life was like. John, it was a terribly story. Your grandfather wasn't a nice man, just as you said. I think the diary should be published with the letters."

He gestured to a chair as he got to his feet.

"Sit down, Adelia. I never heard that she wrote a diary." He reached out a hand and I gave the bound pages to him.

I took the chair he offered, and he sat down, too, beginning to leaf through the pages. After a moment I said, "Your grandmother was a woman of great courage."

"She was, indeed," he answered. "She didn't back away from living, did she?"

"No. I—I wish I could be like her," I said, a little wistfully.

"Give yourself some time," was his noncommittal response. "All right, I think you may be correct. Leave the diary with me. I will read it."

We talked a few moments more, and I returned to my room. But I was unable to sleep when I retired. I kept seeing Ellen's body and remembering her death, and the death of my great-aunt, too. I tried to make sense of it all, wondering if they were related in any way, but they couldn't be. Perhaps Charity was right and Orne Hall was cursed by God. But one of the strangest thoughts I had was that someone had tried to kill me, and I had no idea who it might be; but certainly whoever wished me dead was still in the house. This evening I had talked with John, pleasantly, even with some intimacy, within the confines of his office—yet it may have been him who tried to kill me! It hardly made sense. Why did I not fear him? And Rex; I saw him every day, and he was attentive, kindly, and yet it might have been Rex who sought to take my life.

At dinner, John mentioned the diary, and at the surprise and curiosity they evinced, he told his brother and the others that I'd found it and that it told much of Aunt Jewel's early married life.

Each wanted to read it, and John said they could take turns, and that I was to use it in the preparation of the book.

On the same day, as I later worked on the letters, I came across one to Aunt Jewel from an Edith Pepper. It was an intimate kind of a letter, the type which one close friend might write to another. Apparently the letter was in response to one Aunt Jewel had written to her, for it contained unkind references to Melinda and her common background. "Her people are nobodies, a worthless drunken lot. Your son was a fool to marry her!"

That had to be a reference to John Orne, Aunt Jewel's oldest son, the one who had been killed in a duel over Melinda.

I began to think like a detective, trying to put the pieces together, and always I was aware that someone *did* try to kill me, and that someone was certainly still in the old mansion. A thousand times I asked myself why I did not flee, but it became so simple to answer the question. For where could I go? What would I do? What opportunities existed for me? At the same time, I reminded myself that I would no longer run away from things which frightened me. I'd emulate my great-aunt and I would fight.

The very next day John asked me if I would accompany him on a trip to the nearby city of Rochester.

"I must conduct some business, and I would like the company. I thought you might find the trip enjoyable, and pleasant. You might shop for some new fashions in gowns."

Certainly his invitation startled me, but pleased me as well.

"I would love to go, John," I said. "You are very kind."

He said he wished to leave the following Monday morning. Later the same day I told Rex of the invitation.

"You aren't going, are you?"

"Yes, I think I am," I answered. "Why should you object?"

"I have asked you to marry me. I don't want you making a trip with my brother," he said. His blue eyes showed anger.

"I haven't accepted your proposal, Rex," I said. "You have no right to object," I chided. "Shame on you!"

He changed his tone.

"Don't go, Adelia," he said softly. "Let me tell everyone that we are to be married."

"No, Rex," I answered firmly. "I will make the trip with John since he was nice enough to invite me."

"Tongues will wag," Rex warned.

"Not in John's presence," I retorted, and I knew this was true.

We left Orne Hall early enough to reach Pykerie Junction before the arrival of the westbound morning train due at nine-fifteen. The locomotive came puffing, pulling the train into the station just on time. John assisted me up the high step and we began a most pleasant trip. It was now spring and the trees and fields were greening. John told many interesting things of the countryside as the train sped past farms and villages, and crossed and recrossed the wandering Erie Canal. As we entered the city of Rochester, John explained its origin.

"Nathaniel Rochester started a settlement here in 1812; it became a city in 1834. Now tons of wheat are milled to flour here, and sent on canal boats on down to Albany and thence to New York City. Without Rochester's mills, New York would have no bread," he joked.

It was a new and amiable side of John, whose demeanor usually seemed so stern and forbidding, yet I kept remembering his gentleness with his grandmother, and that time he'd played mumblety-peg with Harlan and me. It was as if he were truly two different men.

We arrived at the station and John hailed a cabriolet, a new kind of a small two-wheeled carriage I'd not seen before. He told the driver to take us to a large department store.

Once in the cab he pressed money on me, telling me to buy all that I might desire.

"I have business nearby and I will meet you at noon. Then we will have dinner," he said.

I protested against taking the money. "There's nothing I need," I said. "I'll just look around."

He would have none of it and he insisted I take the money, which was more than I'd ever had in my hands at one time in my whole life.

At the store we dismounted from the cabriolet, John paid the man handsomely, and we walked to the big store's entrance. We agreed to meet at the same place at noon, sharp.

For two hours I roamed the store, entranced at the lovely things I saw and that I might buy, yet I bought little, for there was so little I needed.

I found some rich-looking goods which I thought would make a lovely gown for Felice and I bought ten yards. There were other trifles that I bought on impulse, including a pretty, but not expensive, stickpin for John to wear on his cravat, a fob made from a gold coin for Rex to attach to his watch, and a toy hayrick for Harlan.

We met at the store's wide entrance precisely at the time appointed, and John tucked the packages of goods under his arm.

"We'll have dinner at Louis's Oyster-bar," he said. "Do you like oysters?"

"I—I've never tasted them. I don't think I could eat an oyster."

John laughed and said it was never too late to learn.

"It is easy when you know how," he assured me.

It was quite the largest restaurant I had ever seen, and the waiters were all dressed in formal frock coats and striped trousers. John was known to the headwaiter and to the other waiters as well. We were escorted to an important table situated by a window that overlooked the city street.

We dined on oysters, which I discovered were tasty when dipped in the highly seasoned red sauce, and on roast beef, which John said I should try rare, served with a rich steak sauce.

146

John became a third type of a man, for he was urbane, confident, a man of many interests, and a man who knew well how to please a lady. We each had a glass of sauterne wine, and later he ordered Napoleon brandy for us to sip with our coffee.

On a sudden impulse, I'd had the stickpin wrapped as a gift, and as we drank our brandy and coffee, I gave it to him.

"Because you have been so kind to a poor, distant relative," I explained lightly.

He unwrapped it carefully, and viewed the pin with pleasure.

"It is very nice," he said. "Adelia, you have excellent taste."

He started to insert the pin in his cravat, but peering down, he did it badly. Without giving thought, I rose from my seat and ran around the table to him.

"Here, you are so clumsy. Let me . . ."

I did place the stickpin with its bright red stone in just the right place in his cravat, and then, in a familiar way, I smoothed lapels of his handsome suit.

"There! You are quite the man around the city, John," I said with a light laugh. I returned to my seat. John stared at me oddly, his dark eyes unsmiling. I wondered if I had offended him by doing what I had done right there in the restaurant, and I flushed, thinking I had been forward.

I felt I had read his mind, and I said, "I'm sorry if I embarrassed you, John."

"Adelia," he said, paying no attention to my words, "will you marry me?"

His words utterly astonished me. He had never indicated that he cared for me or had ever considered me suitable to become his wife.

"John! Have you lost your mind?" I said. "Remember, this is plain-faced Adelia."

"I know who you are," he said, his voice a rumble of irritation. "I asked you a question. Will you give me an answer?"

"Did you mean it? You truly want to marry me?"

"Of course. If I hadn't, I wouldn't have asked. Now, may I have my answer?"

"John, that is hardly the most romantic proposal a woman has ever received," I murmured, and even as I spoke I realized how much this Adelia Dorsey had changed since she had come to Orne Hall. "Why do you want to marry me?" I asked, not without some archness.

He seemed actually puzzled. "So you would be my wife. What other reason could there be?"

"Well," I said as if I were contemplating the possibilities, one finger to my lip, "there are occasions when people have married because they felt some affection for one another."

"You know I have affection for you," he said with some exasperation.

"How do I know it? You've never said so."

"You don't *have* to say some things, Adelia."

"Well, John," I said, surprised at my own temerity, "in this case you have to say it if you want an answer."

For a moment he stared at me, his mouth slowly becoming wreathed in a wry smile.

"Very well, Adelia, I have a great amount of affection for you, and for this and other reasons apparent to anyone of any sense, I wish you to become my wife."

I looked across the table at him and a perverseness prompted me to say to John, "Rex, again last night, asked me to marry him."

John's bearded face hardened and it seemed to me it instantly became as a thundercloud ready to break into a raging storm.

"What answer did you give him?" he asked in a low, deep voice that seemed filled with a fury tugging to be loosed.

"The same answer I shall give you, John. I thank you for the compliment of asking me, but I shall give you the answer that I gave your brother. John, if a man gave you a proposal for a business deal which would ultimately affect your fortunes for the rest of your life, would you say yes or no immediately? Or would you wish to think it over?" I paused and smiled at him gently. "John, you thought it over well before asking me, didn't you?"

I saw a smile touch the corners of his lips, and the hard lights in his dark eyes became gentled.

"So, you want to think it over?" he asked. "And you told Rex the same? All right, I can be a patient man—when I must."

"But I do want to thank you, anyway, Cousin John."

For a moment he stared at me, with that same slow smile on his lips. Then he swished the brandy around in his glass, and lifted it for a small sip. "Adelia," he said as he returned the glass to the table, "you are a changed woman—changed from the frightened baggage who came to Orne Hall last fall."

"I hope the change is for the better, sir," I said archly.

"It is. You've become a grown woman, not a girl."

I thought of his grandmother and what she'd taught me.

"Aunt Jewel made me grow into a woman," I said softly. "I miss her so very much."

"And I," John returned. "Yes, she was a wonderful woman."

We caught the afternoon train at four after we'd spent several hours simply walking around Rochester and going into stores for the fun of it. I was tired, but it had been a wonderful day; it seemed that in many ways I had learned to know my cousin John for the first time. Often I thought of how different the two brothers were—and surely they were both fine men, and a catch for any still unmarried maiden.

On the train I leaned back with a satisfied sigh, my head resting against his shoulder.

"Thank you, John, for . . . for everything," I murmured.

The next thing I knew he was gently nudging me awake. "We're coming into Pykerie Junction, Adelia," he said softly.

"Oh," I said, startled, and I felt my face warm when I discovered his arm was over my shoulder and I was sleeping with my cheek pressed against his broad chest. I sat up and attempted to straighten my gown, and to smooth the

**149**

bodice over my hips. "John, I am ashamed. . . ."

"Adelia, the pleasure was mine," he broke in, and this time he actually grinned at me! "I was sorry we reached the Junction!"

"You should have awakened me. . . ."

"Ninny, I did, just now."

Aaron waited with the team and within the hour we were riding up the lane, headed for Orne Hall.

In the privacy of the carriage John said in serious tones with only a trace of banter in them, "I will await your answer. Of course," he went on, "I may have to break Rex's two legs at the knee!"

"Don't you dare," I cried. "He has nice knees," I insisted, and blushed as John laughed.

But as we drove up the lane to the big house, around the fountain and beyond the east wing, we passed within steps of the place where Ellen's body had been found. I remembered John's acceptance that she had not died of her own hand, but whoever had thrown her to her death was still alive and perhaps he still was near Orne Hall. I looked at John even as I thought of Rex; both were strong enough to throw Ellen from her window. Either might have done it. John's face seemed somber and I wondered if his thoughts were like mine.

"John," I said impulsively, "do you know who caused Ellen's death?"

He turned to look directly at me.

"No, I don't know, Adelia. I wish to God that I did!" He spoke with such vehemence that I was startled, and I withdrew from him. Again, I felt the change in him and the presence of violence which threatened to break out at the moment. But then he smiled. "Don't think of it," he said. "Perhaps we will never know."

Charity, knowing that we would arrive, had delayed supper, so that as soon as we entered the Great Hall, Georgia came from the dining room.

"Charity told me to tell you supper will be ready in twenty minutes."

"Fine," John said good-naturedly. "That will give Miss

150

Adelia just enough time to wash the train dust from her shiny nose."

"And you to brush it from your beard," I retorted gaily.

Once in my room, I removed the coat and changed quickly to a more comfortable skirt and shirtwaist, washing my face and hands at the washstand in the lavatory. As I did so, I thought of John—and of Rex—and I even giggled, sounding silly of course, for I was alone. Only weeks before, I thought that no man would ever desire me—that I was doomed to be an old maid because of my plain face. But in two days I had received two proposals from two fine men.

" 'Tis ridiculous," I said out loud, but I quickly sobered, too, for I must choose between them—or choose to *be* an old maid.

But when I entered the dining room and took my place beside the empty chair of Aunt Jewel, the grief swept over me again and I had to fight that I might still smile at the others.

Of course the supper chatter was all about what we'd seen in the Rochester stores, and about the things that we did in the afternoon. If I thought I detected a brief expression of jealousy in Rex's eyes across from me, well, why not? It was a delicious feeling that a man should show jealousy—should care that much about me.

How could I know that my happiness was to be so short-lived? How could I know that the concern that John showed that day on our trip to Rochester was so soon to turn to coldness and contempt?

After supper Rex asked me to come to the music room with him, for he had a piece by Chopin which he wished to play for me. With a smile at John, I permitted Rex to take my elbow in his fingers and guide me to the Great Hall's balcony, and down the wide stairway to the music room.

"The piece is a nocturne," Rex explained, and he did play it beautifully. But when he finished, he leaned on the pianoforte and asked if I had made up my mind.

"No, Rex," I answered, and then I thought that since I'd told John, why not tell Rex? "Rex, today John asked me to marry him, too."

Rex's face became suffused with color, and his blue eyes turned hard, but he said nothing for a long moment.

"And your answer?"

"The same answer I gave you; I won't make a decision now. I will think it over."

"Don't take too much time, Adelia. It would be unwise," he said, his voice level but its quality carried a threat none-theless.

"I will tell you when I know the answer," I retorted, and I left the music room to return to the sitting room, thinking that I might well do some work. However, I had been in the room only minutes when I knew that someone had again been at the files, and that the letter folders had been searched, and perhaps some removed.

I stood at the file case, my eyes closed, in deep thought, for who would go through the letters and for what purpose? It would be no stranger, for Aaron patrolled the grounds, and no one could enter Orne Hall surreptitiously. But who at Orne Hall would seek to go through the letters? Suddenly I thought of the diary, and with a small cry, I ran to the davenport and opened the top drawer.

I gave a sigh of relief, for it was there. I picked it up and I began to thumb through it quickly. A faint variation in the paper edge stopped me, and I looked at the sheets. One was missing. There was no doubt about it, one sheet had been carefully cut, and the entry made by Aunt Jewel for January 9, 1831, had been removed.

A faint chill seemed to fill the sir of the sitting room as I returned the diary to the drawer in the davenport. Why would someone remove one sheet? And when had it been done? While I was in Rochester?

I didn't know, but I felt a fear and I wondered if I really wanted to know. Perhaps it would be better that I not know.

I tried to remember what had been on that page, reading both the preceding and following pages, but my memory failed me; I could remember nothing. I did recall that John or Rex, I'd forgotten which one, had said that the Erie Canal had been completed in 1825, so that this page must have been written after the canal had been constructed—

and when John and Joshua had been involved in the corruption that accompanied the canal's construction and operation.

I told myself the page could hardly be important now, yet I knew it had been in its proper place the days previous. It must have well been important to someone.

On impulse I decided to show the diary with the missing page to John. I knew that others of the family had surely been reading it during our absence in Rochester.

With the diary in my hand, I left the sitting room and hurried down the hallway to the stairway, and down to the Great Hall. The way to John's room led past the doorway to Rex's bedroom, and just as I walked down the corridor the door opened and Rex appeared before me.

"Adelia," he said in some surprise, "what are you doing wandering around at this time of the night? It's late, you know." He smiled at my sudden embarrassment and confusion, for I'd not thought of the time, I'd been thinking so hard about the diary, and working longer at the letters than I'd realized.

"I wanted to show John some—"

"At this time of night, dear cousin?" Rex broke in with a smile that curled up at the corners. "Couldn't it well have waited until morning?"

"Yes, I suppose that it could," I answered. "I—I didn't realize that it was so late."

"Well, why not show what it is to me, Adelia? You know that I am John's brother, and what you show him shouldn't you show to me also?"

He took my arm and drew me toward the bedroom door.

"No, Rex," I said firmly. "I wanted to discuss something with John, not you! Please let go my arm."

"No, Adelia," he answered. "Please come in a minute and tell me what is so important that you must see John at this time of the night."

"Rex, you're hurting me. . . ."

I struggled against him, but he was too strong, and a moment later, willy-nilly, I was in his room, my back against the door. I was furious at Rex. "Shame on you," I cried. "You are no gentleman, Rex Orne!"

"I've not touched you. . . ."

"You drew me into your room against my will. . . ."

"Curiosity, Adelia. What was it that you wanted to show my brother?" He pointed to the book which I still held in my hand. "Was it because of the diary?" he asked. "Did you find something?"

Why shouldn't I tell him? He was John's brother, and his behavior had been abominable. "A page has been cut out," I explained. "The page was there day before yesterday," I added.

"Let me see. . . ."

I handed him the diary. "January 9, 1831," I explained.

He carried the diary to a chair and seated himself, holding the book to the light that he might more easily examine it. He found the place, and I saw the intensity of his gaze as he examined the two pages that faced the one which was now missing.

Finally, he shook his head as if he were puzzled, and placed the book on the library table beside him. He glanced up at me as I still stood at the closed door.

"Come closer, Adelia," he commanded. "Don't stand at the door as if you were ready to flee."

"Give me the diary, and flee I will," I said angrily.

"Come and get it, cousin."

I did, and when I reached for it, Rex reached for me, and before I could catch my balance, I found myself in his lap, his strong hands holding me tightly.

"Let me go," I whispered in quick fury. "What do you think you're doing? Do you think I'm one of your whorehouse girls from Waterloo?"

I struggled against him and he did release me.

"I'm sorry, Adelia," he murmured, his words contrite, though his tone was not. "I acted the scoundrel, didn't I? All right, Adelia, flee thee to John," he added with a derisive quality to his words.

"I will! Rex, I am ashamed of you," I cried, aware of how tousled I must have become in the struggle against him.

I ran to the door, opened it, and stepped out into the dimness of the hallway, and before I was aware of his presence, I ran into John's arms as he walked down from the Great Hall.

# Chapter X

"John," I cried, and I am afraid my voice expressed astonishment, for I knew instantly that he must well have seen me coming from Rex's room. And I knew how disheveled I must look, because of my brief struggle with Rex. "Oh, John, it—it isn't what you think," I said in faltering tones, for his expression had become fearsome.

"What is it that you believe I think?" he asked politely, the words cold and stiff.

"I was coming to see you, John, and Rex . . ."

"Am I to be pleased that you were coming to my room in the night and were so easily delayed by my brother?"

"It was about the diary; there's a page missing." I knew that I babbled as I held the diary out for him to see. I began to fumble through it, seeking the location of the missing page. "It was there two days ago, John. . . ."

"Good night, Adelia," John said coldly.

I looked into his eyes and saw only the hard and furious anger, though his deep voice remained cold and even. I felt something in me sag and I felt weak, for the accusation was plain in the way his lip curled and his dark eyes widened.

"Ask Rex," I urged, even so knowing the uselessness of my words, for would John believe his brother? I knew better.

"There is no need to ask anyone," John said. "Good night, Adelia."

Without another word he turned his back on me and walked down the hallway to his own bedroom. A moment later I was alone in the dimness, the diary in my hand, my eyes filled with tears. I stood motionless, hurting in a way

I'd not known that I could be hurt, and then I turned and walked to the Great Hall.

I climbed the wide, carpeted stairs slowly, wearily, aware of what John believed of me. The realization was unbearable.

Once back in my great-aunt's sitting room, I woodenly returned the diary to its place in the file, and turned down the wicks of the lamps. In the gloom, lightened only by moonlight through the windows, I went to my own bedroom, undressed, and turned down the wick and got into bed.

For a time I lay awake, staring into the dark of the high ceiling over my head. Inwardly I writhed to realize what John had certainly believed, for I could not deny that I came from Rex's room. Even should Rex attempt to explain—and to take the blame—would John believe? One part of my mind became angry; if John wanted me to become his wife, shouldn't he believe in me? Trust me? But another part scoffed, and I asked myself what I would believe should I have observed John coming from some lady's room at that late hour, his hair and clothing in disarray— and I knew the answer quickly enough.

As for Rex, he probably meant no harm, and certainly he had hurt only my dignity.

I turned and tossed; as if in a theater I saw again the events in the dark corridor, and wondered what I could have said that would have changed the expression in John's eyes. And I wondered, too, at the hurt I felt, for I knew that now his tendered proposal would of certain be withdrawn. When I examined the real hurt, I knew that it was John I cared for more than I had known. Otherwise the pain of my realization of what he must believe of me would not have been so great.

Finally, I began to cry, for it seemed to me that I had lost something that I'd not known I truly desired—lost it forever. John would never forgive me for what he believed had happened. I knew that, now, but too late.

Yet, I did sleep finally, though my dreams were filled with shapes that threatened and filled me with terror and a sense of hopeless, heartbreaking guilt.

I woke before the time to arise, and lay quietly watching the hands of the big clock move slowly toward the time at which I must dress and present myself at breakfast. What would be the expression on John's face? And Rex, how would he behave?

Again, as always, the sight of Aunt Jewel's empty chair at the breakfast table stirred my feelings, and as I seated myself, I asked myself what she would have done. It seemed to me that I drew strength from her, even though she be buried with but a stone marking the place.

I was the first to arrive in the dining room; Georgia appeared with the coffeepot to pour the dark, fragrant-smelling brew into my cup. I seated myself and answered Paul's greeting with my own good-morning, even as my mind still thought only of the event of the night before.

John appeared and took his seat at the head of the table, his dark, somber expression and his cold stare told me nothing except that from him I could expect no warmth or understanding. But pride kept my head high.

"Good morning, John," I said as calmly as I could.

"Good morning, Adelia," he answered, his voice expressing only coldness and contempt. "I trust you slept well."

"Badly," I admitted, and I looked down at my cup of steaming coffee.

Rex and Melinda came into the dining room, followed by Walter and Felice. Further conversation between John and me became impossible. Rex and John talked the plans for the day briefly, and I told Felice of the goods I had brought her from which she might sew a gown.

Once Rex caught my eye as a quizzical smile touched his lips, and then he deliberately winked. Foolishly acting as if guilt prompted my response, I looked quickly at John, and I knew he'd seen the interchange, for his expression became even more grim.

Breakfast over, I went down to the kitchen to find Harlan. He had just finished his cooked breakfast cereal and milk and was still seated at the scarred old table.

"Harlan," I said as I walked to him, putting my hands on his thin shoulders, "I brought you something from

Rochester. Will you come up to the sitting room and I will give it to you."

He squirmed around to look up at me, his lips wreathed in a delighted smile.

"Right now?" He glanced at Charity. "Can I, Grandma?"

Charity told him to go along, and with his hand in mine, we crossed the Great Hall and climbed the wide stairs.

He was pleased with the toy, but I sent him downstairs again. "I have much work to do, Harlan," I explained.

For two hours I did work on the files, though it seemed to me an empty task, and the pain in my heart could not let me forget the thoughts I knew that John had about me. A measure of frustration and inner anger began to form in my mind, and when Rex entered the sitting room, I was in a mood receptive to an argument. Even before Rex could speak, I blurted out, "John saw me come from your room last night, Rex, and he believes . . . you know what he must believe. I wish you to explain I was in your room for only seconds, and that you had been ungentlemanly enough to drag me through the door!"

Rex had the temerity to smile widely.

"Adelia, why should I do that? Let him believe what he will—now, will you give me an answer? Will you marry me, Adelia?"

"No!" I stormed. "I think I hate you!"

"Well, John probably isn't of a mind to marry you now, so what choice do you have?"

"I can go to the almshouse, should I have to!"

"You have a temper, Adelia," he said as he seated himself comfortably on the settee, his long legs outstretched. "You should learn to curb it, if you propose to be a proper wife and mistress of Orne Hall," he said calmly, though the teasing light in his bold blue eyes belied the calm. "You really have no choice, now, do you, Adelia? Marry me you must."

"Must I?" I flared. "Why must I?"

"What other choices do you have?" he asked with sweet reasonableness. "Surely you don't want to waste your life on splendid spinsterhood, do you?"

"Why should it be wasted?" I demanded, furious. "Am I

so useless that lest I be your wife I be nothing? You are shaming me!"

"Not at all, Cousin Adelia; just pointing out the facts." Suddenly his mood changed. His eyes became gentle, as did his voice. "Adelia, I love you. Surely you know that. I want you to become mistress of Orne Hall, to be my wife and to bear my children. . . ."

"What if John should marry?" I asked sharply. "What—would not it be his wife who would become the mistress of Orne Hall? And not me, with the plain face, and . . ."

"Oh, John will never marry," Rex broke in to say with confidence. He laughed briefly. "Not after being so disillusioned by finding you coming from my door."

"If you were a gentleman you would explain that you'd pulled me within, and for just a few seconds."

"Would he believe me?" he asked, his lips twisting in a wry grin. "Would he, Adelia? Would you, if you didn't know the truth?"

"Rex, there are times when I would gladly split your head open like a ripe watermelon," I exploded in frustration.

"Marry me, Adelia, and I will agree to supply you with an ax once a day—and a ripe watermelon for you on which to practice."

"You're making a joke of it," I cried. "I don't want John to think badly of me."

"I want you to marry me, Adelia," Rex said. He got to his feet. "Shall we agree on the first week in June?" He raised one eyebrow quizzically as he waited for an answer.

"We will not agree on anything," I answered sharply. "Now, Rex, please go away and leave me to my work!"

He came to me, and before I could divine his purpose or escape his grasp, his lips brushed my cheek gently.

"I love you when you are angry, Cousin," he murmured, and turned away. I watched him walk to the door, furious but still sensible to the touch of his lips and aware of what it did to my emotions. At the door he turned.

"Have you remembered what was on the page which was torn from the diary?" he asked, with what seemed to me to be elaborate casualness.

"No." I answered, "I have not! Nor am I likely to. Please go away, Rex, and let me work!"

"Very well, cousin," he murmured. "I'll see you at dinner," and he disappeared, closing the door behind him.

For a moment I simply stood in that one spot, looking at the door, and I asked myself what kind of a woman I had become, for the touch of his lips on my cheek had been pleasurable. Yet, not many moments before, I'd been so certain that it was John I loved down deep in my heart—and I'd lost him.

John did not come to dinner, and Rex explained quite casually that his brother had found it necessary to drive to Waterloo on business, but Rex's smiling eyes rested on me knowingly for a moment.

Conversation during dinner was relaxed, yet when the meal was over and I left the table to return to the sitting room and to my work, Rex followed me into the balcony above the Great Hall. "Adelia," he called to me gently, and I did stop, one hand resting on the broad, smooth banister.

"Adelia, will you ride with me this afternoon? It's such a warm day."

The idea did appeal to me, and it sounded as if he meant it to be a peace offering, so after a moment's hesitation I nodded. "Yes, I'd like that, Rex.

"Now?" he asked eagerly.

"Very well, Rex. I'll meet you at the stables," I responded.

I retired to my own room and dressed myself in my riding habit and boots. Rex waited for me at the stables, and my favorite lively sorrel-and-white mare had been saddled for me.

Rex assisted me to mount the sidesaddle, and once my knee was securely hooked over the pommel, he himself mounted and we set off at the canter down the lane that led to the valley. His big stallion was faster and fought the bit, so that soon my smaller mare and I were distanced. I watched Rex skillfully handle the stallion, his hands firm but not hard as he controlled the animal's spirits and its desire to run. I thought that he truly was a fine figure of a man, and in many ways so much preferable to his moody and violent-tempered older brother. Though I felt the hurt at the rejection by John, I told myself not to be foolish. And I found myself debating in my mind, assuring myself that if I did not love Rex, I could well learn to.

When we reached the lane which followed the bluff above the canal and the valley, the horses were willing to reduce their exuberant speed to a walk. It was very pleasant adjusting myself to the swaying motion of my mount, and to be aware of Rex's fine blue eyes resting on me.

"Adelia," he said suddenly, "I don't think you realize just how attractive and desirable a woman you are."

His words startled me, and I laughed heartily at him.

"Rex, you forget I have a mirror into which I frequently peer."

He seemed as if he would say more, but then he abruptly spurred the stallion to a canter and I had no choice but to do likewise.

Once we had reached the valley, and the winding canal, Rex reined his mount to a halt. It was truly a lovely meadow, and I willingly lent my hand to him to assist me down after he himself had dismounted.

We walked slowly along the towpath; at the moment no boats moved on the canal's placid surface, which reflected so perfectly the blue and white of the sky and clouds.

"Adelia," he said softly, "do you think that flower is beautiful?"

He pointed to a spring flower, a little crocus of delicate beauty.

"Of course it is beautiful!" I knelt beside it, admiring its coloring and loveliness.

"Why?" Rex asked from where he stood beside me.

"Why? It just is," I murmured.

"Who said so?"

"I have said so!" I rose to my feet and glanced up into his bold blue eyes, which were somehow softened and had only a gentle glint in them.

"You mean it's natural a flower should be beautiful, just because it is?"

I nodded, not understanding what point he pursued. I

smiled at him, a little impishly. "Are you lecturing me, Rex?"

"Perhaps," he confessed with a chuckle. "Adelia, the flower is natural, so it's lovely. Aren't you natural?"

"Natural I may be, beautiful I am not," I answered tartly.

"I think you are," he said softly. "Adelia, to me you are very beautiful indeed!"

I caught my breath, and my heart rose in my throat. In my entire life I had never heard sweeter words spoken to me, and even though in my mind I scoffed, still I felt my face flushed and warm. I blinked quickly, for tears threatened as I looked into his steady blue eyes.

"You have made me very happy, Rex," I said softly.

He put his hands on my shoulders and drew me toward him, nor did I resist. Without thinking, I lifted my face and closed my eyes; I felt the pressure of his lips on mine, and it seemed to me that surely the battering of my heart on my ribs must shake me apart. For what seemed a beautiful eternity, he held me so, and then when he released me I thought I might faint and I wished my corset had not been drawn so tightly about my waist.

"Marry me, Adelia," he whispered. "Tell me that you will be my wife! For I love you very much."

"Yes," I answered in a voice that trembled with emotion. Of course I loved him! How could I do else after the words he'd said to me. It was as if the heavens had opened, and it was a new universe—as if I had been born anew. I'd been an ugly duckling but Rex's words changed me into a swan!

"Oh, yes, Rex!"

He kissed me again, but lightly, and then he held me in his arms for a moment and I thought that his heart beat with a heavey urgency which matched the fast thudding within my own breast.

Reluctantly, I pushed away his strong arms and stepped back, so that I might look up into his eyes, and the tears did overflow and I felt them race down my cheeks, though I knew that I smiled even as they did so.

He took my hand and we began to walk slowly along the old towpath which had been trod by so many thousands of hooves. A straining pair of mules appeared around the bend, and a canal boat appeared behind them. We could see the steersman at the stern, and at the rear of the beasts a young girl used a switch on the gray rumps.

We stepped aside to let the slow-moving craft pass by, the girl's light voice mouthing the encouraging words used by all canallers to urge the mules into their yokes. The steersman raised a cap in a gay, impudent salute.

"I must go back," I told Rex as we returned to the tow-path. "It's getting late."

"Will it be June?" Rex asked.

"Yes, June," I answered, and for some reason the wonder of the afternoon became just a little marred by my acceptance of the date. A part of my mind foolishly worried at the question: Why June? Why did Rex want it to be June? I told myself not to spoil the moment, but it *was* spoiled, for as I glanced up at Rex, I wondered against my will how many other ladies he had said words of like kind. *What are words?* I asked myself. Anyone can speak them. How do I know if they came from the heart? Mentally I saw myself as if I were standing before a mirror, and I *was* plain, and no man could tell me otherwise.

Somehow the magic of the afternoon dissipated as a fog might disappear before the brightness of the morning sun. I was completely ashamed of my thoughts and I asked myself silently: What is wrong with me!

At the stables, Aaron and Toby came out to take the mounts' bridles in their hands as Rex dismounted, and then I unhooked my knee from the pommel and slid off the back of my mare and down into Rex's arms. For just an instant he held me, and I felt again his sturdy strength.

It was nearing time for supper when we entered the house and returned, each of us, to our own rooms. I changed from the riding habit, and for a moment rested on the soft comfort of my bed, my eyes closed. I would have thought of Rex had I any choice, but I had none, for instead of Rex's fair vision I saw in my mind the brooding, bearded face of John, his dark eyes looking at me accusingly.

"Rex loves me," I whispered, and then for a reason I

myself could not understand, I turned on my side and began to cry. I suspect I was suffering from the vapors which one reads would come upon a maiden when she had received and accepted a proposal.

Suddenly I glanced at the long clock; I would be late for supper if I didn't hurry. I dashed cold water on my face and in my eyes, combed out my hair disarrayed by the pillow, and dressed quickly in my three petticoats and a white-and-yellow skirt below the form-fitting shirtwaist.

When I presented myself in the dining room I was indeed late; all of the others of the family were there, including John. Rex rose as soon as I entered, and with a flourish he escorted me to my place, but then he hesitated and his hand held my elbow.

"I think," he said, in a voice all could hear, "that Adelia should take her place at the head of the table—in *Grand'mère*'s place—for she has today consented to become my bride—and the mistress of Orne Hall."

For a moment no one spoke, and then Felice called out her approval. "You belong there," she said. "You already are the mistress!"

Strangely, Melinda echoed the same thought. "You do everything a housekeeper is supposed to do," she said, and her choice of the word "housekeeper" rankled just a little. Was I not to be more than a housekeeper? Still, I wished that Rex had not announced our engagement so quickly —and I did not wish to take Aunt Jewel's chair at the table.

John's voice, cold and harsh, broke any magic the moment might have had.

"Rex," he said, "are you so sure that your wife will be the mistress of Orne Hall? Would you also take my place?" His words were hard, as was his tone, and no one said anything for a long moment as the two brothers stared at one another. Then it was Rex who broke the silence.

"Brother," he said in a soft, even voice, "don't press me too far."

But John stared only at me.

"Will it be that the ceremony must be soon?" he asked in a manner that was insulting in its implication.

Rex's face reddened and I saw dangerous flecks of light in his eyes.

"Rex," I said quickly, my voice as matter-of-fact as I could make it, "I don't want to sit in your grandmother's chair. I am not mistress of Orne Hall. Let me take my usual place." Without another word, I did slide into the chair at the place I'd been seated since the first day I'd come to Orne Hall.

"Please, sit down, Rex," I said gently.

He did so, and as Paul and Georgia began to serve our dinner of mutton and boiled potatoes, no one spoke. I was aware of the expression of disinterest on Paul's face, but I knew, too, that his eyes had flicked from one brother to the other with an import that escaped me. Did he wish that they should quarrel, or did he hope that they would not? I couldn't tell.

During the rest of our time at the supper table, little was said. Rex appeared somewhat like a sulky boy who had been reprimanded, and it seemed strange to me. So many times he appeared so sure of himself, so willing to assert himself, and yet, when he faced John on an issue, John's implacable stare seemed always to be the critical element, and Rex would shrink in size. I found myself resisting very much John's domineering manner, and his contemptuous words.

Supper over and our cups of coffee drained, we rose and John addressed me directly.

"Adelia, I would like a word with you in my office." He glanced at Rex. "That is, if my brother is willing to permit it?" His voice, filled with cold bitterness, brought a new flush to Rex's cheeks. He looked at me as if to say that everything would be fine before he nodded to his brother.

"All right, John," he murmured.

It surprised me that Rex did not object, for he merely glanced at John, his blue eyes expressing an emotion I was quite unable to fathom.

John led the way and I followed, resenting the manner with which he walked ahead, yet aware of the strength with which his powerful shoulders swung with each stride, and the lightness of his step which one would not expect in a man so tall.

We climbed the three steps to the west hallway, and down to the door of his room. Nor did he open it and then wait for me to enter, but instead he walked in, leaving me to follow him, and to close the door behind me.

Without a word he went to his heavy chair behind his desk and seated himself. Nor did he ask me to be seated in one of the chairs before him. I stood near the door, waiting for him to speak, but instead he took from the holder one of his pipes, packed it slowly with fragrant tobacco, touched a match to it, and drew for a moment. The smoke drifted from his nostrils before he turned to look up at me.

"You may sit down, Adelia," he said negligently, as if it made no difference to him.

"I shall stand," I said stubbornly. "Of what did you wish to speak?" I asked as calmly and steady as I could.

"As you wish," he murmured. His dark eyes were as cold as the blackest winter night, and beneath his trimmed beard I saw that the muscles of his jaws were clamped in a way that suggested an indomitable will and determination.

"I do not wish you to marry Rex," he said coldly.

"Is it any concern of yours, John?" I asked with some pride and spirit. "Is Rex your slave that you may choose for him his wife? Has he no say in the matter?" I tried to keep my voice level, and I discovered that in spite of myself I was speaking with heat and rising anger. "What right do you have to tell me that I must or must not marry your brother?"

"No right," John said, and a wintry smile touched his lips. "Except the right of power. You see, I am able to decide because I have the power to do so. I shall use it."

"Why do you object?" I asked after a moment. I had thought I might love this man, and he had asked me to become his wife and the mistress of Orne Hall. I thanked my good fortune that I had learned of his true nature before I had made that mistake. I waited for his answer. "Why do you care if your brother might wish to marry me?"

"Because he isn't my brother. He is my half brother,"

167

John said, in level tones that expressed no feeling but simply stated a fact.

"What do you mean?" I asked, confounded by his words. Melinda was the mother of both John and Rex, was she not?

"I mean that although John Orne, Junior, was my father, my half brother, Rex, was sired by some dog whose identity was never known." His words carried a message as harsh and unforgiving as any I had ever heard; the manner of John's speaking was that of one who merely recounted the total of a day's cattle sales.

I thought a moment while the impact of John's words made their impression on me.

"May I sit down?" I asked in a small voice. "I think I feel faint."

"It's those damnable corsets you females insist on wearing," John said. "There's no way you can breathe enough air, so you expire to vapors." A kind of smile did quirk up his lips. "However, and nonetheless, yes, you may sit down."

I did so, for indeed my knees felt wobbly and unsure. However, I had nothing to say, and instead I thought of the revelation that John had just made to me. I thought of the months I had been at Orne Hall and I realized I had never seen a gesture or word of gentleness expressed by John toward his mother. Yet, Rex was at times affectionate—I looked up at John and I asked if Rex knew.

"Most assuredly he knows. He also is aware that he cannot inherit, for none of the Orne blood moves in his veins." His smile grew contemtpuous. "And that is why his offering you *Grand'mère*'s chair was insulting, for his wife can never become the mistress of Orne Hall."

"Why do you permit him to remain then?" I asked. "Do you hate him?"

"No, I don't hate him. We grew up as brothers; we shared our youth. We played games, and I extricated him from many an entanglement brought about by his nature." John paused before he went on. "Let me assure you, though I love him because he is my half brother, I know well that his father must have been the greatest liar of all

**168**

time, for Rex, his son, will choose to tell the truth only under a threat of being beaten senseless."

His words brought anguish to my heart, for I remembered Rex looking down into my eyes as he called me beautiful. I stirred, my hands in my lap, as I inwardly cringed, my shoulders drawing together almost as if I were in grief, as well I may have been. But my mind continued to operate, even though I felt shattered by the revelation.

"Why should you care if your half brother should marry a homely woman?" I asked. "What is it to you?"

"I don't want a woman like you in Orne Hall," he said with calculating cruelty. "I know my own desires. I know that you might find in convenient to come to my bedroom some night as you went to Rex's, and I am not an adulterer. I would not sleep with my half brother's wife. So," he added, his voice filled with a contempt that struck me as if with a whip, "I don't want you to marry Rex. I don't want you around Orne Hall after you have completed you work on *Grand'mère*'s memoirs." He paused and went on more kindly. "Nor do I wish you to have hardships. The Orne holdings are great enought that they can see you do not want. You will receive a reasonable stipend each month until your death or until you marry, whichever event occurs first."

Something down deep in me made my spine stiffen and my head to lift until I stared directly into John's face, my own eyes locking his in a battle.

"I came to Orne Hall with nothing, John Orne, and I will leave with nothing," I said in as hard a tone as I could muster. "Now, I want you to listen to me, John, for though Rex may not tell the truth, *I do not lie!* I did not lie before nor shall I lie now. I was on the way to your office with the diary to inform you that the page was missing. Rex happened to open his door and he pulled me inside *against my will!* He caught me down into his lap and his hands were familiar, but I fought him, and I was in his room no more than one minute. Of course I was disheveled!

"Oh, John Orne, your mind is corrupted and unclean! I had once thought kindly toward you, but now I hate you with every fiber of my being! I care not that Rex is your

169

half brother; from what I've learned of the Ornes, his father could hardly have been worse than yours. I shall marry him, for he has given me the honor . . ."

"Wait up, Adelia," John said with a heavy laugh. "All right, I may have been wrong. But you won't marry Rex, for if you do, he will have nothing; he has never done a day's work in his life. He is charming; he can seduce a woman with expert skill. But he is worthless in business. If you marry Rex, you'll never know a moment of peace. You don't think he could remain faithful to you, do you, Adelia? Let me assure you, he could not. Nor can he supply you with food; when you get heavy with his child, where will you get the money to feed yourself and your coming child? And get you with child, he most assuredly will. Nor," he added, "will it be the first time."

"I will leave in the morning; I will go away. . . ."

"Where, cousin, will you go? Do you have a single silver coin to pay for fare on a train? Don't be childish; without money you cannot go anywhere, unless you wish to become one of the women who wait at the villages for the coming of the canallers. And let me assure you, that, too, is a life you are ill suited for."

"You mock me and my plainness, John Orne! Does it please you to be cruel?" I felt angry enough to scratch out his eyes as the import of what he said sank into my thoughts. I rose to my feet as if to do battle.

John appeared shocked and astonishment spread over his face. But this was replaced by a contrite expression. "Adelia, you misread me! That was not my meaning! I meant, indeed, that you were far too fine a woman for that kind of life. I didn't mean . . ."

"Too fine a woman! What did you think of me when you saw me at Rex's door? What did you think of me when you told me with your own lips that you wished to marry me, for me to become your bride, the mistress of Orne Hall? *What kind of a man are you, John Orne?*" If I'd had a sword, I'd have run him through the heart!

I stood before him, my hands clenched into fists, my eyes wide with fury, my chest rising and falling with each quick breath, my throat tight.

He rose to his feet and stared down at me, much as if he was seeing me for the first time. He leaned forward, his hands on the desk top, his dark eyes blinked quickly, and he spoke as if to himself. "By God, you *are* beautiful when you are furious!" He moved his head from side to side as if in disbelief. "Like a savage up-country lynx ready to fight for her kittens!"

I stared at him much as he stared at me, and as if I were a bag out of which the air moved slowly, I felt myself collapsing. John's mouth began to widen, and I heard a chuckle coming from his big chest.

My first reaction was to find something heavy enough to beat him to death, but in spite of myself I felt the infectiousness of his laughter, and I discovered that my lips were curving up into a smile, and then I began to laugh with him!

It was insane, for we both began to laugh so hard that tears came to our eyes. I fell back into the chair behind me, and he sank down into his chair, still howling with idiotic laughter.

Finally, we had to cease, for we were both exhausted, and with only faint eruptions, we looked at one another. But finally, after a pause, I said with a sigh that meant almost anything to me, "I'm still going to marry Rex."

"Don't be silly," John retorted. "He won't marry you; not with the choice I will give him." He hesitated and his lips pursed a moment. "Do you love him?"

"Would I marry him if I loved him not?" I retorted.

"Adelia, I wish I knew," he murmured heavily, and then he sighed. "Women aren't like men. . . ."

"So I have heard," I broke in demurely.

"Men are predictable. Women are not."

"Life would be dull, if it were not so," I commented.

"No, you won't marry Rex, for he will change his mind quickly when I tell him he will have nothing. And I am doing this for you, for you could not bear long to live with a man as faithless as Rex will be. Fidelity to one woman isn't possible for the likes of him."

"You're *too* kind! Nor do I believe you."

"You don't believe what?"

**171**

Though I was less certain than I pretended, nonetheless I would not permit John to play the patriarch to me.

"I don't believe that Rex will refuse to marry me because you cut him off with nothing."

"You don't? Do you wish to put it to the test?" he asked, cynically smiling his assuredness that he was right.

"Of course," I said confidently.

For a long moment John stared at me, and I gave him as good as he sent. Abruptly, he rose and went to the window where the signal cord hung. He gave it a hard pull, and returned to the chair.

In a moment Paul Wiley came to the door and asked if he could be of service.

"Find Rex and send him here," John said shortly. "At once!"

"Yes, sir," Paul said, and turned. He left, closing the door shut with silent speed.

"Prepare yourself for a disappointment," John said, his voice less cold. "I know my half brother better than you do."

I thought of Aunt Jewel's affection for Rex. "Did your grandmother know that Rex was—was not . . ."

"She knew," John said grimly. "But as far as Rex was concerned, no woman could resist him." He cocked one eye at me. "No more could you!"

"You are hateful, John Orne!" I cried. "Did you pull the wings off of dragonflies when you were a boy?"

"I loved dragonflies," John answered. "Didn't you?"

Suddenly I was convulsed with a giggle. "When I was a little girl I was told that dragonflies would light on your lips and sew them shut and you'd never be able to talk again.".

He laughed and nodded. "Yes, I remember . . ."

Rex came into his brother's office, closing the door behind him. He remained at the door, his lips smiling but his blue eyes as hard as agates. "What is it that you wish, brother John," he said in a voice contemptuous and bitter. "I suppose you have been telling Adelia the sordid details of my accidental birth, and of the fact that I will have no share of the Orne fortune? Am I right, John?"

"A little more than that, Rex. However, Adelia, strange as it may seem, believes in your love. She actually thinks you are going to marry her after I have informed you that you will be without a penny from that point on, nor will you be welcome at Orne Hall. However, Rex, you and I know better, don't we?" His tone carried the rasp of complete contempt.

"You're quite wrong, John," Rex said in an even tone. "I don't need your money. I can care for any woman I marry and I love Adelia. I will still marry her, though you deny me my rightful share of the Orne wealth."

"That was quite a speech, Rex," John said thoughtfully. "Am I wrong about you? Do you care enough for Adelia?"

"I do, John. You can't prevent us from marrying."

I felt a glow of pride in Rex, and in the way he had picked up the gauntlet thrown down by his half brother. I rose to my feet and ran to him, and I felt his arms hold me close.

John began to laugh. "Well, I'll be eternally damned," he said finally. "You really mean it, don't you, Rex?"

"I do mean it," Rex answered, his voice filled with determination. He looked down at me. "Adelia, I love you," he said softly.

I closed my eyes, feeling drained by the emotions which had swept through me since I'd followed John from the supper table.

"All right," John said, in a tone that indicated he had made a decision. "You two can marry; you will richly deserve each other, I suspect. On the day you marry I will present you with a thousand dollars, Rex, and on the day you marry you will leave Orne Hall, and you will never return. Do you understand?"

"Why, brother John, I understand very well. But mark my words, I shall return—sooner than you believe I might. I will return with Adelia as my wife." He paused. "And she will be mistress of Orne Hall and sit at the head of the table."

The two brothers glared at one another, and though I still was held in Rex's arms, I had the feeling of being a pawn of no importance in the game the two men played with one another. Nor did I like the hint of slyness that touched Rex's blue eyes any more than I liked the dark contempt that showed in John's downturned lips.

"No," I said. "I shall never try to take the place of Aunt Jewel; it was her place, for she earned it over the years. I am the outsider. . . ."

"You might be surprised," Rex murmured, and then he leaned down to kiss my lips. I clung to him, ignoring John, who I knew watched.

But the joy of his kiss was missing, and I pushed him away reluctantly, knowing that the moments had passed and too many thoughts had been expressed; time was needed to think, to assess, to understand all which each had said.

"I am going to my room," I said with a small smile that betrayed my weariness more than I might have wished.

"Good night, Adelia," Rex murmured. "I will talk to my beloved brother a few minutes. We have much to discuss. Probably more than he realizes."

He released me. I said good night to him, and nodded to John. Some impulse bade me say, "It was an unfair fight, John, and you lost."

"*Touché*—and good night," he answered with a smile of his own.

I went out the door and up to my own room. It was as if I had done battle in a cavalry charge, for I felt utterly exhausted. I undressed and put on a robe that I might be more comfortable. I sat down, then, before the fire and for a while merely watched the coals glowing as aimless thoughts drifted through my mind. The weather was getting so warm soon no hearth fire would be needed. I had to have a bridal gown, and who would pay for it? John or Rex? John had been so sure—nor had I been absolutely certain he hadn't been right. Rex had said I was beautiful a second time. John—John had said I was beautiful when I was angry—how had he said it? Like a mother lynx fighting for her kittens? I saw him in my memory, his dark eyes shining . . .

I leaned back in the chair, my head against the tall back, my eyes closed, and I began to cry soundlessly, the tears

174

coming from the corners of my eyes. A deep pain spread through my body, and the anguish tore me apart, though I moved not at all.

"Oh, John!" I whispered, the sound coming unbidden to my lips.

For I knew in my heart of hearts that it was not Rex but John whom I truly loved, and it was he I would always love.

I cried a long time, and then I removed the robe that I might get under the covers, I whispered, "I'll make Rex a good wife. I promise I will!" What other choice did I have?

# Chapter XI

But sleep would not come; for a long time I lay in the dark with my eyes wide open, staring upward at nothing. More than once I whispered, "Oh, John," in an agony of remorse that I'd lost him irrevocably and foolishly. What was the future which faced me now? Rex and I would wed and with a thousand dollars we'd leave Orne Hall forever. What would Rex do that we might have a home, might live in a small measure of comfort? Where would he take me? Then I remembered his enigmatic claim that he would return with me to Orne Hall soon, and that I would be the mistress, whether John wished it or not. What did he mean? How could he be so sure? I was proud of him that he had stood up to his arrogant older brother, but doubts crept in, for always in the back of my mind I remembered sly looks that had slipped like shadows over his countenance.

But tears would fill my eyes and slide down my temples when I had that feeling of having loved and lost which swept over me, for it was John I loved—arrogant though he be—it was his half brother, Rex, I had promised to marry!

Dawn came after I had finally slept, and Georgia's touch and light voice bidding me awaken came too quickly. I felt drawn and tired, though I hid it well enough from the girl.

"Good morning, Georgia," I said as cheerfully as I might. "Thank you for waking me!"

"Good morning, Miss Adelia," she responded. She started the fire in the hearth, and then left. In a few moments the room warmed as I began my morning ablutions. Then when I was dressed, for it was nearly seven, I heard a light tap on my door, and then Rex's voice calling my name. "Adelia!"

I opened the door and Rex stood there, a small smile wreathing his full lips.

"Good morning, darling," he said gently, and took me in his arms. He kissed me lightly, gave me a quick hug, and asked if I slept well.

"Not very, Rex," I answered, reluctantly bearing his embrace, yet feeling that I must. "It wasn't a very pleasant evening."

He held me a moment, and then released me from his arms. "Did you mean what you said, that you will marry me, no matter if John sends us packing from Orne Hall?"

"Yes," I answered as firmly as I could make my voice sound. "I meant it, Rex. I would not marry you for money, nor will I let John dictate to me whom I should marry."

A conspiratorial smile moved over Rex's lips as his blue eyes crinkled at the corners.

"Well," he said as if it were a secret, "perhaps John will change his mind and you will sit at the head of the table as mistress of Orne Hall the night we return from our honeymoon."

"What do you mean?" I asked, puzzled. Did Rex have knowledge withheld from me? "You believe you can change John's mind?"

"I do," he said, his smile broadening. "I do indeed!"

I permitted him to escort me. As we walked along the balcony over the Great Hall I thought of his words, and I discovered that they gave me no comfort at all. Marrying Rex with the knowledge that I would not see John was one thing, but to believe that we must share living in Orne Hall, with John's presence to remind me of the love I knew I secretly bore him—I doubted if I had the strength to bear it. But I could think of nothing to say.

At breakfast Rex, in jovial good humor, told everyone that he and I would be married the first week in June and that we would honeymoon in New York City.

Only John withheld congratulations; Melinda was most effusive, showing a pleasure that I'd before only observed when she was eating. Felice asked if she might be the bridesmaid, and of course I said that she could. Even Paul, leaning his white head near mine as he poured coffee, offered his felicitations. "I hope you will be very happy," he added.

"Thank you, Paul."

But as I watched him move about the table, filling the coffee cups, it seemed to me that even his best wishes appeared suspect, for wasn't there an expression on his face that suggested something beyond his words? Yet, what could there be? It seemed to me that his pleasure in the prospects of my being wed to Rex was greater than it need be.

Breakfast done and over with, we separated to go about our various duties. Rex left the dining room by the way of the spiral staircase to the kitchen, explaining that he wanted to check one of the mares.

"She seemed a little lame," he said.

As I rose and walked down the hallway to the balcony in the Great Hall, I heard John's heavy steps behind me but I neither slowed my step nor turned until he caught my arm and drew me to a stop.

"Adelia," he said in his very deep voice, "I do wish you the best of everything this life allows. I—I believe you are making a mistake, but if you love Rex, perhaps you may have some influence over him for the good."

"Thank you, John," I said with all the coolness I could summon, although my heart begged him to say more, to tell me that he loved me. But the words he uttered were not the words I wished to hear.

"I shan't relent, however, for I believe it will be best for you and for Rex if you do not remain at Orne Hall. Nor should you take too seriously his boast that he will return, or perhaps not leave. He has no rights in Orne Hall except which I might grant him."

"Would you play God, John?" I asked coldly.

"No. However, I have a responsibility to the family."

"Could it be, John, that *you* are mistaken, and not Rex?"

He shrugged his broad shoulders and smiled briefly. "It could be, I suppose, Adelia. However, permit me to apologize for my thoughts; I do believe you told me the truth about that—that incident."

"Thank you for your too delayed trust and belief," I said. "Now, if you will excuse me, John, there are many things I must do."

He nodded and turned to go down the broad steps to the Great Hall. I continued on to Aunt Jewel's sitting room, intending to continue with my work with the letters, for now that I knew I would be leaving soon, I wished to complete the filing and sorting and typewriting.

In the late afternoon Rex came to the sitting room. "There's an hour left for a ride," he said, his voice gay, his blue eyes alight and dancing. "Come away from your dusty desk, and let's be off!"

"I can't ride in this dress, Rex," I protested.

"Then change into something you can ride in! I'll get me to the stables and see that the horses are saddled. I think I will ride John's stallion."

With that he flung out of the room, and I hurried to my bedroom to change into my riding habit. As I did so I rather wished Rex had not chosen to mount King this day, for the stallion had a bad temper and took some handling. I'd watched John mount him, and bring him to obedience, but John was probably a better and a more aggressive rider than Rex.

King was indeed in fine spirits, as I could well see as I left the mansion and walked down the slope to the stables. Aaron held the bridle of the sorrel mare I often rode, and I saw that the sidesaddle was properly cinched. But Rex had already mounted King, who pranced and threw his head as he chewed on the bit. Rex dug his heels into the animal's girth, and I heard a shout: "I'll show you who is the master!" Rex then saw me and urged me to hurry. "Aaron, give her a foot up! This beast wants to run!"

Aaron did as he was bid, and I carefully smoothed the full black skirt over my knees hooked above the pommel.

"Don't you try to keep up to King," Aaron warned me as he handed me the reins.

"I won't," I promised, nor did I. Rex pounded the big horse's flanks, and landed his quirt smartly on the rump.

179

Instantly King headed up the lane at a dead run. I urged the mare to follow, but of course we were greatly outdistanced. The stallion was well over a hundred yards in the lead when Rex neck-reined the mount so that his thundering hooves pounded the gravel of the lane that led northward, higher along the bluff, and it seemed to me that Rex let the animal run far too close to the edge. My heart seemed to me to climb into my throat as I kneed the mare into a faster pace.

The stallion ran freely, heading with wild speed toward the clump of trees which grew close to the highest point of the bluff high above the valley.

I think I had a premonition, for as Rex and the lunging steed neared the trees, I saw the path led to a narrow ledge barely wide enough for rider and mount to get through between the bluff's edge and the low limbs of a big oak tree.

"Watch out, Rex," I screamed, and then almost as if it was in a movement slowed down so my eyes could see it all happen, the stallion raced past the tree, leaping in long strides—and I saw the projecting limb strike Rex as he raised one hand to protect himself.

I saw Rex torn from the saddle, and then I saw his body arching over the bluff's edge, and I saw him turning over in the air, his arms and legs flailing, as he disappeared from view.

"Oh, no!" I cried, and quirted the sorrel up to the tree so that I might look down. At first I couldn't see him, and then way down below I discerned the motionless figure, sprawled like a broken doll.

There was no way down from the bluff at that point; the only way to reach Rex was around, down the path and then back along the foot of the bluff. I reined the sorrel toward the stables directly, ignoring the path, and as I rode I began to shriek the names of Toby and Aaron—and of John. I laid the crop hard on the sorrel's rump and she ran as if she was terrified.

I saw first Aaron and then Toby run around the corner of the stables; they stared up toward me. I began to scream at them long before they could discern my words. "Rex— over the bluff!" I cried and repeated. "Harness team!"

Suddenly Toby said something to Aaron and waved his arm. Aaron disappeared, and then I rode up on the sweating mare, and, lifting my knee free of the pommel, I slid to the ground, not waiting for Toby to assist me.

"Rex fell from the bluff!" I cried, and pointed back toward the bluffs. "He's hurt—way down below!"

Aaron led a pair of draft horses to a wagon, and began to hitch the harness to the whippletrees. "Aaron," I commanded, "start down the path—we'll have to get to the base of the bluff." I turned to Toby. "Saddle a mount for John, and change my saddle to a fresh horse. "I'm going in for John." Over my shoulder I shouted at Aaron, "Go, now!"

John looked up in astonishment when I burst into his office. "Rex has been hurt—he went over the bluff," I cried. "Toby is saddling a mount for you! Come!"

John said not a word but followed me across the Great Hall and to the kitchen, where Charity waited with pieces of cloths folded, ready to be put in my arms.

Toby had already brought the horses out of the stables and was cinching up the gelding for John. My mount was ready. I waited not at all to be helped; with little care for convention, I lifted my foot to the stirrup and swung myself into the saddle, and even as I laid my knee in position over the pommel, I touched the mare with a crop, and together John and I raced after the lumbering wagon that already was heading down the path to the bottom.

As the wagon turned to the right to follow the bluff, John and I passed it, and hurried on. I eyed the bluff, orienting myself so that I would know where Rex had fallen. As we rode, I pointed to the trees at the highest point. "Up there!" I shouted above the wind. "He must be below!"

John said nothing but urged his gelding to a greater effort, so that when we reached the point below the trees he was fifty or more yards ahead of me.

We both saw the sprawled body at the same time. John dismounted and ground-hitched the gelding automatically, and then ran to Rex's side.

I slid from the mare and followed him, scrambling up

181

the steepness of the sandy slope. I reached them as John listened for a heartbeat.

"He's alive," he said grimly. "His leg is broken, though."

A bit of blood showed at the corners of Rex's mouth, and John took one of the pieces of cloth I held out to him to wipe it away. "He may have a broken rib as well," he said.

"John, will—will he be all right?" I asked foolishly, for how could John know?

"We'll have to wait and see," he said. He straightened the twisted legs. "It's better to do this while he is still unconscious," he muttered. "The steepness of the sand slope saved him—if he'd hit solid ground he would have been killed."

Aaron drove the heavy draft animals up to us at a lumbering speed, and leaped to the ground. "We have to get him into the wagon," John said. "Adelia, we have to protect his legs; you see if you can support them while Aaron and I lift his body. Try to keep them level."

"Yes," I said breathlessly.

John and Aaron stooped beside the sprawled, heavy body, and I knelt beside his legs. "All right," John commanded, "all together!"

We lifted, and from Rex's unconscious mouth a cry of pain issued forth. We began the descent to the wagon, the sand treacherous under our feet, causing each of us to stumble awkwardly. Once at the wagon, John and Aaron slid his shoulders on the edge. "I'll hold him; you get above," John ordered, and Aaron did as he said. "Take his shoulders—slide him along," John suggested.

A moment later Rex rested on the center of the wagon's bed. I took off my jacket and rolled it to make a pillow under his head.

"Aaron," John said, "take my horse and ride into Waterloo for Dr. Horace. Get going," he added roughly. "I'll handle the team. Tie the mare to the wagon."

Aaron did as he was told. John climbed over the seat and grabbed the reins. He turned to me as he snapped the reins. "We won't hurry; he shouldn't be jarred. Hold him the best you can."

"Yes, John," I murmured, and I did so as the wagon bumped over the rough ground, trying to see that Rex's head was held steady, though there was little I could do for his brokn leg; it flopped with every jounce of the wagon.

It seemed as if it took forever for the team to pull the wagon to the lane, and to tug its way up the long slope to Orne Hall.

Toby, Charity, and Paul and Harlan, too, waited, and as we drove nearer I saw that Melinda joined them. I saw their white faces and it was Harlan who called the question they all waited to hear the answer to.

"Is he dead?" he called.

"No," John answered. "Toby, Paul, we must make a stretcher. Get poles. Charity, fetch two heavy coats—anybody's."

He drove the team close to the conservatory entrance of the west wing, Melinda and Harlan following. Toby and Paul disappeared into the stables and returned with a pair of long poles just as Charity came out with the coats.

"Button the coats and slip them over the poles," John commanded.

Toby and Paul did so, converting the poles to a stretcher. They laid it beside Rex's still figure, and then they clambered into the wagon's flat bed. John joined them and they lifted Rex carefully, laying him on the coats between the poles.

It was awkward lifting him from the wagon, but the three men did, and then Paul and Toby carried Rex through the conservatory door, down the corridor to Rex's room, with the others of us following.

Once in the room, the men transferred Rex to the bed, and Charity took charge. "The rest of you go," she commanded. "Adelia and I will do what has to be done before Dr. Horace gets here."

They left, and Charity sent John for heavy scissors, which he brought back in a moment.

"Cut off his trouser leg," Charity said. I must confess I hesitated a moment, but Charity told me to hurry.

It was difficult, and the sight of the compound fracture with the sharp edge of a bone protruding made me feel

**183**

faint. "He's bleeding," Charity murmured and, as I cut away the trouser, she took a cloth and tied it tightly around his thigh, so the bleeding slowed.

Charity took the scissors from my fingers. "I am stronger," she muttered, and she began to cut away his riding jacket and waistcoat. I eased the parts of the cut trousers from beneath his body, and I felt in the pocket there were several items and I thought I should take care that they not be lost. I slipped my hand into the pocket and withdrew a billfold and placed it in the pocket of my riding skirt.

Rex began to moan as Charity worked to cut the jacket away from his broken body.

"He's living," Charity muttered. "I hope Dr. Horace gets here quickly. He's hurt bad."

Every so often she loosened the tourniquet until blood again flowed from the wound. "He will lose his leg if we leave it too long," she explained.

It did seem as if hours had passed before Dr. Horace bustled into the room. Without a word he shed his jacket and went to work on Rex's leg, straightening it, pulling it so that the bones became realigned. "Better he stay unconscious," he muttered.

He told John of the splints he wanted made, and then he ordered me from the room.

"You look like you might faint," he said. "I don't need two patients. There's nothing you can do now."

I did feel faint, badly shaken, and soiled by the blood and by the sand and dirt we'd trampled through and by my ride on the dirty wagon bottom.

The others waited in the Great Hall, and as I appeared they came toward me, questions in their eyes, their faces white.

"I don't know," I answered the unspoken questions. "I'm going to my room to change."

I mounted the broad stairs and then went down the dim hallway to my room. For a moment I stood quietly, my eyes shut, feeling too drained even to start to undress.

I felt the thickness of Rex's billfold in my pocket and I reached down to take it out. As I was about to place it on

184

the bed table, a piece of folded paper fell from it, tumbling to the floor. I remember thinking that it must well have been simply in the fold of the wallet, and not tucked within it. I stooped to pick it up, and as I did so I saw the spidery scrawl of my great-aunt's peculiar handwriting, and I glimpsed the figures 1831.

I was startled and for a moment I held the paper still folded in my hand. This had to be the missing page from Aunt Jewel's diary!

# Chapter XII

Rex was the one who had cut the page from the diary of his grandmother! Why would he do that? For some reason I didn't understand myself, I was reluctant to unfold the page and to read what it contained—afraid, perhaps, that it might be a revelation which would change my life and I didn't think I could stand any more changes. And Rex was fighting for his life in the room below and certainly could not defend himself—if any defense was necessary.

I did unfold the paper, and I read the first entry, which consisted of only two sentences about a purchase of some new material for a dress. The second one, however, concerned her husband, John Orne I, and some unnamed woman.

"He's got her pregnant," Aunt Jewel had written, "and he thinks that it's a great joke. He told me about it, telling me awful details that I dearly wished not to hear. The man is coarse beyond belief; I suspect he raped the poor woman, though there are some females who find him irresistible, and he has his way with them easily. He even showed me the letter the woman had sent him, imploring him to protect her from her husband, who must surely find out soon of the bastard she carried. She wrote she feared for her very life, and the life of the child she carried. She ended her plea asking if he cared nothing about the child she had conceived of him. Little she knew John Orne, for he cares not even for the lawful children I've had to bear him, much less those of some woman who foolishly let him come to her bed!"

I unfolded the page and carried it into the sitting room, where I carefully placed it in the diary between the pages from which it had been cut. Then I returned the diary to its proper place in the file.

Once back in my own room again, I continued to change my clothing, and then I sat down in my most comfortable chair to rest a bit, and to think. Why would Rex wish that page removed from the diary? Who was this unnamed woman? Was she the woman that Joshua and John were supposed to have fought over? It seemed unlikely. I remembered the date, 1831, but it had no significance.

I glanced at the tall clock and I saw that its big face indicated it was nearly six o'clock. Charity might well still be with Rex and Dr. Horace, and it occurred to me that someone should start the preparation of our evening supper, which would most certainly be later than usual. So I rose, left my bedroom, and walked the balcony over the Great Hall to the east wing, and thence down the spiral staircase to the kitchen.

I discovered Paul, protected by a large apron, attempting to organize the kitchen as well as direct Georgia and Holly in their tasks.

"Paul," I said as I left the stairwell, "I'll see to supper. I don't think that apron becomes you, anyway."

I saw the expression of relief which passed over his face. "Thank you, Miss Adelia," he said with a shake of his head. "I don't think it does, either."

"Take it off, and go about your business. The girls and I will get supper ready. . . ."

Holly and Georgia were cooperative, and together we did put together a supper of sliced, fried ham, boiled potatoes, with sour-milk biscuits and cream gravy. When it was ready, I sent Georgia to summon everyone as Holly and I carried the food up to the dining room.

During the evening meal, John explained briefly that Charity and Horace were still working over Rex's broken body, and that he still lived. "It was a terrible fall," he added.

"It's a wonder he still is alive," I murmured, and I saw in my memory the way his body had cartwheeled from the bluff's edge off into the sky, and downward.

After supper I saw to it that the girls, Toby, Aaron, and

Paul were fed at the heavy worktable in the kitchen. Aaron told me that he'd found and brought back the stallion.

"He'd run more'n two mile," he explained. "I found him grazin' out in the east pasture. He gave me no trouble at all."

Once supper chores were finished, I said good night to the girls and Paul, and then I went to the west wing, where I tapped on John's study door.

He bade me come in, and I did.

He sat at his desk, the reflector lamp illuminating the record books in which he had been writing figures in neat columns. He put down the pen and looked up at me, his mouth lifting in a tired smile. He gestured to a chair, indicating that I should sit down.

"How is Rex?" I asked.

"Uncle Horace believes he will recover, though his left leg is broken and may never be well again. He'll be bedridden for some time, however." His smile became faintly twisted. "I suspect that he may not be in shape to marry by early June."

"John," I said, my mind still on the diary rather than on a postponed marriage, "I found the page which had been removed from the diary."

"You did? Where?"

"It fell from Rex's trouser pocket—from his wallet." I paused, and John urged me on impatiently.

"Well, what was on the page? Why did he do it?"

"I don't know why he did it," I answered tartly. "It told about your grandfather bragging that he'd got some married woman with child."

"Was the woman named?"

I shook my head. Did I read relief in the expression in John's eyes? Why should he care? Then I decided that I was indeed losing my meager wits, for I was beginning to suspect everyone of some kind of mischief, even though I didn't know for sure that mischief had been done!

John thought a moment, frowning as he looked at the columns of neat figures before him. Finally he shrugged and shook his head. "It makes no sense to me," he said. "What was the date?"

188

"January of 1831," I answered.

"Forty-five years ago! I can't imagine what could be important about something that happened so long ago. When Rex is able to talk, you might ask him why he did it." His smile broadened. "He might even tell you the truth!"

"Why should he lie to me?" I asked. "He'd have no reason to. Anyway, I should trust him, shouldn't I? I will be his wife. . . ."

John's expression hardened, and he glanced down at his numbers. I knew the interview was at an end, so I rose to my feet. "I thought you would wish to know, John," I said, and added—with a little note of sarcasm in my voice—"I am sorry to have disturbed you."

John looked up quickly. I couldn't divine the meaning of the expression in his eyes, but he said with a quirk to his lips, "You've disturbed me ever since you arrived at Orne Hall."

I could think of no rejoinder, so I left, and as I closed the door, Dr. Horace came from Rex's room. He saw me and put his fingers to his lips, gesturing me to follow him into the Great Hall. I did so, and there he turned to face me.

"Rex is strong, he will survive. I have given him tincture of laudanum, and now he sleeps. When he wakes he will have pain. I have left several papers of powder with Charity, which are to be used as needed to reduce the pain." He took a heavy watch from his waistcoat pocket, peering down to read the time. "It is nearly nine. He should sleep through the night."

"You haven't eaten. Aren't you hungry?" I asked. "I can prepare you something. . . ."

He shook his head. "I must return to Waterloo. Send Aaron in to fetch me if Rex takes a turn for the worse. Otherwise I will see him day after tomorrow."

John came from his office, and Dr. Horace repeated his comments. "Rex will probably survive," he said dryly. "However, he will probably have to pursue his ladies with a game leg. It was badly shattered."

"He is marrying Adelia, and I doubt if she will take kindly to his pursuing ladies in the future, so perhaps it is just as well," John said.

189

The doctor chuckled briefly, and then left through the conservatory.

I glanced up at John. "I will sit with Rex tonight," I said. "Charity must be exhausted."

"Very well," John answered. "I will take your place later, perhaps at midnight."

"Oh, no, I can . . ."

"No, you can't," he answered forcefully. "No, don't argue with me," he added when I opened my mouth to protest.

"Very well, sir," I murmured, and I left him to go to Rex's room.

Charity tried to protest that she could stay with Rex, but I told her to get some rest, and something to eat. "Dr. Horace filled him with laudanum, so he won't wake 'til morning, no matter what might happen, so scat!"

She gave me a weary smile, and then I was alone with the man I'd decided to marry. He was a sorry sight, his leg tied in heavy splints to hold the shattered bones in place so they might knit, his broken head bound also. He lay flat on his back, his breath stentorian in the silent room.

I seated myself in a comfortable rocker by the library table, a pillow at the small of my back, the lamp with wick turned down giving just enough light that I might see, and then I leaned back and closed my eyes.

The minutes and hours passed slowly. Rex slept without moving, the rasp of his heavy breathing the only sound in the large room.

From time to time I glanced at my watch, the chain of which was pinned to my blouse. Precisely at midnight the door opened and John entered.

"He still sleeps?" he asked softly.

I nodded, saying nothing.

"Get you to bed, Adelia," he commanded. "I will sit with him until dawn. Uncle Walter will come then—I've informed him that I expect it of him."

"Very well, John. Good night," I whispered, and left, hurrying to my own room.

I was no sooner in my own bed, the lamp flame extinguished, than sleep overcame me, and I knew nothing until a sound awakened me. My eyes opened on darkness, and I heard the faint click of a door closing.

Then I saw the large shape loom over me, and before I could move, I felt a pillow pressed against my face! I couldn't breathe! I fought and tried to cry out, but whoever sought to kill me was strong and heavy, and it was as if I was a helpless child. No air could reach my tortured lungs and my eyes felt as if they would pop from the sockets, and I thought that surely I was dying.

Only distantly I hard the sound of someone pounding on the doors, but even as I listened everything darkened and I knew no more.

Slowly my senses returned, and though the pillow still lay on my face, I could breathe and the downward pressure had gone. I flung the pillow away, and then I heard the continued pounding on my door.

My air-starved lungs rose and fell as I gasped for breath. I managed to sit up, holding my head.

"Adelia! Are you all right?" I heard the voice of Felice. "Answer me, Adelia!"

"I'm coming," I managed to answer, and I did rise to my feet and make my way to the door. My hands fumbled with the door latch, but the door was locked! I'd never locked it before. I turned the key and Felice pushed the door open. Behind her Georgia carried a lamp high, illuminating my room with light and shadow.

"What is it, Adelia?" Felice cried. "Why didn't you answer? Why was your door locked?"

My mind refused to work quickly. "Someone tried to kill me," I managed to say. "I—I didn't lock the door!"

"Somebody tried to kill you! Who? Where is he?"

"Whoever it was must have gone into the sitting room," I said. I sat down on the edge of the bed, feeling ill and shaken. "I think I am going to faint," I murmured.

"No," Felice said. "Don't faint!" She touched a match to my bed lamp's wick. "How did somebody try to kill you?"

"With a pillow over my face. Somebody very strong—much stronger than I am."

Felice ran to the door which opened into Aunt Jewel's sitting room. She pulled it open, and peered through, holding the light high. "The sitting door was locked, too. Georgia tried it," she said as she took another step forward. "There's no one here—the door's wide open now."

So whoever had tried to kill me with a pillow had escaped through Aunt Jewel's sitting room while Felice and Georgia tried to enter my room from the other door. Everything seemed exaggerated as I looked from Georgia's white face to Felice's. I'd never seen Felice so aggressive as she was now.

"Why would anybody want to smother you?" she demanded.

"I don't know," I answered wearily.

At that moment John came through the door from the hallway. "What is all the noise about?" he demanded. "Are you trying to raise the dead?"

"Someone tried to smother Adelia with a pillow," Felica told him. "Whoever it was went through the sitting room."

John stared down at me, consternation on his face. "Why would anybody want to kill you?" he asked, and I heard doubt in his voice.

"I don't know," I answered heavily, and then I recalled Felice's pounding. "Why did you want to see me? You and Georgia?"

"Charity is awful sick," Georgia said. "Paul told me to wake someone, so I woke Felice, only she came to wake you."

"I know nothing of food poisoning, and I thought you might," Felice explained.

I shook my head to clear it. "Hand me my robe," I told Felice. "I will go to Charity and see what I can do."

"Felice," John said sharply, "you go to Rex's room and sit with him until Uncle Walter comes at six. I will go with Adelia. . . ."

I pulled the robe over my shoulders, and rose unsteadily to my feet. But as I led the way through the hallway, the lamp held high, it occurred to me that John was strong and heavy enough to have held that pillow to my face. It wouldn't have been Rex; his broken leg wouldn't bear his weight for even a brief moment.

Who else but John? Toby was strong enough, as was

Aaron, but why would either of them seek to smother me? But then, why should John?

Charity's dead-white face was bathed in cold perspiration as she writhed with pain on the bed she shared with Paul Wiley. He was frantic, not knowing what to do. Nor did I, except to give her a tablespoon of paregoric.

It seemed to work and she quieted finally, as the clock read just after four in the morning.

"What did she eat?" I asked Georgia.

"What was left over from supper," Georgia answered. "I got it for her with Miss Melinda's help. And the sauce you decided not to put on the table. Remember?"

I did remember—it was a sauce for the ham which I had thought might be old.

After Charity slept, I gestured to Paul and he followed me to the kitchen. I found the sauce in a covered dish, and when I lifted the cover I sniffed. Did I detect an odor that didn't belong? I wasn't sure.

"Smell this," I ordered Paul, and he did so.

"There is a taint," he murmured. "But I don't know what it is."

"Nor do I," I said. "Throw it out, before some other person tastes it. Who made it?"

"Charity, I suppose," he answered. "I don't know, but who else?"

I shuddered, drawing my shoulders close together. "Dispose of it, where it can harm no one," I said.

"Yes, Miss Adelia," he said. "Do you think Charity will be all right?"

"She vomited—probably nothing poisonous is left in her stomach," I said. "Georgia can stay with her for a while."

I returned to Paul and Charity's apartment next to the kitchen. John had left, but Georgia remained. "She is quiet?" I asked.

"Yes," Georgia answered. "She sleeps."

"You, Georgia, sit with her until dawn," I commanded.

I returned to my bedroom and this time I carefully locked both the door to the hallway and the door to the sitting room. I wanted no more visitors that night.

I lay down on my bed, utterly exhausted.

**193**

Someone wants to kill me, I thought wearily. I must leave Orne Hall before I die. I will leave Orne Hall in the morning, forever, I promised myself, a promise I couldn't possibly keep, for where would I go without money?

# Chapter XIII

For the first time since I had come to Orne Hall I slept beyond six in the morning. When I opened my eyes the slanting rays of the morning sun streamed in the window. I was aware that someone tapped gently on the door of my bedroom, and then I heard the faint voice of gentle Georgia call.

"Miss Adelia! Are you awake?"

"Yes," I called as I slipped from beneath the warm covers of the bed. I padded in bare feet to the door and turned the key. I pulled the door open.

"I slept late," I said to Georgia. "I'm sorry."

Georgia's face was pasty white.

"Mister John wants you to come to Mister Rex's room quickly," she said breathlessly.

Had Rex taken a turn for the worse? My heart leaped into my throat as I reached for a morning robe and slipped my arms into it. My feet found the bed slippers and I followed Georgia to the broad staircase to the Great Hall, and thence to Rex's room.

The door stood open and I saw that John leaned over Rex's bed as I entered.

"John! What is it?" I whispered as I ran to his side.

"Yes," John answered, not looking up. "He has a fever; his forehead is hot and he doesn't know where he is."

Rex stared up at me, but no recognition appeared in his glazed glance. He rolled his head back and forth as if he struggled to free himself from the bindings that held him quiet.

"Walter summoned me," John said. "I'm no doctor," he added. "I don't know what to do."

Rex's forehead and cheeks did feel hot to my touch. I quickly removed the covers from his body so that I might examine the shattered leg where the bone had pierced the skin. The bloodstained wrappings meant, surely, that the wound still bled.

"Help me," I directed Georgia and she hesitantly and gingerly approached the side of the bed. "Support his foot!"

As I removed the wrappings, I saw that clearly the wound had abscessed, and the whole area had become reddened with fever. I was no nurse, unskilled in the arts of the sickroom, but I knew well enough that Rex's life was endangered.

"We'll have to get Dr. Horace again, and quickly. The wound is fevered!"

"I'll send Aaron at once," John said and left the room. With Georgia's help, I rebound the wound with clean cloths and then I told her to bring a basin of cool water. "Not cold, Georgia, but just gently cool. And some more cloths."

She did, and I began to gently sponge Rex's face and chest. He seemed to dream, for his mouth kept uttering broken words, and he at times fought to get out of bed and I had to restrain him.

John returned. "Aaron's gone to get Horace," he said grimly. "How is he?"

"He is delirious," I answered. "His mind doesn't know where he is. He seems to be reliving something which happened in the past."

"Perhaps his conscience has been awakened," John said without humor. "Is his life endangered by the fever?"

"I—I don't know, John," I answered. "I'm afraid. . . ."

"We will wait, and hope," John murmured, and when I glanced into his face I saw affection for his half brother in his dark eyes. He glanced up at me, and I turned my face away, for it seemed to me there was an intimate quality to his expression which I as an outsider could not share.

"You love him very much, do you not?" I murmured.

"I love him, but I hate some of the things he has done," John answered. "I blame myself. . . ."

Suddenly I remembered the pillow pressed over my face,

196

and how near I had come to death as someone with strong arms attempted to smother me. Who other than John was strong enough—except Aaron or Toby. Or Paul! Perhaps even Uncle Walter, although I couldn't imagine that he'd ever do anything violent. Yet, someone had.

At times I can be very foolish, and as I studied John's bearded face, and saw the expression on his face as he looked down at his half brother, I felt it could not possibly be he who would try to kill me. *Yet, I didn't know, did I? Could I tell if John lied?*

"John," I said in a whisper, "was it you who tried to smother me with a pillow?"

His eyes widened and I saw astonishment in his eyes, and then he slowly shook his head.

"No, Adelia," he said softly.

"Who could it have been, then? Was it someone who still seeks to prevent the publication of the letters and the diary?"

"I don't know," John answered. He looked down at his brother. "Will he live?" he asked.

"I don't know," I responded, realizing that I parroted his answer to my question. "I know that the fever means the wound isn't clean—there's sickness and pus in it."

We stayed with Rex until noon when the doctor arrived. He examined the wound and shook his head. "He is strong," he murmured. "He has a good constitution. It's up to him. There is no medicine that will heal him."

Dr. Horace stayed for only two hours. "I have other sick people," he explained. "Mrs. Holman in Waterloo is expecting her first child; it will be a difficult delivery and I must be there."

Charity's sickness had left her weak, so I took over the preparation of the meals and the supervision of Holly and Georgia. The days passed quickly, and life soon took on the humdrum of familiar everyday existence. Rex's strong constitution began to take command, and his fever left him four days later. He woke, as weak as a child, his body so quickly emaciated and thinned by the ordeal.

I was with him when he first recovered his wits. I sat by his bed, a box of letters resting on my knees, for I still

197

worked at my task while I stayed in the sickroom. I suddenly became aware that his eyes no longer searched the room vacantly, but were now steady.

"Good morning, Rex," I said cheerfully.

"What's happened?" he asked in a hoarse, thick voice. "Where am I?"

"In your own room," I answered, and I saw his eyes move as he examined his surroundings.

"Why can't I move?" he asked, and I saw pain appear in his blue eyes, made to seem extra large by his thinness.

"Do you remember going riding with me, Rex? You were knocked off of King by a tree branch and you fell from the bluff. One of your legs was broken."

He shook his head and blinked as a frown appeared between his eyes. "I remember—I remember falling. Is—is King all right?"

"The stallion is fine, but you have been very ill, Rex," I said gently. "You've had a fever."

"May I have a drink?" he asked, and I got a glass of water. I held his head up as he drank greedily.

"I have no strength," he murmured as I lowered his head again to the pillow.

"You'll get your strength back," I assured him cheerfully. "You'll be pursuing pretty ladies in no time at all."

For a moment he didn't answer, but continued to stare at me; he seemed to be thinking hard, as if he slowly collected his wits.

"A married man shouldn't pursue pretty ladies, should he?" he asked.

For some reason I caught my breath and I realized that I had deliberately refused to think that when Rex recovered we would be married; I realized, too, there had been a time during which, in my mind, the question had been not *when* but *if*. For a moment, I could think of nothing to say. Rex was still very ill, though the fever had left him, and it was hardly the time to make plans.

"Rex," I said gently, "you tend to getting well. Then we will worry about your pursuing pretty ladies."

Later John came to the room, and I saw the delight in his eyes that his brother recoginzed and spoke to him.

"Brother John," Rex whispered, "I took a fall."

"You did indeed," John answered. "It was right clumsy of you, Rex."

I gathered up the box of letters and rose to my feet in preparation for leaving Rex with John. "Are you hungry, Rex?" I asked.

He nodded. "I am famished," he said. "I am weak as a newly born kitten," he added to John.

"I will see that you get some broth," I told him, and I left the room.

I took the box of letters to Aunt Jewel's sitting room and then I did go to the kitchen and told Charity, who was up and around, her usual self, to fix some thick broth for Rex.

"He is awake, and himself, and he is hungry," I explained.

"Bless the Lord," Charity cried out, and a wide smile wreathed her face. The expressions on the faces of Holly and Georgia reflected Charity's as each exclaimed her gratefulness.

As I returned to Aunt Jewel's sitting room, I mused that Rex had many admirers among the ladies, even at Orne Hall. I sat down at the davenport and began again to sort out letters.

I'd been at the task for an hour, so it neared suppertime when I came to the letter which was destined to change the course of my life forever, and which would make it all clear to me why Rex wished me to be his wife.

It was a faded letter addressed to Aunt Jewel's husband, John Orne I, and it was signed "Joshua." I saw it had a return address of Newton, where I'd been born and had lived most of my life. It was an explosive letter, and it opened with a vile, obscene curse which I won't repeat. But Joshua damned John to the eternal tortures of hell, and then told him why.

> You took my wife to your bed, after sending me to Albany. You got her with child and this you know. You forced me to leave Orne Hall, and now let me tell you this! Your child, blood of your blood, has been born, and I swear to you that I will make of her a

miserable slave, I will sell her into whoredom, I will cause her to live a life of filth, for filth she is, spawned of your dirty loins! My hate and my curse will follow you all of your life. You are stronger than I am, and you have driven me away and taken from me what lawfully is mine, and may you and your seed forever be cursed. . . .

The letter was long, and as I read it I felt ill at the violence of it. It was only when I had finished reading it and held it in my lap that I gradually thought of myself. It was my grandfather who had written the vile letter to Jewel's husband. No! I felt the blood rush to my head as I realized *he was not my grandfather! My mother's sire had been John Orne! It was his blood which ran in my veins, not that of Joshua, his brother.*

Now I knew why my mother had been estranged from her father, why he had hated her so much and had caused her so much suffering when she was a girl—suffering which I knew so little about, for my mother rarely spoke of her parents.

Suddenly I gasped, for the skein of events abruptly rearranged themselves. Rex had cut the page from the diary so no one would read of John Orne's flagrant infidelity. Rex must not have known of the letter I had just discovered. But now I knew why Rex was so sure that he and I would return to Orne Hall, for it was I, not he, in whose veins coursed the blood of John Orne! It was I who would inherit a portion of the inheritance, and as his wife, all I possessed would then be his, would it not?

"Rex wants to marry me because he knows I am one of the true heirs," I said aloud, and my illness increased. Was it not the worst cruelty to which a woman might be subjected, that she be married only for her inheritance, and not for herself? Rex had said he loved me, but as I viewed his wavering nature I knew it was not so.

I put the letter away, safely, not in the file, but well hidden in my own room. I would not marry Rex, and I would tell him as soon as he seemed truly out of danger. I would then show the letter to John, and seek from him enough money to establish myself elsewhere. I would repay him, too, for I wanted no part of the stained inheritance of John I. Surely, John would give me the money when I told him what I had discovered. But even as I made my plan, I hated myself for it, yet what choice did I have?

Encouraged by the knowledge the diary and the letter had given me, in the weeks that followed I went about the task of completing the manuscript.

Rex recovered rapidly and was soon able to come to the dining room on crutches obtained for him by Dr. Horace. I always sat in my usual place, aware of the empty chair which had been Aunt Jewel's. Rex appeared to be quite cheerful, though John's expression remained glum, and I would often feel the weight of his dark eyes on me. Uncle Walter and Felice seemed to withdraw into their own private concerns, and Melinda continued to gain weight, so that she became still more grossly fat. Of course, she had been virtually useless in the sickroom, but now that Rex was recovering she spent most of her days sitting with him in his bedroom. Frequently, I would feel her blue-eyed gaze on me at times when I was busily eating and looking elsewhere. But unlike John with his gloomy expression, Melinda appeared to be happier as each day passed. It puzzled me, for with her overweening affection for Rex, I thought she'd hate the girl that Rex might marry. But then, if she knew that John I's blood ran in my veins . . . The thought made me blink and wonder. Of course she would be delighted that Rex and I would marry, for her future was tied to that of Rex and she would then have reason to feel secure.

But what if Melinda didn't know that John was aware that Rex was sired by someone not an Orne? That he could not inherit because of her indiscretion? She might not know that it was not a secret to which only she was privy.

The tangled web made me dizzy when I thought of it.

One day in late May, after our evening supper, I walked beside Rex as he hobbled on his crutches back to his room. We slowly crossed the big expanse of the Great Hall, passing the fireplace, which was no longer needed for warmth, and suddenly Rex spoke of our engagement.

"We'll be married in June as I planned, Adelia," he said with a grin. "Can you wait that long?"

Now the time had come when I had to speak out. "We will talk of it when we reach your room, Rex," I said, and I could hardly prevent some grimness creeping into my voice. "There is much to discuss."

"There's nothing to discuss," he retorted. "We will be married as planned."

I said nothing until we were in Rex's room and he had again stretched out on the bed, for his leg pained him when he was forced to sit in a chair.

I closed the door and then I went to stand at the foot of the bed. I looked directly at the man who pretended to love me. "Rex," I said, "I cannot marry you, for you do not love me."

His face showed his surprise at my words. "Why do you say that?" he asked. "Of course I love you and you will become my wife."

For a moment I sought the proper words. "Rex," I said slowly, "I know it was you who removed the page from the diary. I know why. You are not a descendant of your grandfather, and you cannot inherit. You know it; and you know, too, that your grandfather was the sire of my mother—and I am of his blood. As your wife, all I would possess would become yours—including my share of the Orne inheritance. You don't love me, Rex," I said with scorn in my voice. "You want my inheritance, and that is why you were so sure you would return to Orne Hall, in spite of what John had said."

Rex's face became suffused with color and his angry blue eyes glared at me as if he would destroy me.

"Why else would I marry a homely female like you?" he asked, his lips sneering. "When there are women of real beauty who would marry me at once . . ."

"Would they, Rex, if they knew you were a pauper?" I asked, hitting back.

"You'd best think again, Cousin Adelia," he said, harsh threat in his voice. "So I would marry you for the inheritance. What other reason would a man marry a creature like you? Take care or you will become a spinster like Felice."

"Rex," I said, "you are overlooking something. Aren't there many men who will wish to marry me, homely though I be, when I claim my rightful share of the inheritance? Are you the only man who would marry me for the money I shall have?"

"John will never consent. . . ."

"I will obtain a lawyer. . . ."

I had raised my voice, and the words I shouted I could hardly mean, for in truth I would prefer to be a spinster than to marry a man who sought only my inheritance. Abruptly, I closed my mouth and walked to the door. There I turned back. "Rex," I said, my voice more normal, "I will leave Orne Hall as soon as I complete my task."

I left, and as I approached the Great Hall's staircase, I met Melinda as she descended. She was so grossly fat that I stood aside, yet I was astonished at the lightness of her foot as she came toward me.

"How is Rex?" she asked. "Is my son feeling well?"

"Well enough," I answered. "He may well have much to say to you," I added as I climbed the staircase.

I went to my bedroom and, as I had always after someone sought to smother me, I closed the doors and locked them securely.

The sun had not yet set, as the spring days had grown longer. For a time I stood at the window looking north at the edge of the bluff and at the valley beyond. It had been barely six months since I had come first to Orne Hall. I wondered if I was the same woman who had entered the Great Hall for the first time so long ago. I remembered my first meeting with John in the Great Hall as he'd warmed his back at the fireplace. And then my meeting with Aunt Jewel, a woman I had learned to love so very much.

I heard a tap on my door, and then, when I unlocked it and swung it inward, I saw that John stood there.

"May I come in?" he said soberly.

"Yes," I answered, and gestured to a comfortable chair. "Please, will you sit down?"

I seated myself in my rocker, and then he, too, sat down.

I noted that he carefully left the door well open. A quizzical smile curved his lips as he looked at me, and then he began to fumble in his jacket pocket. "May I smoke, Adelia?"

"Of course," I answered with a nod. "I—I like the odor of good tobacco, John."

He took his time, taking out a pouch of Virginia tobacco and packing it with deliberate care in the bowl of the pipe. Then he lit it with a sulphur match, and the smoke swirled slowly in the air above him and between us as he looked across at me.

"Adelia," he said slowly, "I suppose you will marry Rex soon, and I—well, I want to wish you every happiness. And, Adelia, I—I am withdrawing my objection to your returning with Rex. You and he can have Orne Hall; I will deed it to him and to you, and I will leave. I will see that there is sufficient money. . . ."

"Have you talked to Rex since supper?" I broke in to ask.

He looked at me in surprise, his dark eyebrows lifting. "No, I have not. Why? Would it make any difference?"

"It might, John," I said grimly. "I told Rex tonight that I would never marry him, and that I would soon be leaving Orne Hall."

"Leaving Orne Hall? Why? Why, Adelia?" He made a gesture with his hand, as though indicating the whole of the mansion. "This can be your home! I will give it to you and Rex. You—Adelia, it is right that you be the mistress of Orne Hall. . . ."

"Why?" I asked quietly.

"Because *Grand'mère*—your aunt Jewel—loved you so much, and because you are so much like her; no one should ever sit in her place but you, Adelia. It would be her wish!"

Was he lying? Did he know my secret, that a portion of John I's inheritance was rightfully mine should I choose to demand it? I had no doubt of my ability to prove it.

I rose to my feet with quick determination. "Come," I commanded John, and I walked to the door that led to Aunt Jewel's sitting room. I unlocked it, swung it wide, and went through, knowing that John had risen to his feet and that he followed me.

I went directly to the file and first I withdrew the diary. John stood at my elbow, his teeth still clamped on his pipe, his dark eyes watching me. I opened the diary and took out the cut page and handed it to him without comment. He took it, and glanced at it and then at me, for of course he had seen it before.

"Yes?" he said in a questioning tone.

"Just a moment," I said, suddenly remembering that I had hidden the letter in my bedroom. "I'll be back." I went to the bedroom and recovered the letter.

"Read this," I said in cool, level tones. "You will understand why I must leave Orne Hall forever."

He took the faded letter from my fingers and unfolded it carefully.

I watched the pupils of his black eyes as they scanned the badly handwritten letter, and I knew precisely when it was that it dawned on him why I had asked him to read it.

When he'd finished the letter, he folded it slowly, saying nothing, and then handed it back to me. "You'd best keep the letter safe," he said slowly. "According to John Orne I's will, you are one of the inheritors of the Orne holdings. Adelia, you are a very rich woman."

"Don't be absurd," I said sharply. "I have no interest in the Orne holdings. John Orne, your grandfather, was a hideous man, and I am ashamed that his blood flows in my body, nor do I wish any of his ill-gotten fortune."

"Why did you show the letter to me, then?"

"So you would understand why Rex wanted to marry me, and why I would rather die than sell myself in that manner."

He looked at me intently until I began to flush with anger. Then he turned and walked to the settee before the wide fireplace. He seated himself, his long legs stretched out comfortably before him, and I saw that he puffed on his pipe as if in slow deliberation. "Come and sit, Cousin Adelia," he said after a moment.

I did as he suggested, but I chose the rocker where I had

205

seated myself so many times when Aunt Jewel was still alive.

"You have nothing to fear from me," I said with a little defiance. "I shan't give you any trouble, if—if you will loan me enough so that I can go to some place and find some kind of a suitable position."

"Doing what, Adelia?"

"I am well read and I know my numbers. I might tutor some children of a wealthy family. Perhaps I am qualified to become an upstairs maid. . . ."

"You'd make a very bad upstairs maid," John interrupted to say. "You are much too arrogant. Milady would dismiss you in less than a fortnight. . . ."

"I will find something," I said stubbornly. "The manuscript is nearly ready for the printer. I will leave as soon as it is delivered."

"Whoa, Cousin Adelia," John said, and I saw his lips turned up in a smile. "Why don't you marry me and you will be the real mistress of Orne Hall?" He turned toward me, one eyebrow cocked up.

For a long moment I simply stared at him while my mind churned at his words.

"Cat got your tongue?" he asked finally.

"Because, John," I said slowly, "as long as I might live I would never know that you didn't marry me because of this letter and the page from the diary." He started to say something, but I held up my hand to silence him. "You see, John, even if you should be foolish enough to tell me you love me, I still would never know. Rex said he loved me, too, you know, but in the end he cursed me. He'd never loved me."

"Adelia," he said gently, "I will accept your verdict if you tell me that you bear me no love. If you don't love me, I'll never speak of it again."

My heart caught in my throat, for I knew I must answer, and that I must lie. It was the only way, for what I said was true; my doubts about why he married me would mar irreparably any marriage we might have. Oh, I was tempted! I would be secure, would I not? Women must compromise; Aunt Jewel had been purchased as if she were a mere slave to be bought and sold, but she had met life courageously. Still, wouldn't it have been better for her had she been able to marry someone with whom she could make a good marriage?

When I remembered my own beautiful mother and hateful father, I knew I wanted no compromises.

"John, I do not love you," I said in a clear, even voice. "I do not wish to be your wife. I just want to leave Orne Hall and find a position where I may earn my keep."

For a long time John stared into my eyes, as if studying to determine if I lied or spoke truthfully. Finally he sighed and shook his head. He slowly rose to his feet and from his great height he looked down at me. "Very well, Adelia. I will loan you the money as you wish." He paused as if in deep thought. "Adelia," he said finally, "Orne Hall is a better place because you have been here. I hope with all my heart that you will find happiness somehow, somewhere." He hesitated. "I must go to Albany, and I will be leaving within the hour. I will be gone perhaps a week. When I return we will make arrangements, however you wish them." His lips lifted in a sardonic smile. "You can wait that long before leaving?"

"No," I answered. "I will be gone when you return."

"Very well, if that is your wish," he said gravely. "Wait here, please. I will return in a moment."

He left the sitting room, and I sat in the rocker, stiffly erect, my head held up. I told myself that I would not let John or anyone else know what feelings overwhelmed me at the moment. And when John returned he carried a thick envelope which he placed in my lap.

"There is enough for you for the time being. I want you to promise you will let me know if all goes well with you—and that you will let me know if you need anything. Will you promise, Adelia?"

"Yes," I said, "I promise."

He walked to me, picked up the envelope of money, and dropped it carelessly in the settee. Before I knew it, he had drawn me up and into his arms, and as I looked at him, he lowered his mouth until his lips pressed hard on mine. My arms, unbidden, clung to him and I fought the tears that would fill my eyes against my will. The kiss lasted long, and my heart truly broke when he released me.

"Good night and goodbye, Adelia," he said in a deep, husky voice. "And God bless you!"

"Good night and goodbye, John," I said in a voice that shook in spite of my effort to hold it steady. "And God bless you, too."

He left and I picked up the envelope and walked unsteadily to my own room. I locked the door behind me, and then I threw myself upon my bed, breaking into heavy sobs that shook my whole body, for I knew that I truly loved John Orne, but I knew that I had sent him away. I would never see him again. I cried a long time and then finally sat up and I glanced at the envelope, little caring what it contained, but when, later, I opened the flap, I saw it was more money than I'd ever known in my life, but still it meant nothing to me.

I put the money in a safe place, determined that when I should leave my room hereafter I would lock it carefully. Then I went to bed to lie awake a long time as I thought of the long, dreary years which stretched ahead of me endlessly. "Oh, John," I whispered as the pain of losing my love pierced my heart like a sharp, shiny knife. I felt as if I dreamed of nothing but had slept little when I heard the tapping on my door, and heard Georgia's voice calling, bidding me to rise.

"I hear you, Georgia," I answered, and slid out of bed and walked in my nightgown to the door. I unlocked the door and told Georgia I would be down to breakfast.

It was a strange meal, that morning's breakfast. Only Georgia smiled an answer to my greeting. Melinda eyed me with cold blue eyes as hard as an agate marble which Harlan might have. No good morning escaped her lips, nor did Rex even look up when I took my seat across from him. His crutches stood against the wall behind him as he ate silently.

I saw Felice and Uncle Walter each glance quickly at me, and than return their attention to the eggs and sausages Charity had prepared for our breakfast. Of course

John's place stood empty at the head of the table, though no one remarked on his absence.

After breakfast I went back to the sitting room to complete the preparation of the letters and the diary. I knew the editor of the publisher would arrange the letters as he saw fit; and I knew that the names in the letters would surely destroy some of the great families along the length of the Erie Canal—families whose fortunes were based on the corruption, graft, and worse during the period of the canal's construction, and of its operation, too. The letters and the diary told the story well.

I'd worked for perhaps an hour when Melinda appeared at the sitting-room door. She glanced around quickly, as if to assure herself that I was alone.

"Yes, Melinda?" I greeted her. "Is there something you wished to talk to me about?"

"There is something I must show you," she said urgently. "Something you don't know about, and you should."

"All right, Melinda," I said patiently, "what would you show me?"

"Meet me in the cellar in"—she glanced at the clock on the mantel—"in thirty minutes, at fifteen minutes after ten."

"Why?" I asked suspiciously. "What is there that you can show me which you can't bring here?"

She showed sudden indifference.

"I don't care, Cousin, if you come or not. It is something I thought you should see, but if you don't care . . ." She shrugged her heavy shoulders as if to say it was of no importance to her.

"Very well," I said after a moment. I could spare the time, couldn't I? "Will it take long?"

Again she shrugged. "Five minutes," she answered. "Will you meet me?"

"All right, Melinda, I will meet you—at ten-fifteen in the cellar. But why not now?"

"I have to get it ready," she said evasively.

A sense of foreboding swept over me, but I told myself not to be a ninny, for what could happen to me? Melinda could do me no harm. . . .

She left and I returned to my work, putting her out of my mind for the time that was left.

At ten-fifteen I closed the davenport's cover and left the sitting room. I crossed the balcony and went down the hallway to the spiral staircase which led to the first-floor storeroom, and thence to the cellar. I thought that I was foolish not to bring a lamp, but Melinda would surely have one if she was to meet me there.

Of course I met no one, and as I went down the steps into the cellar I saw Melinda's lamp. She held it high over her head in the entry to the large room, as she waited for me. I felt a shiver as I descended the last steps of the staircase, for it was cold and dank and dark in the cellar. She carried a ball of heavy twine in one hand.

"Yes, Melinda, what is it you wish me to see?" I had little curiosity now, and wished only that I'd not let her persuade me to come down here, which I knew now was a silly thing for me to do.

"It is in there," Melinda said, and pointed to the heavy door at the far end—the one with the ancient padlock that probably hadn't been used for many years—but now it stood open.

I was reluctant to go to the door. I hesitated beside her, waiting for her to precede me, but she motioned me forward.

What am I afraid of? I asked myself silently. I'd take a look at what Melinda thought I'd wish to see, and I'd return to my room. In another day I would be gone from Orne Hall forever.

I peered down and I saw from the rays of the flickering light of Melinda's lamp that it was a tiny, bare room dug downward a half dozen steps with only an earthen floor, but I saw naught else.

"I see nothing, Melinda," I said, leaning forward that I might better examine the walls.

All at once I felt Melinda's hand hit my back and I catapulted down the steps, my arms flailing wildly as I sought to catch my balance. But I could not and I fell to the earth, my face scratched by gravel. My head hit the far wall; a thousand lights flared in my brain, and I knew nothing.

When I again opened my eyes the first thing that I saw was Melinda sitting on the bottom step of the little room, the lamp resting on the earthen floor before her.

"Melinda," I cried. "You . . ." I tried to move and discovered I could not, for my wrists were bound and so were my ankles. "You've tied me up! Why?"

"I have to, Adelia," Melinda said. "Don't you see, I have to? If Rex married you, you'd take him away from me, and I couldn't let you do that!"

"Take him away? . . . Melinda, I am not going to marry Rex! I . . ."

"I don't believe you," Melinda said, and I saw that her blue eyes were wide and staring. Had she lost her wits?

"It's true, Melinda," I said. "You wouldn't hurt . . ."

"That's what Ellen said, too," Melinda interrupted. "She tried to pretend that she never——that Rex had never come to her room, but I saw him! So I knew she lied."

"*You* killed Ellen!" I whispered, and I felt as if a cold hand had been placed on my body. "You threw her body out of the window!"

A crafty smile wreathed Melinda's fat lips.

"You're insane," I cried. "Melinda, untie me. . . ."

"No," she answered. "I'm going to leave you down here, and when they want to know what has happened to you, I'll tell them that you packed your suitcase and you went away with some man!" A change came over her features, and she looked unhappy. "I don't really want to do it, but I have to."

Melinda looked so strong, her arms so heavy. "Melinda," I whispered, "it was you who tried to throw me over the railing from the balcony, wasn't it?"

She nodded. "If you hadn't caught the newel post it would have worked, too," she said. "You aren't very heavy."

"And you tried to smother me!"

"If only Felice hadn't come to the door," Melinda said, her expression becoming angry. "She had no right to interfere."

I closed my eyes a moment, trying to think. It seemed to

211

me that everything was becoming so terribly clear. "Did you poison Charity?" I asked.

"That was a mistake," she answered. "I wanted you to taste it. It probably wasn't strong enough, anyway."

"You—you aren't going to leave me here, are you, Melinda?" I whispered. "Come, please untie me. I won't take Rex away. . . ."

"I don't believe you," she repeated.

"Why did you smother Aunt Jewel?" I asked wearily. It had to be Melinda, of course. Everything fit perfectly. It was she, too, who had removed those letters from the file drawer, of course.

"She was going to send me away—away from Rex," Melinda said angrily, her blue eyes flashing. "She said I couldn't stay at Orne Hall any longer. She said I was crazy, so I had to do it, didn't I?"

"Melinda," I said gently. "Rex loves you; he would never leave you. . . ."

But she didn't hear me, for she suddenly giggled. "John, my husband, was killed in a duel. He thought the man was Rex's father, only it was the wrong man!" She laughed as if it were a great joke.

The heavy twine with which she'd tied me cut into the flesh of my wrists and ankles; she'd drawn the binding so tightly it hurt. A sense of doom descended on me, for Melinda was truly mad, was she not? I thought that I was going to be ill as I looked into her fat face and glaring eyes, for she was surely insane.

Suddenly I thought of Rex and Harlan, and that once I thought I'd seen similarities in their features. "Melinda, was Rex Harlan's father?" I asked.

Melinda nodded and then frowned. "She ran away," she said, but her eyes looked at me craftily, as if she thought I might not believe her.

She leaned forward and reached a fat arm toward the lamp. "I'm going to go back upstairs," she said conversationally. She laughed lightly as she heaved herself to her feet, the lamp in her hand. "You are a very nice lady, but you shouldn't try to take my Rex away from me," she said. She turned and started up the stairs. She laughed again, and then I saw her reach the cellar and turn to close the heavy door.

"Melinda," I cried, "don't leave me. . . ."

But she swung the door closed, and then I lay in the pitch darkness. I heard the faint bang of the padlock and latch, and then I heard nothing; nor could I see anything.

For several moments I thrashed wildly, screaming at the top of my voice, as I sought to free my bound hands and feet. But my wild twisting only drew the binding twine more tightly, and finally, near exhaustion, my heart pounding, I lay back and fought to think clearly. I must be calm, I told myself firmly.

I brought my two nearly numb wrists to my lips, and with them I sought to discover how the tie was made. I could tell that the twine was knotted on my wristbone, and I began to tug at it with my teeth. A hundred times I gave up and lay back, my shoulders aching, but each time I returned to the knot, and finally I felt a strand give!

A moment later my hands were free! I rubbed my wrists to restore circulation and my fingers began to tingle. My fingers explored the knots in the twine which bound my ankles—it took a long time but finally I pulled the twine free from my legs, and I was no longer bound. Unsteadily, using the stone wall for support, I pulled myself to my feet. I stood in the pitch darkness, some inner instinct telling me that to scream more would be useless, though I felt hysteria rising in me, and it was only with great effort that I choked back the sound from my throat.

Then I called at the top of my voice, "Melinda, let me out of here! You've carried your joke far enough!" But I heard no answer. She had surely gone by now, leaving me to die. I walked carefully toward the steps and upward, stumbling, my hands touching the walls as I moved. I pushed against the heavy door, and of course there was no movement. I was locked in, and again I fought against the hysteria that threatened to turn me into an insane person, mindlessly scrabbling around in the darkness. I fought the wild terror down, and slowly I turned around that I might sit on the steps and wait.

"I will be missed at dinner," I told myself calmly. Soon

someone would search the basement and open the door. It wouldn't be long. I simply had to be patient.

But in the total darkness I had no way of knowing how slowly or how quickly the time would be passing. It seemed to me that I'd been waiting for hours and not the faintest sound penetrated the darkness of the tomb-like room, and I had the feeling that I was slowly suffocating.

Once I climbed in the darkness up to the doorway, and I hammered with my fists, thinking, hoping desperately, that someone might hear me, but after a few moments my arms became too weary and my hands so painful I could no longer continue. My chest rose and fell as I tried to draw air into my lungs. How long had it been? Had no one missed me? I went to my knees, seeking some opening. At the very bottom of the door I felt air moving against my fingers, yet I could see no light through the thin crack.

I tried to think rationally, though my thoughts veered away and I felt growing hysteria. But I fought that, too, for in that direction lay madness. I tried to think of Melinda, the mother of John and Rex. Why did she want me dead? I had never done anything hateful to her. She had no reason to wish me harm, did she?

I let out a little cry of desperate fear, for suddenly I knew why no one sought me and no one had come to the cellar! Melinda would have removed some of my clothing from my roon and hidden it, and when the search was originally mounted, she would have announced that I had fled. Perhaps she might even have loosed a mare, sending her flying to give her story credence. How else could she prevent my being found except to give reason to call off the search? I could imagine she might tell of someone having come for me, of my running away with some unknown man.

I began to sob quietly, for then I realized that certainly I would die down in this hole in the cellar, and no one would find me until my body had decomposed. Only my bones would be left!

My life was over and all I could do was await death!

## Chapter XIV

Was there no way out? I sat, shivering with cold, my arms drawn tightly across my bosom. What was I to do? I tried to think of other things, of pleasant things. I remembered Aunt Jewel and the things she endured. But she survived, because she would not give in to her husband, nor to anyone on earth! What would she do were she in my fix? What *could* she do?

I stared in the darkness, trying to visualize the little dungeon as I'd seen it so briefly when Rex had shown it to me, and then in the instant before Melinda had thrown me down the stone steps to fall on my face on the dirt floor.

The dirt floor! Suddenly I felt hope surge through me, for it the floor was dirt, couldn't I dig under the walls? At least I could try—it was better than sitting here waiting for death and I knew it might be long and torturous as thirst and perhaps suffocation would finally overcome me and cause my death.

I would fight, and if I died, at least I wouldn't die a coward! I closed my eyes and for a moment I prayed fervently to God to give me strength, and then I rose and stepped carefully down to the dirt floor one foot at a time. I encircled the room, my hands moving over the rough face of the stone walls. I tried to visualize where the little dungeon must be, and it seemed to me that I should best dig at the far end, and if I should succeed I would come out into the open world beyond the house walls instead of under the Great Hall floor. Even so, a part of my mind scoffed, for it would mean many feet of digging, and I knew not how deeply the walls might be set in the ground. I felt a growing horror of being confined in a small tunnel, but was it

215

worse than this nightmare? At least I could be doing something!

I went down on my knees, and with my fingers I sought to dig; the earth was tightly packed, and it was only with difficulty I was able to bring up a single handful, yet it was a start! I threw the dirt away from where I dug, and started again.

It was wearying work, and in only minutes my back began to hurt, but I kept doggedly on. As I worked, each handful of dirt making the opening a little larger, I thought about my days at Orne Hall. Why did Melinda wish to destroy me? What would she gain by it? I tried to see in my memory how Melinda had acted in the months past. I knew, of course, that she cared far more for Rex than for John, her firstborn. Perhaps she had truly loved Rex's father.

I remembered her way of looking at me, and I began to realize that Melinda had been jealous of me, and I knew that she was afraid I would take Rex away from her. That had to be it! Melinda's mind had somehow failed, and she'd thought of me as a threat to her. Perhaps she thought if Rex left Orne Hall with me, then John would force her to leave Orne Hall, too.

A new thought came into my mind: Did Melinda know what Rex had found out—that I was an heir to the Orne wealth? Even as I dug in the dry dirt, I shook my head, for none of it made sense.

The hole widened as I labored. I knew that air had to be coming from somewhere, otherwise I should have, by now, been suffocated, though I'd found no opening except under the door, either by sight or by my hands. I found I could work but a short while before my back would pain me beyond endurance, and then I would have to rest.

During one brief period a new terror was added to the almost unbearable horrors which already beset me. An animal scurried over my body and then was suddenly gone. I screamed and screamed and I thought my mind was shattered—but when I could scream no more, I knew it was a good rather than a bad omen; if a rat could escape from the dungeon, so could I! So, even though time after time

216

the thought pushed into my mind that it was hopeless, and I might best simply lay back and await death, I continued to dig.

And I was encouraged, too, by the fact that deeper down the earth seemed easier to move, though my nails were all broken and sores had been opened by the bruising of the many stones.

I found a flat rock and with almost childish delight I grasped it, for one edge was fairly sharp and I could dig with it much more easily than with my hands!

The hole became so deep that I knew I had to enlarge it, for I could not easily reach the bottom. I began to do so, but the periods I could work without resting became shorter and shorter, even though I knew not how long they were. I began to use the number of times I would draw the flat stone toward me and finally I began to time myself. Ten draws with the stone, and then rest. I was afraid to lie down on the dirt floor, because of the rat which had once scurried over my body, so I sat upright, and I would feel the thuds of my heart pounding in my chest. When it had beat a hundred times, I would then resume my digging.

It seemed that I had been working for days, and thirst had become an agony. More than once I wailed in the darkness, "I can't go on!" But in the end I did, for what else was there for me to do? Yet each time I returned to the digging my hands moved more slowly and my mind began to wander, and sometimes I wasn't sure where I was. I would be with my mamma and she would be holding me in her arms and comforting me. I would hear her soothing words and I would cry, my face pressed against her bosom. But then suddenly it would be Melinda, and she would be choking me!

It was during a period of mind-wandering that I suddenly realized that I had been scraping with the edge of the flat stone but I was getting no more earth; a funny sound assailed my ears as the stone dragged over something of different texture.

It brought me back from my wandering thoughts, and my hands reached down to the bottom of the hole, which was quite deep now. In the darkness they fumbled; whatever they felt wasn't dirt! It felt like cloth, goods caked with earth, but surely some kind of cloth.

Feverishly, with both hands working, I brushed and dug the earth away. I felt the edge of the material, and then I felt something else. At first I knew not what it was, but then as my fingers explored, they felt strands of something—hair! It had to be hair! The other things I'd touched . . . suddenly I retched horribly and backed my body away from the hole. I couldn't stop the horrible dry retching. The blackness seemed to change and I knew I was falling, falling . . . falling.

My mind slowly awoke from the sleep that had overtaken me, a sleep into which I had escaped from the horror of my discovery, for I knew my clawing hands had uncovered a body—one that had long been buried in the dirt floor of the little dungeon.

Finally, I opened my eyes and saw again the darkness and I became aware of the rapid beat of my heart and again the feeling of suffocation assailed me.

I fought down the hysteria and tried to think clearly. Whose body had I discovered? I thought of Alice, Harlan's mother, the daughter of Charity and Paul. She had disappeared. Aunt Jewel had said that one day she was there, and the next she was gone. Is this the place to which she had gone? To a lonely grave, here in the darkness? Had she died here, as I must surely die? And then, later, had some murderer buried her body, where it was destined to remain forever? Had Melinda tricked Alice into the basement as she had me and pushed her down the stone steps into the dirt, leaving her to die?

I began to sob in the darkness, but no tears came to my eyes, for they were dry—as dry as my tortured throat. I remembered again the touch of the cloth—stiff with dirt and years—and in my mind's eye I saw it, thin and stiff as a piece of cardboard.

Suddenly I remembered the tiny space under the door where I'd felt the faint movement of air; no light came under it, for the cellar was dark, too. But what if someone came into the cellar? What if whoever he was could see something different? Perhaps the cloth was white, or had been. What if I could push it under the door through the thin space? Would someone ever see it in time to save me?

Feverishly I crawled to the hole and, though both the stench and my thoughts of the contents made me ill, I reached down and tried to tear off a piece of the stiffened goods. It was difficult, but the material did finally tear, and with a feeling of revulsion and hope combined, I climbed on my hands and knees up the steps to the door. With my fingers I sought the space, and with both hands and finger-tips guiding it, I tried to push the piece of goods under the door. But the material crumpled. I tried again and again at different places, and then in one spot it seemed to me the cloth did move under the door. As carefully as I could with my trembling weak fingers, I pushed the material forward, moving it from side to side, until finally I could move it no more, for it crumpled in my hands.

Then, still on the stone steps, I lowered my head until it was cradled on my arms. I closed my eyes.

It is finished, I thought. I can do no more!

A strange kind of peace swept over me and I wondered if I were dying. "It isn't so bad," I murmured through parched lips that no longer hurt.

"John," I whispered, "I love you," and then pain did come, for I was dying without ever having an opportunity to say goodbye! John would never know how much I loved him! I began again to cry, great dry sobs shaking my body, and I wished with all my heart that it had been different.

But when my weary body could no longer cry, I finally rested without moving, my body on the steps, half lying, half sitting.

I think I will go to sleep, I thought. My body seemed to be floating and I wondered if my soul were being transported to heaven.

I knew not how long it had been that I had lain without moving, for time no longer meant anything to me. There were moments when I knew where I was, but I felt no compunction to move, nor desire to return to the hole and to dig deeper. I couldn't touch or remove the body of whoever lay buried there.

Most often I thought of John, and I'd see him in my

mind, his bearded face, his dark intense eyes—the gentleness of his smile. I remembered his sweetness to Harlan and how the boy loved him. I saw him before the mantel in the Great Hall, warming himself before the glowing coals in the hearth.

I heard his voice teasing me, harsh as it was at times, gentle and rumbling at others.

I remember whispering, "God, please! Care for him, protect him from harm!"

Then nothing until I heard voices, but they were just a part of my dreams, were they not? I didn't lift my head, not even when I heard the clicking sound, and then the creaking of the old door.

But there was a yellow ray of light on the step beside me and I heard John's voice cry out, "Oh, my God!"

But it was just a dream, wasn't it? I'd had so many. It was just another sweet dream that I heard footsteps, the cry of Charity's voice, and that I then felt strong arms under my shoulder and under my knees. I dreamed I was being lifted up, and it was John's strong arms around me, holding me, carrying me. It was one of the nicest dreams. I hoped it would last and last.

I looked up into John's bearded face, and I saw he was crying, tears streaming down his cheeks. I tried to ask him why he cried, but no words could come from my dry throat or past my cracked lips. So I closed my eyes contentedly, even as John carried me up the spiral stairs.

Everything did become mixed up, for I felt myself being lowered into a bed, and a part of my mind said it wasn't a dream at all, that I was alive. John was there, kneeling beside the bed, and Charity from the other side unbuttoned my bodice jacket.

"Oh, Adelia! My God. . . ." John whispered.

I tried to smile. Georgia came into the room with a glass of water. John lifted my head and touched the rim of the glass to my lips. I felt the cold water in my mouth and I swallowed convulsively, for it was the most wonderful taste in the world.

"Not too much, not too fast," Charity warned.

I cared not that John was there when Georgia got my

soiled clothes from my body and pulled a nightgown over my head. Nor when Paul brought a bowl of soup and again John supported me while Charity put the spoon to my lips and the delicious liquid slipped down my throat.

I felt so warm and comfortable, the feather comforter up about my throat, my hair spread out on the pillow. And I knew it was no dream, for I was truly safe and sound in my own bed in my own room. I knew that John sat in a chair close to the bed.

"You—you won't go away?" I whispered. "I—I'm afraid to be alone."

"No, darling," he answered, and he took my hand in both of his. "No, I will never leave you alone, never."

Later I opened my eyes. "John, I love you," I said distinctly. "There's a body down there. I—I found it when I was digging." Suddenly I giggled with brief, foolish hysteria. "I was going to dig my way out!"

"I know," John answered. "Go to sleep."

"Yes," I said obediently. "You—you won't turn down the lamp, will you? I—I couldn't bear it if I woke up and it was dark!"

"No, sweetheart, the lamp will be bright. . . ."

So I slept. Later John said I slept for twenty-seven hours, waking only when Charity would bring nourishing soup which she would spoon into my mouth as John held me.

Finally, I opened my eyes, and the first thing I saw was John's face as he sat in the rocker, leaning toward me, his elbows on his knees.

"John?" I asked foolishly. "Is it really you?"

"Yes, Adelia. You're safe now."

"I—I thought it was a dream."

"Don't think about it, darling," he whispered.

"John, it was Melinda who locked me down there. She pushed me so I fell down the stairs, and then she closed the door and I was in the darkness."

"I know," John whispered. "Melinda is gone, now. So is Rex."

"What will happen to her?" I asked.

His eyes closed and I saw the pain in his expression.

"She will never stand trial for murder, but my mother—

**221**

she has lost her mind. She—she is insane. But she told us everything."

"I'm sorry," I said softly.

"Perhaps her mind was destroyed long ago, but we didn't know it," John said after a long pause.

"She killed Ellen?"

"Yes, because Ellen and Rex—she thought Ellen would take Rex away from her."

"And Alice? Was it Alice's body I found?"

"Yes. Rex is Harlan's father—Alice threatened to expose Rex, to force him to marry her. Melinda tricked her as she tricked you."

"Why—how did you find me?"

"I'd come back—Adelia, I knew I couldn't give you up that way. I was a fool. I loved you too much. And when I discovered you were gone—perhaps with some other man—I didn't want to live. Melinda had hidden your clothing and your suitcase. But Harlan wouldn't stop looking; he didn't believe you'd gone—he said he'd never give up. It was he who went to the cellar to hunt for you, and he saw the piece of cloth under the door and came back up to call me. I went down; the padlock was closed and we had to chisel it free. Then I found you!"

"I'm glad," I whispered. For just a moment the memory of the darkness overwhelmed me and I began to tremble uncontrollably.

John took my hands in his and held them tightly. "It's over!" he said again and again.

Of course, I will never completely recover from the horrors of that experience. Even now, years later, I can hardly bear to be alone in the dark, and only the warmth of John's strong body beside me gives me strength and courage.

Yes, we were married before the days of June were spent, but we live in Waterloo now. Rex is somewhere in Europe, nor do we hear from him. Melinda is in an asylum; John visits her there frequently, but I can't make myself go with him.

Charity and Paul came to Waterloo with us, and we live in the big house John had built just off the main street, and

222

Harlan, now a strong youth, is becoming John's right-hand man. My sons, too, will probably go into the business.

Vandals destroyed much of Orne Hall, and a fire started by lightning completely gutted it. Only rarely do we drive out to the estate, and when I see its red turrets against the skyline, I still shudder and I feel cold.

But John puts his arm around my shoulder, and once more everything is fine. Then we drive back to Waterloo in our motorcar, the dusty road at times following the placid Erie Canal. We see, as always, the slow-plodding mules drawing the barges piled with merchandise around the bends, under bridges, past towns with noisy taverns. . . .